The Mason's Mark:
Love and Death in the Tower

by

M. S. Spencer

The Mason's Mark: Love and Death in the Tower

Cover Art by *RJ Morris*

The Wild Rose Press, Inc.
PO Box 708
Adams Basin, NY 14410-0708
Visit us at www.thewildrosepress.com

Publishing History:
Previously published by Secret Cravings, 2014
First Crimson Rose Edition, 2016
Print ISBN 978-1-5092-0766-4
Digital ISBN 978-1-5092-0767-1

Published in the United States of America

Dedication

To Lawrence and Barbara,
Kelly and Keith,
Fonece and Leonard,
Clint, and Charles
Who built my dream house while I wrote this book.

Chapter One
Linked In

"Now, Claire, are you perfectly clear on your role?"

The petite redhead, intent on brushing the lapels of her smart khaki blazer and adjusting the large button that read *Docent, Masonic Memorial*, jumped a foot. "Er, yes, Mr. Quinn, I think so. I've memorized everything in the guidebook."

"Good. Remember, you are not expected to be an expert on Masons, just on this building. If a visitor asks you a question about the Masons and freemasonry you can't answer, simply direct them to the gift shop. Harry can help them find appropriate reading material. Don't worry about all the details." He paused and allowed himself a tiny smile. "Especially the ones about masonic rituals."

"Yes, Mr. Quinn."

"All right, off you go. The next tour begins at one-thirty. If you run into difficulties, call Nigel, our tiler. He'll be at the front desk. Have you met him?"

Claire recited from memory. "Tiler—he who guards the door to the lodge room while the lodge is in session. Yes, I've met him, Mr. Quinn." Not that she'd liked the young man. He had a furtive way about him—yesterday she'd seen him fold his newspaper just as though he had a *Penthouse* tucked inside. For that matter, she thought, with that prematurely balding ping-pong ball of a head and the thinly disguised remains of a bout with acne, she doubted he'd have any luck with a non-Photoshopped female.

Claire found her way to the front entrance of the enormous masonic temple, reciting various facts under her breath. A number of people milled around, alternately fanning themselves and gulping water from liter bottles. Like the eye of the storm, a family of four in Amish dress stood very still in the center, the slender female with eyes downcast, her two small children hanging on her skirts, the man lanky and grim. His wispy blond beard straggled over the white shirt buttoned up to a wobbly Adam's apple. He wore a severe black jacket and a wide-brimmed, black hat. Claire wondered if Amish men were required to wear hats indoors. And to be hot. She felt a drop of perspiration dribble down her back and wished for the fortieth time that she didn't have to stand in front of the revolving doors, soaking in the searing humidity of a Washington August.

Two little boys raced around squealing and touching things they shouldn't. Claire cast about for their keeper. *There.* A pony-tailed young woman, much too well-endowed for the purple tube top she wore, paced the floor chattering into a cell phone. Claire checked her watch. *Showtime.* She moved to the hall leading to the elevators. "Ahem. All those here for the tour, could I have your attention?"

As one unit, the Amish family swung around to face her. When the budding juvenile delinquents ignored her, she raised her voice. "Ma'am. Ma'am?" The purple-clad woman looked at Claire but did not stop talking into her phone. "Are you here for the tour?" When the woman nodded, she pointed at the boys. "Do those belong to you? If you're planning to use your cell phone, your children must be kept on a leash during the tour."

The woman blinked at Claire. One of the Amish children giggled, prompting a glare from her father. The object of attention snapped the phone closed with an angry click. "Luther Malloy! Frank! Get your buns over here."

"Yes, Ma." The boys strolled over, staying just out of reach of their mother's hand.

Two people came through the revolving door, arguing in loud voices. A tiny woman with short, astonishingly orange hair, grumbled, "But Bob, you promised after the Jefferson Memorial we could take a break. My tootsies are killing me."

Her companion, a rotund little fellow not much taller than she, said mildly, "This won't take long, Polly. I thought you'd be interested since your grandfather was the Worshipful Master of his lodge." He wiped a wet brow with a soggy handkerchief. "At least it's cool in here. Hotter 'n Hades out there. Tell you what, we'll go down to Joe Theisman's for pizza and a cold beer after the tour."

"Well…okay, so long as it's air-conditioned." Polly took a long swallow from her water bottle. "Wish I'd remembered my pocket fan. And I thought Missouri was bad in August!"

Bob grinned. "It's not the heat, Polly. It's the humidity."

"Yeah, yeah." They caught sight of Claire and walked over. "We have tickets for the tour. Are you our fearless leader?"

"Er...yes, I am. Why don't we all gather at the elevators?" The other sightseers floated off toward the gift shop, leaving nine with Claire.

She took a deep breath and brushed an errant auburn curl behind her ear. It felt a little strange towering over all but the Amish man. At five feet two she rarely got a chance to look down on people. "Good afternoon and welcome to the George Washington Masonic National Memorial. I am Claire Wilding, and I'll be your guide today." She launched into her lecture. "Inspired by the lighthouse of ancient Alexandria, the Memorial honors George Washington as the guiding light for America and reflects freemasonry's tenets of brotherly love, relief, and truth. Built over a period of forty-eight years, the building is three hundred and thirty-three feet high. It has three sections—the ground floor, which houses the Grand Masonic Hall, the main floor, where we are now, and the tower. There are nine levels in the tower."

Bob piped up. "I heard the rooms get smaller and smaller and the elevator rises on an incline to get to the top."

Ooh goody, my first question. Got this one cold. "That's correct. The two elevators are sixty-one feet apart on the first floor, but only four and a half feet apart by the time we reach the ninth floor. They ascend at an angle of seven and a half degrees."

With a solemn face, Bob asked, "So, do we all have to lean backward to keep from falling out?"

Claire gaped at him and for a minute wondered if he were right. *Mr. Quinn didn't say anything about strapping us in. Better sound confident here.* "No, of course not."

Bob shot a triumphant glance at Polly, who sniffed. Claire continued. "The room in which we are standing is the Memorial Hall. Note the spectacular murals on either side, painted by Allyn Cox. That one depicts George Washington laying the cornerstone of the U.S. Capitol building. If you look closely, you'll see he's wearing his masonic apron and holding a silver trowel. These items are on display in the room to my left."

Everybody dutifully sent eyes right to the painting, wavered, then swiveled to the opposite side where the gift shop stood. Bob opened his mouth and Claire raised her voice. "We'll get to that in a minute." She almost choked on the last word. Her carefully memorized speech couldn't stand any interruption. *If I lose the thread now, I'm doomed.*

"In the other mural the father of our country is depicted attending Christ Church in Philadelphia. Above the murals are stained glass portraits of such notables as the Marquis de Lafayette, Benjamin Franklin, and Elisha Cullen Dick, George Washington's sponsor and physician. At the far end, past the eight green granite pillars, stands the magnificent bronze statue of George Washington by Bryant Baker. The doors to the right and left of the statue lead to the Memorial Theatre. A beautiful semicircular auditorium, it is available for public events. To our right and left"— she threw her arms out like a stewardess pointing out the exit doors—"are the North and South Lodge Rooms, where visiting lodges meet."

Polly asked, "What do you mean, 'visiting'? Are these things portable?" She inspected the marble pillars as if looking for hooks.

Claire warmed to her subject. The last two weeks of cramming were paying off. "In freemasonry, the word 'lodge' actually refers to the members themselves—they meet as a lodge. So Alexandria-Washington Lodge number 22 meets in the South Lodge Room. We usually refer to the entire building as the Masonic Temple or Memorial."

Little Luther, spellbound by Claire's lecture, seemed unaware that his brother had tied his shoelaces together. After the inevitable pratfall, trading of punches, and half-hearted scolding from the parent, he asked, "So how old is this temple anyway?"

Pleased at his interest, however short-lived, she answered, "Not that old, actually. It opened in 1949 as the third home of the Alexandria lodge. The Grand Lodge of Pennsylvania warranted the first in 1783. Then in 1788 several prominent men, including Washington's sponsor, Dr. Dick, petitioned to establish a new lodge through the Grand Lodge of Virginia, and asked George Washington to be its Charter Master. The original building stood on what's now Market Square."

"Market Square? Ain't that where they hold the farmer's market every Saturday?"

"Yes, Mrs. Malloy. The first building burned down in 1871, along with many irreplaceable Washington memorabilia. The lodge took up quarters in the present City Hall, where they stayed until this building was ready for occupation."

Luther and Frank took advantage of Claire's momentary pause for breath to topple a large ashcan, spilling sand and cigarette butts all over the marble floor. No one stirred while Claire ran through the docent manual's chapter on emergencies in her head.

Finding nothing, she stepped with what she hoped was dignified composure over the can and motioned toward the gift shop.

"Let us pass through here and enter a replica of the original lodge as it looked in 1802, when General Washington presided as Charter Master. Will you all please follow me?"

Her retinue gingerly skirted the mess. All, that is, except Frank, who plowed right through it, kicking up sand and whistling. Claire led them into a clean, bright room. The wood floor gleamed. Black Windsor chairs lined the walls. Luther ambled over to a glass case. "Hey, Frank, lookee here!"

His brother came over and peered in. "Sheesh, what's this? Looks like junk from somebody's garage."

Claire bit her tongue. The Amish man leaned over them and spoke in a thick German accent. "It says this is the silver trowel Washington used for the groundbreaking of the U.S. Capitol. Next to it is his masonic apron."

"Ah, like in the painting." The others gawked at Mrs. Malloy, who apparently had in fact been listening.

Polly tugged at Claire's sleeve. "My father never told me anything about his…er…organization. Why *do* Masons wear aprons?"

Frank yelped, "Yeah, are Freemasons girly girls?" His brother gave him a noogie.

Claire hoped her tone contained a sufficient dose of disapproval. "Masons wear aprons during rituals to commemorate the origins of freemasonry in the guild of stonemasons."

"I believe"—the Amish man's cold blue eyes glinted under his pale brows—"that stonemasons wear an apron to hold the heavy mallets and chisels they use—implements only a very strong man could handle."

Mrs. Malloy pushed the staring boys to one side and drawled, "I thought the Masons were a men's club. You know, guys who wear funny hats and throw wild parties. Strippers jumpin' outa cakes. Other…stuff. That's why they got no windows in their clubhouses."

One, two, three. "I'm afraid you've been misled by old stereotypes and rather…er…picturesque fancies. Freemasonry is primarily an association dedicated to self-improvement."

Bob snickered. "You hear that, Polly? No fun and games here. Just *self-improvement.*" He guffawed.

Mrs. Malloy continued to fume. Claire heard her mutter angrily, "Strippers. That's what Dad told me. *Hmph.* Bet she's covering up."

Claire hurried on. "Many of its adherent groups— like the Shriners—are well-known for their charitable work."

"That's right—the Shriner Hospitals! But wait…" Polly frowned, eyes uncertain. "Or do they run the circus?"

Mrs. Malloy nudged her. "Yeah—I been to one of those. These big fat fellas drive around in teeny little cars. It's high-larious." She snapped her gum, grinning reminiscently.

Bob interrupted, "I think the Shriners sponsor both the hospitals and the circus."

His wife considered the idea, her brow furrowed. "Well, they can't do both. I mean, those are big projects, and—"

Claire cleared her throat. "Right now we're

discussing freemasonry in general." Surprised by her own assertiveness, Claire straightened her shoulders. "We will get to the different sub-groups as we continue the tour."

"Okay, sure."

"Sorry."

The Missouri couple seemed a little more contrite than necessary. *Are they laughing at me?* Claire plunged on. "The origins of freemasonry are somewhat obscure, but it's generally believed to have evolved from the customs of stonemasons who built the great cathedrals in the Middle Ages. Hence their principle symbols are the square and compasses, tools of the masonry trade."

"Don't forget the apron," said Polly's companion, an undercurrent of sarcasm in his voice.

Polly pinched him. "You crack me up, Bob."

"Let's move on, shall we?" Claire herded them toward the door. "Now we're going to take the elevator up the tower. Each of the tower's nine levels is dedicated to a different theme. The top floor opens onto an observation platform and we should have a few moments at the end of the tour to enjoy the glorious vista of Alexandria, the Potomac River, and beyond it, the monuments of Washington. After that we'll head straight down to the ground floor where the restrooms are located."

The group dutifully followed Claire and squeezed into the elevator. Giggling in the back followed by a frightened squeal told Claire that Luther and Frank had discovered the joys of teasing girls. The doors opened on the third floor to reveal a large room filled with glass cases.

"This floor, which is the lowest level in the tower, is called the Grotto, and consists of exhibits dedicated to other appendant organizations, most prominently the Mystic Order of Veiled Prophets of the Enchanted Realm—"

Luther squealed. "Mystic? Prophets? Grotto? Golly, it sounds like something from my Dungeons and Dragons game."

His brother kicked him. "You big dummy, they're zombies. Right, Lady?"

Claire toyed with various forms of torture, but settled on a mild reply. "The Grotto is similar to the Shriners—a social and philanthropic group."

"Are they Freemasons?" It was the tall Amish man who spoke.

"Yes. All of the philanthropic orders like the Shriners and the Grotto are Masons, but not all Masons are Shriners, and so on."

"I see." The answer seemed to intrigue him.

When the ten minutes mandated for pretending to peruse the exhibits had passed, Claire announced, "Next we'll be visiting a museum devoted to George Washington. The Masonic Memorial houses an impressive collection of artifacts, some of which were donated by the Washington family and some rescued from the fire in 1871 that destroyed the first lodge. Please be sure to check out Dr. Elisha Cullen Dick's pocket watch. He was George Washington's close friend and presided over his death bed."

As they filed out on the fourth floor and automatically turned right as all human flocks do, Claire surveyed the room. The black and white parquet floor sparkled. Around three sides ran a balcony, filled with small alcoves and paintings. The light from a porthole window flooded the room. As she headed toward a bust of George Washington, a shadow moved behind a column. She took a step toward it, but Mrs. Malloy's voice stopped her. "Frank, Luther—you be good, hear? I'm gonna sit down for a bit."

Claire watched, horror-struck, as the woman plunked down on the Chippendale chair Washington had used as Worshipful Master of the Lodge. The yellow tape meant to prevent access to it lay in tatters on the floor. She had lunged forward, one hand stretched out to grab the transgressor, when the shadow flitted across her vision again. Feeling like a spectator at a tennis match, she spun around. *There.* Shaking a finger at the woman and barking "No!" in her most imperious voice, she rounded a pillar. Sure enough, a man stood there by a small bookcase built into the wall.

During Claire's training, Mr. Quinn had ground into her the absolute prohibition against unauthorized individuals wandering around in the Tower. *Oh God, I hope I don't have to call for backup.* "Sir? Can I help you?"

The man jumped and turned to her, his eyes wide, giving Claire the opportunity to admire two very large orbs tinted a luminous tourmaline green. His mobile face sported a Roman nose of reasonable proportion, a strong chin only slightly marred by a salt-and-pepper stubble, and the high cheekbones of an Aztec chief. His tan was not so deep as to seem artificial. Claire had raised her eyes to behold a head of wavy, chocolate brown hair when he began to speak. His sonorous baritone—a cross between Dean Martin and Elvis Presley—captivated her and she found herself humming

"That's Amore" under her breath.

"No, thank you…er…" He peered at her chest. Her hand went protectively to the bosom that drew most eligible bachelors' attention until she realized he was trying to read her name badge.

"Um…Claire. Claire Wilding. I'm the docent here." She indicated her troops, at least two of whom were attempting to wreak irreparable damage on each other with a wooden staff carved in the likeness of John the Baptist. "Who are you?"

He smiled suddenly, revealing brilliant white teeth. His whole face lit up, and Claire swallowed hard. "I'm Gideon Bliss. And in case you're wondering whether I'm here lawfully, the answer is yes." He stuck out a large hand, calluses prominent on his trigger finger. They reminded Claire of her father's hands. "David— Mr. Comfrey—gave me permission to visit the museum." His eyes glinted with little flecks of gold and humor.

Claire found herself at a loss for words and not just because he'd invoked the name of the Worshipful Master of the Alexandria-Washington Masonic Lodge. She sank into the depths of his verdant eyes, while the mellifluous voice rolled over her. Just before she nodded off, he stopped speaking. She shook herself. "Oh, I see. Well, I'll leave you to it." *Sheesh, Claire, are you shooting for the most pitiful female in Washington award?*

Bliss hadn't moved. "You say you're the docent here? Could you help me find something?"

Claire dropped her eyes and mumbled, "Uh…"

"I'm sorry, what did you say?"

"Um…this is my first day. I…I doubt if I can help

you."

He chuckled. "So you didn't actually mean anything by your first question."

"My first…Oh, well, you know, that was sort of…rhetorical. I mean, no one is supposed to be here. Other than me. And of course them." She waved at the group, who had now begun to congregate by the elevator doors. All except for the two boys, who were nowhere to be seen, and their mother, who continued to sprawl blithely on the President's priceless antique chair.

Her abrupt answer seemed to annoy Bliss. "I see." He turned back to the bookcase and pulled a large, dusty leather tome off the shelf. Claire spent a painful second staring at his rigid back and finally tore herself away, visions of emerald eyes filled with admiration at her beauty quickly evaporating.

"We'll be heading to the fifth floor now." She raised her voice to a decibel suitable for command. "I need everyone with me in one minute."

To her astonishment Luther and Frank zipped around her to stand waiting, hands clasped behind their backs. *Must be in Catholic school.* Their mother heaved herself out of the chair, leaving behind an ominous creak, and joined the rest.

As they rode up, Claire resumed her lecture. "The next floor is home to the lowest level of the York Rite, the Royal Arch. We'll see depictions of the building of Solomon's first temple and of initiation ceremonies into the rite."

Bob said in a puzzled voice, "Are we still talking about Masons?"

The Amish man echoed his question.

"Freemasonry?"

Claire smiled. She was on firmer ground here. "Yes. It's a bit complicated, isn't it? In a nutshell, a new Mason must pass through three degrees—Entered Apprentice, Fellow Craft, and Master Mason. Once you rise to the level of Master Mason, you may seek initiation into the York Rite, which in turn has three grades—Royal Arch, Royal and Select Masters, and Knights Templar. After that, the Knights Templar also has three orders to which you can aspire—Red Cross, Malta, and the Temple. Every order or degree requires study and presentations on subjects of importance to freemasonry." She took a breath. "We won't get into the Scottish Rite just yet."

Both men gazed at her gravely. "Thank you."

As Claire expected, the golden angels atop the model of the Ark of the Covenant drew the most attention. The little Amish girl shyly touched a wing. When a curtain closed abruptly over it she snatched her hand away and whimpered. From the other side of the room Polly shouted, "Hey, what are all these coins?"

Claire joined her. "They're mark pennies. Some lodges strike tokens or pennies with special markings unique to the lodge, which they give to a newly initiated Master Mason. He in turn inscribes his own identifying mark on the coin. This case contains marks from the Pennsylvania and Delaware lodges. And these over here were donated by Grand Orient lodges—as the lodges of Europe are called."

Bob came up and studied the coins, pinned like so many butterflies to the wall. "Are they real? I mean, are they legal currency?"

"No, although they symbolize the pay that

stonemasons once received for their work. A few rare ones can be very valuable."

The Amish mother laid a gentle hand on her husband's arm. "Werner, they look like the coins you showed me from the old country, don't they? Didn't you say your grandfather called them marks? He must have been a Mason."

The man pulled his arm away, his face tight. Claire watched them, surprised at the vehemence with which he answered. "You're mistaken, Jemimah. Those coins are real Deutsche marks. Papa brought them from Hamburg. They were called marks in the nineteenth century, yes, but they are real money. Not like these useless tokens." He gestured with contempt at the walls of pennies.

A crash behind them diverted Claire's attention to the broken remains of a sign requesting that visitors keep their children under control and a chastened Frank.

And so it went through the floors. Claire dutifully recited her lessons at each stop, accompanied by more and more disruptions from the holy terrors and less and less enthusiasm from the tiring adults. When they finished viewing the eighth floor Claire pressed the button to call the elevator. "Now we're going to the top level and the smallest room in the Memorial, where you'll see an exhibit of the Tall Cedars of Lebanon—"

"You mean there are *trees* up there?" Frank sniggered.

"No, the Cedars is another charitable organization. Like the Grotto or the Shriners—"

"Oh, yeah, the zombies."

Luther shoved his brother. "They ain't! They're

dragons!" Frank bit his arm and while Luther hopped around yowling, asked with a radiant smile, "So, are they *zombie* trees?"

Claire gave up. "Yes." The boys fought each other to the front.

Everyone stuffed themselves onto the elevator. Claire knew she only imagined it got smaller as they went up, but the space seemed much closer. And smellier. She noted aromas of sweat, bubble gum, cheap drugstore perfume, and something else—a nice clean scent. It seemed to come from the Amish family. *Of course—they probably bathe once in a while. Not like Frank and Luther…or their mother.*

"From the top floor we can walk out onto an observation deck, where you'll be treated to a panoramic view of northern Virginia and the District. You'll be able to see clearly how Alexandria was laid out by its founders, as well as important buildings like the Pentagon. Many helicopters traverse these skies, ferrying dignitaries from there to the Capitol or the White House." Claire put a finger out to press the button marked "9," but missed it when the little cell began to shake. As the others grabbed the handrails, she searched frantically for the emergency button. Before she could hit it, the vibration stopped.

Several people gabbled at once. "What the hell was that?"

"Felt like an earthquake!"

"Oh my God!"

"Is this tower earthquake proof?"

The Amish woman burst out, her voice cracking with fright. "Did anyone hear that sound?" Her husband rounded on her, then paused when he saw her face.

"What sound, Jemimah?"

"I…I heard a scream."

Claire opened the doors. "Did it come from this floor?" She peeped out, hoping no one would notice her hands trembling.

"No." The woman touched her husband's arm. "Werner, it came from above us."

The man nodded and pressed the button. "Let's go see."

Silence fell as the elevator grumbled to life and rose. It opened on a small, elegant room paneled in burnished wood. White steps guarded by tiny golden lions led to a replica of King Solomon's throne. All seemed quiet.

"It must have been your imagination, Jemimah."

The woman said nothing but when Werner turned away she raised her eyebrows at Claire as if to say, *I don't think so.*

Claire considered Jemimah. Slim, about five feet tall, her pale skin was free of makeup and her dress obviously homemade, possibly from a discarded checkered tablecloth. Her eyes, however, held a tawny, feline glow. "Mrs.?"

"Kurtz."

"Thank you. Mrs. Kurtz, remember that we're over three hundred feet high. Most likely you heard a seagull's cry. We have many here. They come up the Potomac." Satisfied with the explanation, even if Jemimah wasn't, she continued, "This room is sponsored by the Tall Cedars of Lebanon, another social and charitable group affiliated with the Masons. This exhibit is a reconstruction of Solomon's throne room, as imagined by the Masons." Claire waited for comment, but no one seemed particularly enthralled any more. "Are you ready to go out to the observation platform?"

The atmosphere brightened considerably, and Claire stepped out onto a narrow walkway that circled the tower. The ninety-degree heat gave her a good thwack across the forehead, and she backed up a step, eliciting a colorful oath from Polly. The boys immediately began to climb the scaffolding. For once their mother recognized the need for action and, in a lightning quick gesture, took hold of the seats of both trousers and pulled them back.

Bob and Polly moved to the balustrade. Properly awestruck, they pointed out the various sparkling white monuments in the distance to each other in high, excited voices. Jemimah kept her back sealed to the wall and her eyes closed, grasping her children's hands tightly. Meanwhile Werner walked around to the other side. Claire stood at the door waiting. The wind picked up and blew the damp curls off her face with a loud whooshing sound.

A minute later Kurtz stuck his head around the corner. "Miss Wilding? Could you come here please? Alone?" He made the odd request sound perfectly natural. When Claire joined him, he stopped by a pylon and pointed a long finger at something on the ground. Claire craned her neck around his thin back to see what it was. And screamed.

Kurtz pressed a hand over her mouth. "Be quiet, you fool!"

Claire struggled, finally wrenching the hand away. She couldn't take her eyes off the thing on the ground. *Dead. It's…he's dead.* She opened her mouth to scream again but paused when she saw Kurtz's face. It was distorted with fury, and terror twisted her lungs into a double helix. *He killed that man. He's going to kill me.*

When she took a step back, he pinioned her arms. "Stop," he hissed. "Wait." Something in his voice made her obey. He whispered, "The killer might still be here. We don't want to alarm him. Or the women." Claire nodded feebly. He pointed behind her. "You go that way. I'll go around the other way. Check above you."

She did as she was told. Nobody seemed to be hanging from the rafters or clinging to the flame-shaped finial. A helicopter whirred a short distance away, painted in camouflage colors. As she came around the south side Frank and Luther attempted to pass her. She spread her arms wide. "Sorry, boys. The other side is closed for maintenance."

They met up with the group by the door. Werner shooed them all in and pressed the ground floor button. The elevator stopped only once on the sixth floor. A little man with the expression of a cornered rabbit got on. He didn't make eye contact with anyone, and no one seemed in the mood to chat. He departed at the main level, and the rest went on to the ground floor. Werner sent his brood off to the bathroom and turned to Claire. "Jemimah forgot her hat in one of the exhibits. I'm going back up to get it. You had better call the police."

Polly and Bob were heading toward the stairs to the main entrance when Claire called. "You two—please don't go just yet."

They looked at each other. Bob snapped, "Why shouldn't we? We already paid for the tour."

"I know, but we have a...slight problem. Would

you mind…er…sticking around for a minute?"

Bob shrugged, and they sauntered back. Luther tugged at Claire's sleeve. "Ma'am? Did that man tell you to call the police?"

Kurtz shot Claire a look through his near-white lashes that said, *Don't waste any more time*, and got on the elevator. Claire led the others to the main level and left them in the portico while she walked over as casually as possible to the reception desk. "Nigel, could you please ring up nine-one-one? Thanks."

The tiler, a chubby young man wearing a mustard-colored blazer that didn't suit him, sat reading a copy of the *Washington Examiner*. He looked up. "Excuse me?"

Claire's heart bumped hard against her ribs. "I said, call the police. Now."

He eyed her a moment, then began to dial. Claire turned to the knot of anxious faces. "I'm afraid I have to ask you all to stay."

"Why?" Bob sounded unhappy. Polly shifted her weight from foot to foot, a grimace of pain pasted on her round face.

"Because…because—"

Just then Kurtz materialized and put a hand on her elbow. "Because we have found a dead body in the tower and we have to wait for the police. Any questions?"

His craggy face, immobile as a rock wall, brooked no dissent. It worked well. No one said a word. In the silence Claire heard the faint wailing of a siren.

Chapter Two
A Severed Link

Claire dragged herself up the steps of her townhouse. A day-old newspaper lay on the top step. She opened the door into the tiny hall and slipped on a pile of catalogues left by the mailman, landing hard on her tailbone. Something mewed. Under the stool Claire used as a hall table cowered a small, gray cat. "Sorry, Ichabod." Rubbing her sore bottom, she plopped on the loveseat that took up three-quarters of her living room and swung her feet onto a cardboard box filled with books. The telephone rang.

"Claire! You're finally home. Where have you been?"

"Is that you, Mother? Where are you?"

"I'm in Paris. Didn't I tell you?"

"Uh, no, you didn't. How long will you be there? You promised to help me unpack and decorate."

"I know. That's why I'm here. I saw the loveliest Edsel-Adams online, and I wanted to check it out in person."

"What's an Edsel-Adams?"

"What's an—oh, I forgot you don't keep *au courant* with the latest artistic fashions. Isaac Edsel-Adams is absolutely *in,* my love—he insists on using oils and spits on artists who settle for acrylics. Literally. He actually spits on them. He's very entertaining."

"Sounds rude to me."

"Yes, well, one man's rude is another man's eccentric, I suppose. Anyway, you would like his stuff—very colorful. It will spruce up those drab walls and help guests cope with the lack of seating possibilities."

Claire rolled her eyes, thankful her mother couldn't see her. "I distinctly remember you calling my new place cozy."

"Cozy? What a plebeian word. As always, Claire, I was attempting to be supportive. You should have seen through that."

Claire checked her watch. "Look, Mother, I just got home. I need a drink. I had a very bad day…"

"I see." Inducing guilt in Claire was child's play for her mother, even from the far shore of the Atlantic Ocean. The sweltering August air turned suddenly frosty.

"I'm sorry, but on my first day as docent at the Masonic Temple I really didn't expect to find a corpse."

That shut her up.

Claire heard rapid breathing as her mother absorbed the news. A minute later a suspiciously calm voice said, "I beg your pardon?"

"A body. A dead man. On the observation deck. Actually Werner found him."

"Werner?"

"It's a long story. How about if I fill you in when you come over to help me move in?" *Two can play the guilt game.*

"I'm afraid that's not possible at the moment, dear. I do have my laptop with me. The Georges V has finally condescended to install wi-fi in the hotel, so I should be able to sniff out what's happened. I'll be home in a couple of days."

"I hope so, Mother. I need you here."

"All in good time, dear. All in good time."

"Yes, Mother." Claire replaced the receiver and heaved her aching body out of the seat. She was heading toward the kitchen when the phone rang again. She picked it up and took it with her. Ichabod pranced ahead and sat pointedly facing the back door. She let him out, then, as she dropped ice cubes into a plastic tumbler and searched under the sink for her bottle of Jack Daniels, she clicked Talk. "Hello?"

"Claire? I just got an email from Mother."

"Oh, hi, Edwina."

"What the hell's going on? She wrote something about a corpse?"

Claire took a long swallow of her whiskey to stall for time. "Okay, here's the thing. We discovered a dead man in the Masonic Temple, on the ninth floor. I mean on the observation platform. I called the police. They came. They took statements from everyone in my group—"

"Group? As in tour group? Oh my God, this was your first day as docent, wasn't it?"

"Yes."

Her sister clucked. "Go on."

"We had to go back up with them—"

"Them?"

"The police. And the criminal investigation people. To show them the…the…thing." Claire closed her eyes, remembering the awful sight—worse, if anything, the second time.

"How did he die? Heart attack?"

"I don't think so. He looked all—bent. Like most of his bones were broken."

"That's very strange. Who was he?"

"No idea. The only other witness, an Amish man, said he'd never seen him before either. When they let us go they still hadn't made an identification."

"Did you get a good look at him?"

Claire had a vision of a swarthy face and polyester-covered body twisted like a pretzel. "Too good."

"Ack—sorry!" Edwina paused. "Had he been there long?"

"How would I know?"

"Yes, yes, you're right." Edwina always knew when to back off. *Not like Mother.* "Did they at least promise to keep you informed?"

"They didn't say. Right now I don't care."

"Okay, I understand." Edwina paused and Claire heard her shuffling pages. "Are we still on for lunch tomorrow?"

"Yes, I'll meet you at Pizza Paradiso at one, all right?"

"Perfect. Get some rest." Edwina rang off.

Claire poured herself another drink and went upstairs to her minuscule study. It looked out over a garden about five feet square—quite a change from the sprawling Potomac estate where she'd lived with Lincoln. *At least this house will be easier to clean.* Certainly not easier to entertain in, but then she didn't expect to throw any more parties, despite her mother's decorating plans. She touched the tiny gold vial she wore around her neck, all that remained of her husband. *Three years.* She'd had twelve idyllic months with him before the disease spread three and a half years ago and could no longer be denied. She scowled to scare off the grief and turned on her laptop. *Three years alone is long enough. Mother's right, I have to move on.*

While she waited for the computer to boot, she unclasped the locket and set it on the desk. She regarded it for a long moment, then, taking a small Italian leather box from the drawer, she laid it gently inside and put the box back in the drawer. A slight movement caught her eye. In the garden below, Ichabod crouched, his eyes glued to a black squirrel. Her grandmother had always said black squirrels were good luck, so she knocked hard on the window to break his concentration. Oblivious, Ichabod charged. The squirrel scampered over the fence, its tail slashing arrogantly, unconcerned. Equally blasé, if not as honestly, Ichabod licked a paw and stalked toward the house.

The little cat had condescended to accompany her to her new place. He'd shown up one night about a month after Linc died and gradually insinuated himself into the household. Six months later she found she couldn't sleep unless he lay curled at the foot of her bed. His tawny eyes reminded her of Lincoln's, soothing her in those hours when her sorrow threatened to overwhelm. Day after day he lay purring next to her, nursing her back to health. It took two years before she was ready to leave the home she and Lincoln had made together. A year after that she found this doll's house in Old Town. Watching Ichabod, a stillness descended upon her. The fan whirred slowly in the background, cooling her temples, wafting the moisture-laden heat away. *Something's changed.* She breathed out, letting her body go limp. *I've been freed.*

She felt around for her heart and found it beating

calmly right where it belonged. *Linc's given it back to me.*

Heaving a tranquil sigh, she clicked on Drudge Report and scanned the news headlines. Nothing on a dead body in Alexandria. She searched the major news outlets. Apparently the only corpse of note was that of a freakish sea creature washed up on the coast of Australia. The local *Patch* newspaper mentioned a disturbance at the Masonic Memorial but provided no details. She looked out the window and visualized the man as she'd first seen him. Greasy black hair a tad too long, his olive complexion and large nose reminded her of Al Pacino or maybe one of the Sopranos. He wore a gray suit shiny with age. The cuffs of his white shirt were frayed and his shoes scuffed. His eyes were closed, and he lay in an awkward position as though he'd simply crumpled in place.

The police detective, a Lieutenant Angle, had asked her a few questions—if she knew the victim, if she'd noticed anything out of the ordinary—*you mean, other than a bloody corpse?*—if she knew the other witness, Werner Kurtz. Apart from the elevator shaking, she had nothing to tell. She couldn't confirm the scream Mrs. Kurtz claimed to have heard.

"We'll probably need to follow up with you after the preliminary interviews, Miss Wilding. Would that be acceptable?" The man's soft gray eyes had held her gaze. About forty-five, he was still thin as a pole with no hint of body fat. A thatch of unruly mouse-brown hair stood straight up, no doubt due to his habit of running his fingers through it at frequent intervals.

"It's *Mrs.* Wilding."

He drew on his glasses and checked his notebook.

"Oops, sorry. My sergeant wrote down 'unmarried.' I apologize."

"No, that is accurate—I'm a widow."

"Ah." He wrote something down.

When he looked up again, Claire had made out the vestiges of a relieved smile. With a sinking heart she had recognized the initial stages of attraction. *Oh dear.*

Claire woke up from her reverie to find a blank screen staring at her. *Who was the dead man? What was he doing there?* Impatience frayed what was left of her nerves—after all, a man died on her watch. It seemed unfair not to be kept informed of the status of the investigation. She pulled out her cell phone. "Mr. Quinn? Yes, yes, I'm fine. I was wondering if you could use me tomorrow. Yes? Great…What? Oh, I'm thinking, jump right back on the horse, you know…Yes. I'll be there at ten. Thanks, Mr. Quinn…Say, did you hear any more about the victim?…No? Oh, they made you leave as well. I see."

Damn. Well, at least she'd be on the scene tomorrow. There was bound to be someone dumb enough to tell her something.

****

Bill Overbrook, the junior warden, halted when he saw Claire and dropped the book he'd been carrying. "Oh, Mrs. Wilding, Peter didn't mention you were coming in today." He seemed at a loss. "It's been so crazy these last couple of days, what with the police and all…" He trailed off, apparently unaware of Claire's role in the affair.

"Please call me Claire, Mr. Overbrook."

"What? Oh, certainly." He stopped, lost in thought. Finally, he barked, "And you may call me Bill. Now, you're aware of the…of the unfortunate situation we're in? That we had a death here?"

"Yes, Bill. I was here. Have there been any new developments?" *Might as well ask.*

He shook his head. Claire noticed the movement had absolutely no effect on his neatly combed hair. *Toupee? Motor oil?*

"They haven't told us anything. That is, except that we can't hold any events until they finish gathering evidence." His eyes grew moist. "We have a lodge meeting coming up next week. I do hope the brothers will understand." He nodded to himself, the woman standing before him forgotten. "Oh, and what about the organ concert scheduled for Saturday? They could refuse to let it go on! The Grand Lodge of New Jersey—I mean *all* the Chairs—will be here and they'll be expecting to hear the fifty-thousand-dollar organ they donated. Oh dear, oh dear." He wandered off down the hall, bumping into a column before veering toward his office. Claire heard him muttering, "I don't know what the Master will do. I just don't know. Don't know…"

A uniformed policeman approached as Claire stood uncertainly in the hall. "Mrs. Wilding? Mr. Quinn said you'd be in today. Lieutenant Angle would like to have a word. Would you come with me please?"

Claire tried to keep her voice from quivering with excitement. "Of course. Lead on, McDuff."

The cop eyed her. "It's McDowell, ma'am. Not McDuff."

"Er, yes." At the elevator she hung back. "I don't have to…to…"

"Go up to the crime scene? No, ma'am. Detective

Angle is conducting interviews in the library. Overbrook said we wouldn't be disturbed there since the librarian is off today."

Claire didn't have time to wonder why McDowell described the observation deck as a crime scene before the elevator stopped at the fourth level. The doors opened to reveal the fellow she'd accosted in the museum the day before. He smiled at her, a shaft of fluorescent light pinging off his perfect teeth. Today he wore an open-collared Brooks Brothers shirt and jeans, barely concealing an award-winning swimmer's physique. He hadn't shaved since their last encounter. Tucked under his arm Claire saw a thick, leather-bound volume. "Well, hello," he said. "Nice to see you again. Going up?"

The policeman made room for him. "Would you mind letting Mrs. Wilding here see the lieutenant first, Mr. Bliss?"

"Not at all." He held up the book. "I've got plenty to keep me busy."

They got off at the sixth floor. McDowell indicated a bench and Bliss and Claire sat down. The policeman went through the door marked *Library—By Appointment Only* and closed it carefully behind him.

"I hear you had an incident here yesterday." Bliss's tone was casual, but Claire noticed his knuckles shone white against the book's spine.

"Yes."

"I must have missed it."

"Really?" *You missed twenty cops spread out in the building searching for clues? You missed the eight cruisers and the ambulance?* "Why are you here, then?"

He cocked his head at the door. "I gather they want to know if I saw anything unusual, but I left early yesterday. I've been so engrossed in my research I didn't hear what had happened until a policeman showed up this morning in the museum. He told me a corpse had been discovered on the top floor."

"That was me."

He looked her over with an appreciative grin. "Funny, you look way too chipper to be dead."

"I mean, I found the body."

"Ah." He put the book down and leaned toward her. His slight tan lent a fulvous glow to his cheekbones. She caught a whiff of lime and something aromatic...*bay*? He gazed into her eyes. "Tell me about it."

It wasn't hard to confide the whole story. He listened gravely. When she'd finished, he laid a large hand over hers. "Miss Wilding..."

The door opened and McDowell nodded at Claire. "Detective Angle is ready for you, Mrs. Wilding."

She stood. Bliss touched her elbow. "Mrs.?"

For once Claire was happy to explain. "I'm a widow."

"Ah. May I see you again?"

The simple request could not be refused.

****

"There you are. I couldn't see you way back here. I've been standing out on King Street waiting for you for ten minutes." Edwina drew Claire to a stand and hugged her. "How are you holding up?"

Claire extricated herself from her sister and the aroma of chocolate fudge that always hung about her. Edwina had inherited their grandfather's sweet tooth, not to mention his ample girth. To Claire he had bequeathed her thick russet curls and cerulean eyes as well as a Calvinist guilt complex and a tendency to argue. She signaled the waiter. "It's not been easy. The junior warden is in a state of near panic and the police—"

Edwina put a finger to her lips as a young man with heavily tattooed arms approached. "Hey there, I'm Joey, your devilishly handsome server." He grinned. "What'll it be, ladies?" He distributed their menus.

Claire looked it over. "What's this 'cask' ale, Joey?"

"The Oskar Blues? It's...well...let me get you a taste." He went off, ignoring the outraged look on Edwina's face.

"He didn't take my order! I'm dying here."

"Relax, Eddie. Here he comes." The waiter set a shot glass before Claire. She took a sip. "*Mmm.* What gives it that slightly bitter aftertaste?"

"It's mainly from the hops, ma'am. Aging the ale in a wooden barrel also gives it an oaky flavor." He grew animated. "Cask ale is actually a living ale—it goes through a secondary fermentation and then we tap it directly from the barrel. It's unfiltered and pure—*real* beer."

Claire blew out her cheeks. "So I've been drinking imitation stuff all these years? Who knew? I'd better have a mug. Edwina?"

"Iced tea. Unsweetened." Joey headed toward the bar and Edwina leaned across the table, eyes alight. "All right, spill. Who's the dead guy?"

Her sister made a pretense of studying the menu.

"Dead? Guy? Who?" Edwina prompted.

Claire gave in. "They don't know yet. He had no identification on him."

"*Hmm*." Joey arrived with the drinks. "Let's order first. I'll have the onion soup and a small salad." He wrote it down and looked expectantly at Claire.

"I think the Hungry Man special—that's the double hamburger with blue cheese, right? It comes with fries and coleslaw, right?"

"Right." He winked. "Will you be wanting the banana split served at the same time?"

"Ha ha, Joey. You're a card. Maybe later. Bring me another Oskar's with the meal, would you?"

Edwina opened a packet of saltines and carefully broke one in half. Claire watched her, an amused smile playing on her lips. "Don't think you're fooling me with that 'small salad' crap, Eddie. I happen to know you have most of a twelve-by-fourteen sheet cake at home. Not to mention the tub of Rocky Road."

Her sister ignored her. Chewing thoughtfully on the cracker, she said, "What did he look like? The dead man?"

Claire frowned. "He looked, well…shabby. Old, worn clothes and shoes. Unshaven. I'm thinking maybe he was a homeless guy who snuck in."

"Homeless? How would he get all the way up to the ninth floor without someone stopping him? And why would he bother?"

"How would I know?"

"And"—her sister picked up the other half of the cracker—"that doesn't solve the main mystery. How did he die? If he was murdered, who killed him? There had to have been a second man somewhere. You're sure you didn't see anyone?"

Claire, in the midst of a large gulp of ale, choked. "Murder? Who said anything about murder?"

"It was all over the news. 'Man Found Dead Atop Mysterious Masonic Tower!' 'Ritual Murder Suspected.' 'Masons Mum on Memorial Massacre!' They're having a field day."

"That is so totally untrue." Claire's newfound loyalty to freemasonry surged. "And so prejudiced. The Masons don't have any such thing as ritual murder. It's ridiculous."

"Are you saying the guy wasn't murdered?"

"Well…"

Joey brought their meals. As Claire poured ketchup and Tabasco sauce over her fries, Edwina sipped her tea. "If he wasn't murdered, what did the police want from you?"

"Lieutenant Angle wanted me to go over what I saw one more time." Claire glanced at her sister and lowered her voice. "He asked me to keep it quiet, but the papers have it half right. The man was beaten to a pulp and shot."

"Shot? So…it *was* murder then."

Claire couldn't help herself. "You don't suppose having all his bones broken did the trick?"

Edwina had seen every episode of every CSI show, including the spinoffs, and fancied herself more than an amateur sleuth. "Doesn't matter what I think—the killer must have believed a deathblow was required. Or he's crazy. Maybe a serial killer…" She lapsed into happy thoughts of murderous rampages and dramatic collars.

"Edwina? Your soup's getting cold."

Her sister shook herself, sat up and, tipping her bowl, took a dainty spoonful of the rich, brown liquid.

"Did the detective ask about a second man?"

Claire shook her head. "No. I didn't see anyone anyway." She bit into her cheeseburger. "Maybe Gideon saw something."

Edwina stopped with her glass halfway to her lips. "Gideon?"

Oops. "Do not—I repeat—do *not* tell Mother. I met a man."

"Gideon. Great name. What does he do?"

"Funny, he didn't say. He's working in the museum at the temple—you know, the George Washington room?"

"He must be an archivist or professor or something. What's his last name?"

"Bliss."

"Sounds like an ice cream flavor." Edwina plunged her spoon down through the thick cheese layer in the little brown crock, and retrieved a ladleful of onions. "Wait a minute. *Gideon* Bliss? The senator?"

Claire dropped her burger and the insides spewed out all over the plate. "Senator? A United States senator? Are you sure? How come I've never heard of him?"

Edwina jiggled the ice in her empty glass at Joey, who trotted over and refilled it. "I guess you haven't been following the news much since Linc died. You do remember that Charles Mather, the junior senator from Connecticut, was expelled for decamping with Senator McNichol's wife last year?"

"Of course I do. It's just the kind of juicy scandal Washington loves. The media dogs gnawed at it twenty-four-seven, successfully suppressing the news that their beloved president had ordered the IRS to harass her political opponents."

"I'd forgotten about that—didn't she send armed agents to confiscate the Cardinal's sacramental wine, claiming he was dispensing alcohol without a license?" Edwina tittered. "She met her match in Cardinal O'Reilly, didn't she? He converted all ten agents to Catholicism, and got them to testify before Congress about the president's abuse of power."

"Meanwhile, in a brilliant feat of investigative journalism, the *Washington Tribune* unearthed Mather's high school sweetheart and Beth McNichol's nanny and got *exclusive* interviews with them."

"So you remember that much. Well, Gideon Bliss won a special election to fill Mather's seat." She stared dreamily into her bowl. "He's supposed to be a real hunk."

Claire grabbed the picture tubing down the river of her mind of a rugged face and white teeth, a lock of espresso-colored hair dribbling becomingly across his forehead, and brought it down to center stage to admire. "If it's the same guy, yes, yes, he is."

"And you have a date with him?" Edwina's eyes were searching.

"Tomorrow night."

"Good. It's about time you got out. Maybe you can find out what Mystery Man's hiding while you're at it."

"Hiding?"

Edwina finished her salad and took a sip of tea. "According to local gossip, he lives alone in this huge house in Old Town. Never goes to parties. All his charitable donations—of which there are many—are made anonymously. They say half the house is filled with books."

"Doesn't sound like a politician to me."

"Right. His opponent tried to make something of that during the campaign—that Bliss wasn't 'likable.' You know, not the kind of guy you'd want to have a beer with."

"So how did he win?"

"Are you kidding? You've seen him! Plus, he has oodles and oodles of money."

"Ah."

"Once he started doling out free champagne at every rally, he won in a landslide. His slogan was 'New Englanders Deserve Better Than Bud.' "

"Didn't he get in trouble with the Budweiser folks for that?"

"Nah. Free publicity. Besides, his opponent's name was Bud. Bud Turlew."

Claire laughed. "So he has a sense of humor. That's a surprise. He seemed so serious this morning."

Edwina called for the check. "Well, you hardly met him under circumstances where jokes would be appropriate."

"I guess. We'll see tomorrow night."

Edwina picked up her purse. "I'm going to the ladies' room. Say, how come the police were questioning him about the murder? Didn't you say he was in the museum?"

Claire blinked. "I don't know. It's probably routine."

"You might want to ask him…or them."

Chapter Three
Linking Up

"Look, here comes the *Cherry Blossom*. Must be a wedding party or something." Gideon pointed at the sternwheeler as it inched slowly toward the dock. Lights twinkled fore and aft, and people on the upper deck leaned over the railings heckling the guests dancing below and dropping things on them.

"An August wedding? A bit warm for that, but she's probably booked up during the graduation season." Claire leaned back into the shelter of Gideon's arm and squirmed on the hard bench.

Gideon looked down at her and touched an auburn curl. "You cold?"

"A little," she lied.

"Looks like the Chart House is still open. Would you like a nightcap?"

Claire, who at that point would have jumped at any excuse to prolong the date, chirped, "Sure."

As they walked the few feet from the pier up the winding steps to the restaurant, she reflected on the evening. She couldn't exactly remember what they talked about, or what she ate, but the adjectives swimming around in her head included intoxicating and delicious. And awesome. Gideon seemed complex and unsettling, but she couldn't have pinpointed what he did to give her that impression. His rich baritone scudded across her brainwaves, for all she knew declaiming poetry. He reminded her of Alfred Noyes' "The Highwayman," a poem she'd memorized as a drama queen of thirteen.

> *The wind was a torrent of darkness*
> *among the gusty trees,*
> *The moon was a ghostly galleon,*
> *tossed upon cloudy seas.*
> *The Road was a ribbon of moonlight,*
> *over the purple moor,*
> *When the highwayman came*
> *riding, riding, riding,*
> *The highwayman came riding*
> *up to the old inn door.*
> *He'd a French cocked hat on his forehead*
> *a bunch of lace at his chin,*
> *A coat of the claret velvet,*
> *and breeches of brown doeskin.*
> *They fitted with never a wrinkle*
> *His boots were up to the thigh,*
> *And he rode with a jeweled twinkle*
> *his pistol butts a-twinkle*
> *His rapier hilt a-twinkle,*
> *under the jeweled sky.*

She could just see Gideon in red velvet and lace, tapping his whip. *Thigh-high boots and breeches. Gulp.*

"Stop!"

She opened her eyes to find Gideon's hand the only thing protecting her nose from her cheesecake. "*Urp.*"

"Claire, you're falling asleep. I think it's time I took you home."

She made a plucky effort to turn humiliation into self-deprecating laughter, but knew she had failed when

Gideon stood up without looking at her. He said nothing on the way home, the only sound the slight and incongruous beep of the GPS unit on the dashboard. In an effort to distract herself, she checked out the car. Long, sleek, and crimson, it hugged the road like a child hugs his teddy bear. Gideon had told her it was a McLaren 12C Spider—a car only the very few could appreciate, let alone afford. With a top speed of 204 miles per hour, it could go from zero to sixty in three seconds. Plus it had a really cool retractable hard top. She'd said it felt like riding in the space shuttle.

When they reached Prince Street, Gideon found a parking spot directly in front of her house, no small feat. *Just one more way he's special,* thought Claire glumly. He walked her to her door. She unlocked it and turned to thank him, but he was already on his way to his car.

Ichabod greeted her with a snarl.

"I know. I forgot to feed you. Come on, Icky." She found a can of cat food and emptied it into his bowl. Then she poured herself a large glass of water and took it to the living room to conduct an analysis of the soiree.

So at any point did I come across as even semi-coherent? She tried to hack through the warm, fuzzy blanket of the evening. Gideon had been the perfect gentleman, ordering foie gras and champagne, pointing out the constellations with obvious expertise, helping her in and out of the car. It all seemed so…unreal. *Like he was acting a part. Too perfect.* And he'd sucked her in like soda through a straw. She slapped her forehead, forgetting that she still held the glass. Water sluiced across her face and ran down her front. She mopped it up with some tissues and vowed to hit the antique stores that weekend. *I've got to get a coffee table. Preferably one with cup holders.*

The doorbell rang. With the disintegrating tissue pressed to her face, she stood on tiptoe to check the peephole and looked straight into an unblinking sea-green ocean. *Gideon.* After a minute she remembered to open the door.

He stared at her with concern. "Are you all right?"

Claire pulled the tissue away and noticed black streaks on it. Her mascara must have run. *Oh no, I bet he thinks I've been crying.* She rubbed her eyes, hoping that wasn't making it worse. "Fine. I spilled a glass of water, that's all."

"Oh." He stood, shifting his weight from one foot to the other. "Um, could I come in for a minute?"

She pointed at the living room and backed away, then turned and leapt up the steps. A quick look in the mirror confirmed her suspicions. *I look like something Ichabod's been playing with.* She fixed her face, wrung out her blouse, and returned with renewed aplomb.

Gideon filled the small space. Claire sidled around him and sat on a packing crate. He looked around the room. "So…er, have you just moved in?"

"Yes." It struck her that he was more uncomfortable than she and drew strength from that. "About a week ago. Sorry about the mess. Won't you have a seat?"

He dropped down on the loveseat but immediately sprang back up. He patted his rear, flummoxed. "Why am I wet?"

Claire put a hand to her mouth to suppress the giggle. "Ooh, I'm sorry. I forgot. That's where I spilled the water. Here, let me."

She retrieved a towel from the kitchen and began to dab at the dark blotch on his khakis. He stood it for a minute, then put a hand under her chin and lifted her up. "You'd better stop doing that. This is hard enough for me." He blinked. "Do you...do you know how beautiful you are?"

The question threw her. How to respond? *Yes? No? Tell me more?* She decided to let him talk.

"Your eyes are the color of the deepest part of the Caribbean Sea on a cloudless day. I could sink into them and drown." He touched her brow. "And these little cinnabar ringlets framing that soft, creamy face..." He wrapped one around his finger. "Wind one up tight and it could strangle me." He took her hand. "Your fingers—so slim and delicate, like little stilettos. Sharp enough to gouge an eye out."

Claire stepped away from him, bewildered. "You make me sound like a vicious animal. Why?"

His hands dropped to his sides. "Because I sense how dangerous you are."

"Dangerous?"

"To me. Claire...I—" He gazed at her helplessly.

Someone had better take charge. "Come with me."

"What?" He seemed distracted—*perhaps working out another ghoulish metaphor?*

"I want to show you something."

"Okay."

Gideon let her take his hand and lead him upstairs. Since he had to duck his head to avoid hitting the lintel of the miniature door, he missed the part where Claire stripped off her skirt and blouse and tossed them aside. She stood before him, a translucent blue lace bra and panties the only thing between her and the touch of his fingers on her tingling skin.

He gazed at her, perfectly still and silent.

Claire waited as long as she could, then gently unbuttoned his shirt. She unbuckled his belt and pulled the chinos down, When she reached his socks, Gideon pulled her up. "I see where this is going."

She arched an eyebrow. "Would you like to help?"

He ran his hands over her shoulders, down to her waist, then around to her ass. "You haven't left me much to do."

"Only the best part."

He sighed. "I knew it would come to this." A minute later Claire's last line of fabric defense lay in tatters, Gideon's shoes, socks, pants, and assorted other items lay strewn about the room, and the two of them were locked in a frantic embrace, limbs intertwined in a complex filigree pattern. Claire's desire exploded, shattering the cloistered walls built up over three long, empty years, years without the feel of a man's hard body, of his hands, of his penis. She lapped him up, reveling in the joy of uninhibited pleasure, banishing all rational thought. Gideon made her feel both delicate and wanton. Whatever he had feared must have lost its power, for he was not shy in his efforts to bring her to the edge. When his fingers and his lips had finished their work, his cock slid slowly and inexorably inside, nudging her to orgasm. Like Sisyphus pushing the boulder up the hill, Gideon drove her steadily to the tipping point, his eyes locked on hers, his hips rocking, lifting her, goading her, until she fell, rolling joyously back down, taking him with her.

A while later she stirred and tried to roll over.

"Um."

"Um?"

"You're lying on my thumb. It's twisted."

"Oh, sorry, I'll get up."

"No, no, don't. Just move one inch…there."

"What are you doing? Gideon!"

"Me? My thumb found this lovely opening. I'm inserting it. Just to stretch it out."

"*Mmm.*"

"Does that feel better?"

"*Mmm.*"

"I think I'll just…yes, now that finger can stretch out too. Ah." Three fingers began sliding in and out, palpating Claire's quivering flesh. She arched her back and rose off the bed to allow him greater access. Gideon laughed softly. "I'm glad to see you're getting into the spirit of my calisthenics program."

With his other hand, Gideon pushed her onto her side. His fingers pulled out, leaving her vagina gurgling. "Other parts of me need some exercise too though." Before she could speak, his head plunged down and a rough tongue took up where the fingers had left off. She opened her thighs wide and pushed his head down. His lips rode hers, licking and sucking.

A tide rose in her, rolling over his mouth like waves on a beach. She held his head tight, wanting to swallow him whole. "I'm coming. Oh God, I'm coming." Her hands flew up in the air, and she surrendered, her body taking control.

As she rested on the down slope, Gideon crawled up her thighs and over her stomach, stopping to nip her breasts, circling the nipples with his tongue. His penis pulsed against her leg. She touched it. "I suppose there are still more parts of you that could use a workout?"

"As a matter of fact…"

****

She woke to his fingers caressing her cheek. She reciprocated. "Now do you believe I'm not some rabid Medusa ready to strangle you?"

He rolled on his back. "I'll concede. No silken garrote, no nails raking my back, no thumbs pressing on my windpipe. I would say, definitely an enjoyable experience. Which I wish we hadn't had."

Claire sat up, pulling the sheet under her chin. Setting aside the sting of his words, she asked, "Why?"

He kissed her nose. "Because, sweet thing, I promised."

"Promised? Promised who?" She jumped up, pulling the sheet with her, launching Gideon onto the floor.

"Ouch!" He got up, ripped the sheet from her hands, and wrapped it around his middle. Lying back down on the bed, he said, "If you come back, I'll tell you."

Goosebumps erupting under the cool breeze from the ceiling fan, she mustered the last dollop of dignity and said, "I prefer to stand."

"All right." He pulled the pillows under his head and let his gaze linger on her breasts. "Nice view, I must say."

She sat. "Promised who? Oh my God, you're married!" Disappointment quickly superseded the guilt, begetting more guilt.

"Married? No, no. Well…sort of. You see, I…uh, promised my mother."

"Your *mother*?" Claire looked him over. Judging

by the laugh lines and the slivers of silver in his hair, he had to be at least forty. "Aren't you a little old to be in thrall to your mother?"

"Hey, no trash-talking my mum, if you don't mind. It's just that, she's in Paris and—"

"Paris? That's strange."

"Why? It's a perfectly ordinary city…well, I mean, it's not like she's traipsing around Thimphu or something. Not *strange.*"

Claire toyed with the idea of pretending she understood this little cognitive detour but doubted it would ring true. "Thimphu?"

Gideon had lapsed into thought. "It's just that…it's just…"

"One thing at a time, Gideon. Thimphu?"

He closed his eyes and muttered, "Capital of Bhutan. I know the capital of every country in the world."

Curiouser and curiouser.

He roused himself. "Where was I?"

"You promised your mother. Or did you first want to expound on the origin of this fascinating feature of your portfolio? Say, you could use it as a pickup line. Bring it up casually in conversation, something like"—she trilled—" 'I'll bet you a beer I can tell you the capital of Sarawak, pretty lady. You game?' "

He threw a pillow at her. When Claire picked it up from the floor she noticed two yellow eyes shining under the bed. "Ichabod? Have you been there all this time?"

For answer the cat made a beeline for the door. Claire threw the pillow at the man lying splayed on the bed, hoping to hit a sensitive part. Instead he rose and began searching under the piles of discarded clothes. "Aha." He lifted up a pair of khaki trousers and began to pull them on. "I'm serious, Claire. We shouldn't have done this. I shouldn't have, anyway."

Not having anything to say in response, she took her bathrobe from its hook and tied it on, wishing it were a silk peignoir instead of a ratty pink fleece wraparound with holes in the elbows. "I'll make some coffee."

She had bagels and cream cheese and a bowl of sliced kiwis and blueberries on the counter when he came down. He looked around for a chair. She pulled a folding stool from the closet. "I haven't had a chance to shop for furniture yet."

"I'm fine." He took a bite of bagel and chewed thoughtfully. "Thanks, this hits the spot."

Claire poured him a mug of coffee. "You were explaining?"

He sighed heavily. "Mother is in Paris, getting Dorcas to sign the papers, and she made me promise not to…you know…until the divorce is final."

Claire immediately understood. "Not even casual?"

He contemplated her, his face grave. The gold flecks flickering in his chrysolite eyes reminded her of a stalking jaguar. "We're not talking about casual, are we?"

The question hung in the air, but she couldn't bring herself to answer. *Not yet.* Instead she passed the bowl of fruit to him. "Tell me about Dorcas."

"Dorcas? Ah, how to describe her? She is…a troublesome woman."

Claire sipped her coffee. "Let me guess. She left you, then changed her mind. By that time you'd moved on, but she clung to the love you once had, stringing out the separation as long as possible."

He put down his bagel. "Right on the money. I guess it's not such an original story after all. Anyway, she won't deal with me, so Mother volunteered to go to Paris to try to talk some sense into her. Dorcas has thrown every spatula into the works—"

"Spanner."

"That too. She's used every tool at her command to gum up the business. Mother fears if I met someone— had a relationship—that she'd twist that around and use it as another excuse to deny me my freedom. So I promised."

Claire thought of a locket and a dream cut short. Only yesterday she'd been at peace. Now her heart clunked against her ribs in a fair imitation of dread. She'd only known this man some forty-eight hours, but already he'd squeezed his way into her affections. She rose and put her mug in the sink.

"You should have told me."

"I tried." His lips twisted. "What can I say? You overpowered me. I did state you were dangerous, didn't I?"

To hide the sudden pain in her eyes she bustled around as best she could in the tiny space. "Well, we can't undo last night, but we can forget it ever happened. You'd better go."

"But…" His shoulders sagged. "Okay." He held out a hand. "Friends though, right?"

Slowly she moved toward him. As her fingers reached out to shake his hand, he pitched forward and caught her lips with his. Her arms went around his neck, and he held her in a desperate grip. They broke apart. He didn't say a word but pivoted and sprinted out the door. She heard an engine start up.

****

"You're telling me you never got around to asking him why the police interviewed him? Wasn't that the whole point of accepting the date?" Edwina's accusing eyes raked her sister.

Claire signaled to the bartender. He sauntered over and leaned on the bar. "Another JD, Claire?"

"Thanks." She knew Edwina would eventually worm the evening's events out of her, but saw no reason to expedite the process. "We talked about a lot of stuff. We just never got around to that topic."

"Excuse me?" Her companion's tone crackled with skepticism. "You're a witness to a murder, and it doesn't come up in the conversation?"

"I wasn't a witness, Edwina. The man was dead when we found him. And Gideon didn't even know about it until the next morning."

The glass missed her sister's mouth by a millimeter, allowing a thread of water to course down her chin. She wiped it away impatiently. "He told you that? And you believed him?"

Claire refused to encourage Edwina's penchant for theatrics. "The police haven't declared it a murder yet. Nor have they identified the man, so at this point Lieutenant Angle says they're acting on the theory that he was a bum and maybe died of exposure."

"Leaving aside the obvious fact that it's impossible to die of exposure in Washington in August, didn't you tell me he'd been shot?"

Oops. "I...I forgot about that. Still, it could have been a robbery. See, he'd made his way up to the observation platform, and while he was sleeping some creep stole his wallet. And shot him when he resisted."

"Resisted while asleep? And then where did the thief go? There's only one entrance to the observation deck. You would have seen him."

"Not necessarily. He could have snuck out while we were in the Cedars exhibit and taken the other elevator down."

Edwina put her glass down. "I've been in the Cedars room, Claire. I know how small it is. Do you really think a strange man could have waltzed in from the observation deck waving a firearm, called the elevator, and gone down while you were there? With a group of—how many?"

Claire counted on her fingers. "Nine. Maybe he did it when we were on the eighth floor."

Edwina was relentless. "You told me that Amish woman heard a scream when you were in the elevator on the way to the ninth floor. That had to be when the guy was killed. The murderer would have had to come in from the observation deck, call the other elevator, and jump on it before you arrived on the ninth floor. Unless you're postulating that the killer himself screamed?"

Claire downed her whiskey. "My own sister, I love you dearly, but enough. This is in the hands of the police now. They'll deal with it."

"Okay, okay. But if we're only talking about a mugging, why did they want to talk to your Gideon?" Edwina did not attempt to keep the triumph out of her voice.

Claire stood up, threw a twenty on the bar, and retrieved her purse. "I don't know. I've got to go—I have some studying to do. If you solve the crime, give Detective Angle a call. I'm sure he'll listen to you."

She saved the grin until she reached her car. She'd kept Edwina on the murder long enough to avoid talking about her dalliance with Gideon. *I outfoxed her this time.* Until this divorce thing was straightened out she didn't need any advice other than what she'd already given herself: *Forget him.*

****

"Thanks, Boris." Claire tipped the pizza delivery boy and took her prize back to the living room where the television blared. It being August and Congress in recess, the local news station had no choice but to obsess on the mystery.

"The police still have no leads in the case, Colin." The reporter tossed back her Jennifer Aniston hairdo and continued with barely disguised scorn. "Some in the community are calling for the FBI to take over— someone *professional* who can handle a case of this complexity."

Colin, as sleek and tan as only a weekend on Aruba could make him, slipped on his "more to be pitied than censured" face. "In fairness, Shannon, it's only been five days. Chief Martingale may not have the strongest track record in solving homicides, but let's give him a break—this one's a doozy. Have they identified the body yet?"

"No, although they're guessing he's a foreigner."

"On what basis?"

"Detective Angle states his clothes were…let me see here…" She licked a fuchsia lip and turned a page. "Yes. They were made in Peru. Although I don't know why that would mean anything. Aren't most of our clothes manufactured in third-world countries nowadays?" She plucked at the low-cut dress the studio insisted she wear. "In those horrid sweat shops?"

After making sure the Made in Thailand label was tucked inside his tie, Colin ginned up a nugget of righteous indignation over the evils of cheap foreign labor. "They had better not be, Shannon. That would be outrageous." When Shannon shuffled uncertainly before the camera, he changed course. "Did the detective clarify the purpose of Senator Bliss's presence? We know he's been assigned to the Homeland Security Committee. Could he be involved in the investigation?"

Shannon jumped at the chance to entangle a celebrity in the scandal. "The police claim he just 'happened to be in the temple' and had no connection to the events there." She produced a knowing smile. "But then they would say that, wouldn't they?"

Colin shrugged. Claire wondered if his brain was too busy dwelling on important stuff—like if his roots were showing—to have enough brain cells left to deal with actual news. "Well, keep us posted of any developments. Thank you, Shannon." He swung around to face Camera Two. "And now to the weather…"

Claire shut the television off and went back to the book on freemasonry Harry had sold her. The origins of the order were lost in the Middle Ages, although theories, both incriminating and laudatory, abounded. At some point the "operative" masons—the men who actually worked with stone—were subsumed by the "speculative" masons—prominent businessmen and politicians who gradually turned the organization from a guild into a social and philanthropic enterprise.

Because their rituals were secret, the Masons were dogged by allegations of Satanism and bizarre rites, but as far as Claire could tell only those little cars the Shriners drove in parades were truly weird. The more she read, the more the myths dropped away.

As to the organizational structure, it was simple but a bit obscure. The broadest division lay between the Grand Lodges—based in the United Kingdom and the United States—and the Grand Orient—based in Europe. There seemed to be low-voltage but continual tension between the two groups. The book talked about "irregular" and "regular" lodges. Claire resolved to ask Mr. Quinn. She had to be careful not to offend though. He tended to answer some questions easily and with others he clammed up. So far she hadn't been able to ascertain which questions trod on forbidden territory and which didn't.

The telephone rang. "Mrs. Wilding?"

"Yes."

"Detective Angle here. Would you mind coming in to the Masonic Memorial tomorrow morning? We have a few more questions."

"Not at all. Have you identified the victim yet?"

"No. We're hitting dead ends everywhere. He had no identification on him, and no one has come forward to identify him, nor has anyone filed a missing persons report matching his description."

"I didn't see his photo on the news. I thought that was routine?"

"You must have missed it. It's been on every local channel, plus all the appropriate websites. We may have to go to Interpol. You're sure you didn't recognize him?"

Claire thought back to that day and her first sight of the victim. A rumpled suit, no tie, no socks. She put him in his late sixties. A grayish complexion was visible underneath the luxuriant black moustache, although that might have been due to the fact that he was dead. When she first saw him, he lay face up, one leg and one arm twisted beneath him. His mouth was open as though he hadn't had a chance to close it after he screamed. *Or was he still screaming when he died?* "Positive. I've never seen him before."

"Well, we'd still like to go over the scene with you one more time. Perhaps you'll remember something. It could be as simple as an odd noise or unexplained door left ajar. Something out of place. Is ten o'clock all right? We're on the ninth floor."

The ninth floor. Oh dear. "Mr. Overbrook said you closed the building to events? Does that include tours?"

"For the time being, yes." His tone was dry. "Can you come?"

"All right."

He rang off. Claire went to bed wondering if they had asked Gideon to return as well. *You wish.*

Chapter Four
The Freemasonry Link

When Claire arrived, Angle greeted her and ushered her back onto the elevator. He punched "G" and waited silently as they rode to the ground floor. Leading her to an unmarked door, he said with a hint of resentment, "Mr. Comfrey—the *Worshipful* Master—has provided us with temporary quarters for our investigation. Won't you come in?"

It looked to Claire as though the Master had grudgingly cleared a supply closet for the police. A battered desk and two rickety chairs had been squeezed in next to a couple of pails and a shelf filled with toilet paper. The only light in the windowless room came from a bare fluorescent bulb. Angle sat and indicated the other chair. He smiled warmly at her, his gray eyes twinkling. "You look well, Miss…Mrs. Wilding."

She observed his freshly cut hair and starched white shirt. *For me?* "Er…so do you, Detective."

He seemed to take her reply as a positive sign and pulled out his pen with a flourish. "Okay. Let's go over the discovery one more time, shall we?"

Claire described the scene as she had so many times before. "I wish I could help more, Detective. Did you talk to Mr. Kurtz?"

"Werner Kurtz? Yes, we managed to catch up with him and his family before they left for Pennsylvania.

He had no more to offer than you did. Mrs. Kurtz claims to have heard a scream when you were in the elevator heading up to the ninth floor, but no one else did. Kurtz says he walked around the corner of the observation deck, saw the body, and immediately went to find you. No one was hanging around in the Cedars exhibit when you came off the elevator, correct?"

"Yes. I mean, yes, correct."

"And there were no other...*er*...extraneous persons in the building during your tour?"

"No. Except for Senator Bliss in the museum. Oh, wait. I forgot. The librarian got on at the sixth floor."

"He did?" Angle checked his notes. "That would be Timothy Treadwater?"

"I think so. Monday was my first day as a docent. I hadn't yet been introduced to everyone."

"How did you know he was the librarian?"

Claire started. *Did he just pounce?* "He came out of the library. That's all there is on the sixth floor and no one is allowed in without an appointment. Who else could he be?"

Angle made a note. Apparently this tidbit struck him as significant. "Did he ride up with you?"

"No, he rode down with us to the main entrance. After we...we..."

"I see." Angle bent toward her, tapping his pencil on the desk. The sound echoed in the tiny space. "Did you tell him about the body?"

"No. Mr. Kurtz didn't think we should say anything until we'd called the police. He thought it would be better not to frighten the others."

The detective sat back. "I see. Did Treadwater stay with you while you waited for us?"

She shook her head. "He walked out the front entrance."

"Oh, he did? And this would have been about four o'clock?"

Claire tried to remember. "It must have been."

He closed his notebook. "Thank you very much, Mrs. Wilding. I'll be in touch."

As Claire walked out, she tried to decipher the rather abrupt dismissal. *Did I say something wrong?* She started up the steps to the main floor. Gideon stood at the elevator doors.

He straightened when he saw her, a blush creeping over the tan. "Oh, er…Claire. Hi. Just heading up to do a little work in the museum." He held a book under his arm. Claire remembered he'd carried a similar one the day she'd met him.

She pointed at it. "I don't think you're supposed to remove items from the museum."

He looked down in surprise. "What, this? This is my book. I want to compare something in it against…against something here."

Is it me or did his eyes just get shifty? "What kind of something?"

"Oh, um…" He slipped the book into his briefcase. "George Washington is a hobby of mine. There are items in the museum that have yet to be catalogued by any outside specialist."

"Really? Mr. Quinn gave me a detailed inventory of the collection during my docent training. Are you saying the Masons are hiding something?"

"No, no. It's just…well…some items could use more clarification. Fill in the gaps, you know. Only a few years ago the lodge discovered all kinds of papers they didn't know they had." He pressed the elevator button without looking at her.

There's something fishy going on. Claire had an inspiration. "I'll come up with you then, shall I?" She hopped on.

Discomfort and possibly guilt raced across his handsome features. "I just remembered. I have to stop at the library first." He pressed "6" and spent the trip staring at the ceiling.

Across from the elevator lay the library. Gideon knocked. A man opened it. "Mr. Treadwater? I believe Professor Nutley called about me."

Treadwater, a slight man with a friar-like tonsure of lusterless hair, pushed his bifocals up his nose and peered at Gideon. Claire came out of the elevator and stood behind him. "I don't remember any such call, Mister—"

Gideon drew up to his full six feet three and regarded the librarian with lofty forbearance. "Bliss. Senator Gideon Bliss."

"Oh." The little man began to gabble. "Certainly. Right this way. I'm so sorry. I do not take calls from Professor Nutley. He…" Treadwater led Bliss into the library. Claire started to follow, but the librarian gave her a supercilious stare and shut the door.

Okay, that's it. I'm going home for a nap. It looked like the day had very little potential for lifting her spirits. A murder mystery likely to remain unsolved, a man who made her heart go pitty-pat ignoring her, a door slammed in her face—what else could go wrong?

After twenty minutes of circling the block, Claire finally found a parking spot five streets away. As she reached her door, the telephone began to ring. Tripping over the packing crate, she dropped her purse on her toe, knocked over her favorite lamp, and only managed to grab the receiver on the seventh ring. "Claire, is that you? Where were you? I was about to hang up. It's Mother."

What was that about nothing else going wrong? "I know it's you, Mother. Are you still in Paris?"

"Yes, and I'm so glad I am. I found the most adorable little set of Staffordshire puppies—they'll be perfect on your mantel. You do have a mantel, don't you?" Her voice wavered with unaccustomed doubt.

"Yes, I do. You've seen it, Mother—remember? You've been here. You should also remember that I hate porcelain figurines."

"You do? Oh. Well, I'll keep them then."

Claire smiled indulgently. She recognized an oft-utilized little ploy.

"Dear? Are you still there?"

"Yes, Mother."

"I actually called you for a different reason. I went to the most fascinating luncheon. It was at the Princeton Club here—Susie took me. You remember your cousin Susie? Did you know she's been named director of Alumni Affairs for all Europe? Isn't that marvelous?"

Great. Another successful relative. And *she lives in Paris.*

Apparently, Claire's mother decided to save that particular guilt trip for a long weekend, for she went on. "Anyway, I sat next to this lovely lady. She's a little older than me, but has kept her looks quite well considering. Of course, she's let her hair go gray, but I guess that's the fashion now. Personally I wouldn't do—"

"Mother? The lady?"

"Yes, yes, I'm getting to that. She's from the States as well—Connecticut actually—but is here in Paris on business. She told me the whole story, poor thing. Apparently her daughter-in-law is this harridan who refuses to sign divorce papers for her son even though she ran off with some other man. Awful. I can't imagine."

Claire took a moment to retrieve her heart. "Um, Mother? What's the lady's name?"

"Oh, now see, you keep interrupting me and I've forgotten. What was it..." Claire heard fingernails tapping. "Elation? Ecstasy? No, that doesn't sound right..."

"Could it be Bliss?"

"Aren't you clever, dear. *Exactement*. Oh, here's her card." She read, "Andromeda Miller Bliss. Quite a mouthful, isn't it? She said she had to come across the pond because this Dorcas creature won't talk to anyone but her."

"Did she succeed?"

"What? Oh yes. The woman talked to her."

"And signed the papers?"

"That I don't know. The luncheon presentation began, and we were shushed. That's why I hate those affairs—you're forced to sit through an endless parade of bombastic speechifiers who drone on and on while you're trying to eat your dessert. And they're horrified if you don't appear utterly rapt at their rants and laugh uproariously at their pitiful jokes."

Claire had heard this particular tirade before and waited her mother out. When she heard the telltale intake of breath, she cut in. "Will you see her again?"

"Andromeda? We're having tea tomorrow. Just the two of us. So we can talk without all this hoopla."

"Would you call me after?"

"Why, dear?"

"I think I know her son. We met this week."

"Oh dear, I hope you aren't involved. He's still married, you know. Claire, tell me you're not!"

"I'm not, Mother. And I know all about his divorce. Goodbye, Mother."

****

No further word came from the police, and by Monday Claire decided it would probably be safe to go back to work. Mr. Quinn was happy to see her.

"I'm so glad you could make it, Claire. We're so backed up—we had to cancel several school groups last week due to…due to…"

"Yes, Mr. Quinn. I'm glad we're back to normal." *Or whatever this is.*

"Yes, yes." He wiped his brow with a monogrammed handkerchief. "Worse still, the other docent—Zoe Maguire—told me she felt a cold coming on." He peered a little nearsightedly at Claire. "Have you met her? No? She just started as well. Her mother's a particular friend of mine and I said I'd give her a trial run and…now, where was I?"

"Zoe has a cold." She had all day—no point in rushing the poor man.

"That's right. Can you relieve her? She started about half an hour ago, so you can probably catch them on the fourth floor."

Claire half expected to see Gideon in the museum, but the place was deserted. She found the fifth floor equally empty. She pressed "7" but instead, the doors opened on the sixth level. An interesting tableau met her astonished eyes. Gideon, Mr. Treadwater, and an unfamiliar older gentleman faced each other in a tight circle.

The older man stuck his chin out and yelled, "I have every right to be here, Timothy. You can't keep me out!"

Treadwater glared at him, lips set in a thin line. "Not while I'm in charge, Frederick," he hissed furiously. "I'll never let you back in. Not after what you did to me."

Gideon fluttered his hands over the tops of their balding heads, distress mottling his features. As the doors closed again, she heard him say, "Calm down, Treadwater. You and Professor Nutley can't let old feuds stand in the way of—"

Hmm. Claire had no time to think about the meaning of the little scene. Zoe met her on the seventh floor, a motley group of teenagers trailing after her. They did not appear engrossed by their surroundings.

"Are you Claire? Wudderful! I'b so glad you cad take ober by tour. I'b foreber gradeful." She pulled a heavily used tissue from her pocket. "Hab fun!" She grabbed the doors before they shut and, waving the tissue at Claire, hopped onto the elevator.

The children—a class from T. C. Williams High School—were doing time, or rather summer school, so Claire went straight to an account of the lurid myths associated with freemasonry and gushed melodramatically about jewels supposedly hidden in secret caches in the lodges. She saw no reason to explain that the "jewels" were the Masons' insignia of office and their value merely symbolic.

As she sent the chattering students off to their bus, Gideon appeared in the hall, arguing fiercely with the older man she'd seen in front of the library. "I promise you, Fred, I'll straighten this out. Comfrey has pledged all the support I need." He shook his head. "You could have been a little more diplomatic, though."

"Diplomatic? With that little twerp? Do you know what he did to me in 2008?"

"No, what?"

"He published a critique of my doctoral thesis on the Knights Templar. Christ, I wrote that forty-five years ago! Of *course* new facts have come to light since then. But no, he had to pick the paper apart line by line, as though that were real scholarship. Git." The professor gave a malicious snort. "I'm not sorry I blackballed him on that appointment to the historical commission. Serves him right."

Gideon said mildly, "Well, it's all water under the bridge now, Fred. After all, you're a tenured professor at Georgetown and Treadwater is…well…"

"In a position to shut me out of one of the best resources on George Washington in the country."

Gideon laid a soothing hand on the man's arm. "I told you, I'll fix it with David. We'll go in when Treadwater isn't around. I really need your help." At that moment he caught sight of Claire and waved. "Hi there." When she made as if to leave, he called, "Wait!"

He ran after her. "Claire, there's something I want to tell you."

She stopped short and his shoes hissed on the terrazzo floor as he skidded to a halt before her. She waited for his panting to abate. "What is it?"

"I…uh…talked to my mother. In Paris."

"And?" *Let me guess.*

"She told me she met your mother at some luncheon or other."

"I know."

He drew back. "You do? She—"

"Bliss! Are you coming or not?" The professor's lecture hall voice echoed through the chamber. Apparently United States senators held no terror for him.

"Just a minute, Nutley." Gideon caught Claire's elbow. "Can I see you tonight?" he whispered urgently.

"I don't know, Gideon."

"It's important. I won't..." He reddened. "I won't importune you, if that's what's worrying you."

Claire hoped the disappointment at his words didn't show on her face. *I guess spending a few minutes platonically admiring his attributes wouldn't hurt.* "All right."

He blew out his cheeks. "Great. I'll come by around seven? Thanks." He strode back to the professor and they continued to confer in low voices under the murals, unmoved by George Washington's enormous face as it stared gravely down upon them.

****

"Damn, I did it again."

Claire stretched luxuriously and purred. "You sure did, mister. I thought you promised not to importune me'?"

Gideon rose from the bed and padded to the bathroom. "Oh, Mizz Spinmeister, I beg to differ. Once again, you have lured me into your wicked, sensual web. I'm going to have to start lugging a bodyguard around with me."

63

"Doesn't the Secret Service protect you?"

"Me?" He shrugged. "A junior—probably temporary—senator? Nah. They only guard the First Family, the Cabinet, and the candidates. I'd have to pay for my own security detail."

Claire rolled over on her side and made a pouty face. "Is widdle Giddykins afraid of the big, bad girl?"

She opened her mouth to laugh and found it covered by a large, strong hand, replaced immediately by large, soft, lips. Fingers walked down her neck to her breast, paused a moment to fondle it, then moved on to her belly. "What warm skin you have, my lady."

He traveled a little further down. Claire pushed herself onto his exploring fingers. "*Mmm*, what wet skin you have, my lady." He ducked his head and replaced the finger with his tongue. "*Mmm*, what—"

She pulled his head closer. "*Shhh*. Don't talk. Just do. Me."

A few minutes later she lay on her side again, eyes closed, breathing in the scent of lovemaking. She heard footsteps. "I've got to go, Claire."

She opened her eyes. "But you haven't told me what you wanted to talk about!"

Gideon patted her bottom. "Again, your fault." He sat on the bed and pulled his shoes on. "I told you my mother is in Paris, right?"

"Yes."

"Trying to get Dorcas to sign the divorce papers, right?"

"Yes." Claire held her breath. He didn't sound very upbeat—had she refused? Something rumbled in her stomach.

"Well, she has made a new acquaintance."

"My mother."

He stopped. "I forgot you knew. How did you find out?"

"Mother called me."

"Did you...did you tell her about us?"

All of a sudden Claire felt like the "other" woman and she didn't like it. "No, I didn't." *Maybe I should have.*

As though he guessed her thoughts, Gideon said gently. "It's only for a little while. When the divorce is final I'll shout your name from the rooftops—or from the top of the Masonic Memorial. That is"—his voice dropped to a mumble—"if you wish."

Claire had to wait for the rush of emotion to wash over and out before she could answer. The memory of Lincoln and a whirlwind romance spilled onto the scene. She hadn't hesitated then. They'd met at a Christmas party at the Monocle on Capitol Hill. Nick the maitre d' introduced them. "Lincoln, you'll want to meet this newly minted Republican. She needs reeducation in the ways of the right, and probably protection from her Virginia family, who've been Democrats since Andrew Jackson." They were married on New Year's Eve. Eighteen months later he was dead and she swore she'd never leap off a cliff into anyone's waiting arms again.

"I...don't know, Gideon."

Gideon slammed his fist into his palm. "Damn! Why couldn't Dorcas just slouch off into that good night? Why must she be such a..."

"Harridan?"

He twisted to look at her. "That's an interesting word. Not a bad description of her. Anyway, Mother of course had no idea that I knew her new friend's daughter, and I didn't disabuse her. Let's hope they don't become bosom buddies just yet."

"No." *I guess.* For a short minute Claire wondered if their mothers becoming fast friends might be useful.

Gideon kissed her nose. "I have to go home and get some work done. Tomorrow's Treadwater's day off and I'm meeting Professor Nutley at the temple."

"Is that the man you were talking to this morning?"

"Yes." Gideon abruptly turned and headed toward the door. "He's an…er…old friend."

"What were you three arguing about anyway?"

"Oh, nothing. Access to the library. Just research. Nothing." Without looking at her, Gideon left the room. She heard his feet pounding down the stairs. *In an awful hurry all of a sudden. I wonder why?*

****

Claire spent the following day buried in docent duty. Mr. Quinn insisted they reschedule all the tours that had been canceled, extending the memorial's hours to accommodate them. She hadn't made it home until ten on Tuesday, and was back at the temple at eight the next morning for the first tour.

"And that's how the Masonic Memorial came to be built."

A young man scratched at the pimple on his chin. "Miss? Are you saying that the Lodge built this enormous concrete tower nine stories high because they wanted a fire-proof building?"

Claire often stumbled over this point. It didn't make much sense to her either. "That was the initial reason, yes. As I told you, the original Washington Alexandria Lodge burned down in 1871, destroying much of their collection of Washington memorabilia. The committee charged with raising funds for a new building didn't want to risk the loss of any more precious artifacts."

"So they wanted a vault and they got a temple."

The youth's girlfriend, who had hitherto spent more time on her iPad than paying attention, piped up. "It sorta grew like Topsy, huh?"

Apparently *Uncle Tom's Cabin* was on the eleventh grade summer reading list. "I guess you could say that. Now if that's all, it's closing time. If anyone needs to use the restrooms, they're down that corridor."

As the group shuffled out, their teacher nipping at their heels like a border collie, Claire trotted over to the bookstore. "Harry, do you have the second volume of that history of freemasonry for me?"

"Oh, dear, no, I'm sorry. There's been a surprising run on them lately. I sold the last one to a man just an hour or so ago. I can order more if you like."

Maybe freemasonry is required summer reading as well. "Yes, please. The public library has very little on the subject. Oh, speaking of, I'd like a copy of that brief history of the memorial you showed me. I've got to figure out how this building 'grew like Topsy.' "

"What?"

"Never mind."

Harry went to the brochure rack and twirled it, muttering. "Nope, that's gone too. Oh, I remember, the same guy who bought Volume Two bought it as well. In fact, he walked out with two hundred dollars' worth of stuff. He even took my scale model kit!"

"Must be writing a book or something."

Harry shrugged. "Didn't look the bookish type.

Dark. Hooded eyes. Never cracked a smile."

"Interesting. What was he wearing?"

"Let's see." Harry screwed up his eyes. "No tie. Cap. Grayish suit and shirt."

"Grayish face too?" Claire thought she was making a joke, but Harry didn't laugh.

"More like a faceless face."

"Oh." A little tingle went up her spine. "Queer. Like a cipher."

"Yeah, or the perfect spy."

Claire shook off the sudden chill. "Well, please do order that book for me. I'll see you tomorrow." As she opened the glass door, a pale-faced man with short-cropped blond hair almost ran into her. She caught a whiff of a fresh citrusy cologne and an impression of military bearing. His black leather shoes shone in the dim light. *He looks like the German colonel in that movie I watched last week.* The man said nothing, but stepped aside to let her pass.

As she came out on the front steps, a vast circular driveway with an enormous topiary of the Masonic square and compasses in the center stretched out before her. A crimson sports car turned right off King Street, drove up the hill, and headed around the building toward the parking lot. She looked closer. The sleek lines of a three-hundred-thousand-dollar, one-in-a-million car. A McLaren. *Gideon.* She knew that the side entrance had already been locked. *What's he doing here?*

She followed the sidewalk and reached the corner in time to see the door open and a man stick his head out. The lamppost blocked most of his face. He crooked his finger at Gideon, who climbed the steps and slipped inside past him. Claire stopped, confused. *Why is Gideon sneaking in after hours? And where did he get that gray hat and raincoat?*

She walked slowly to her car. As she got in, a sedan started its engine and pulled out of the lot. Through the window Claire glimpsed a familiar face. Detective Angle.

Chapter Five
Conjugal Links

"You can only stay an hour. Sammy has soccer practice, and it's my turn to carpool."

"That's all right, Eddie. I just wanted to bring Mother's postcard over." Claire dropped a card on the table. "I don't understand why she can't spring for two, one for each of us," she grumbled.

"It's using up the two stamps she hates. She hoards them, you know. I think it has something to do with the Great Depression. Anyway, why buy two identical postcards?" Edwina picked it up. "Oh Christ, it's a photo of ceramic dogs."

"Probably the ones she tried to foist on me."

"You let her have them, I hope."

"Of course."

"She's so transparent." Edwina pulled her little mop of a dog onto her lap. "By the way, I spoke to her yesterday. She was going on and on about Giselda's grades so I told her about you and Gideon to distract her."

"You told Mother about Gideon? I can't believe it, Edwina. You're my sister—if I can't count on you to keep things from Mother, who can I count on? Now she'll be constantly on my case."

"You know that's not possible. She's still in Paris after all."

Claire glared at her sister. "And your point?"

"You sound an awful lot like a girl with a story to tell. Last time we talked you had had one date with the good senator. Anything to confess?"

Claire toyed with the idea of admitting her recent encounters—her sister was always a good listener and generally supportive of her romantic attachments. That is, until she married Lincoln. Edwina had never explained the early dislike she'd taken to Claire's husband. It had thrown a pall over their formerly frequent socializing, but it hardly mattered now. *I need her advice.* "We…er…had another date."

"I see."

Claire sighed. From the look of comprehension on her sister's face she knew there was no need for further elucidation. Edwina stood up, and the little Yorkie tumbled to the floor. "Oops, sorry Toby. Is my pwecious okay? Did Momma scare oo?"

The terrier shot a look of canny triumph at Claire as though to say, *This should be good for at least one treat and a walk.* He whimpered. Edwina scooped Toby up and carried him into the kitchen, whispering guilty apologies.

Claire followed her. "Edwina! You haven't told me what Mother said about Gideon?"

"What do you think she said? I quote, 'Tell her this—Watch your step, child. You know what happens when you jump into cold water with your eyes closed.'"

"She said that? What the hell does that mean?"

"She means Lincoln of course."

Claire shook her head and pulled a bottle of water out of the refrigerator while Edwina fed Toby tidbits from a plate of liver paté. "This is nothing like Lincoln.

It's true that I'm ready to move on—it's been three years after all, Edwina—but this time I'm in no hurry. I do like Gideon…" She paused to let the lump in her throat dissolve so she could deliver the lie smoothly. "He's very…nice and we enjoyed our…dates." She took a quick swallow of water. "Anyway, it's not like it could turn into anything serious—he's still married."

"Yes."

Claire looked up quickly. Something in Edwina's tone struck a cold note. "What is it?"

Her sister put the paté back on the counter, prompting a growl from Toby, then pulled a stool out and sat down facing Claire. "I think it's about time you learned the truth. I swore on Mother's Queen Elizabeth purse that I'd never tell you, but that was against my better judgment." Claire gasped. Only the most serious oaths were taken on the embroidered clutch their mother had carried when she had tea with the queen. Edwina spoke slowly. "Now that Dad's gone I can do the right thing. If you're truly ready to move on, that is."

Suddenly Claire wished the water would turn into wine. A little voice told her she would need a dose of alcohol. "I'm listening."

"Lincoln was married when he met you." Edwina's gaze was steady, her eyes empty of expression.

"No."

"Yes." Edwina tossed another chunk of paté at Toby. He caught it in midair. "Things were happening so fast between you and Linc. Dad and I were concerned. Lincoln seemed to be pushing you awfully hard. Remember, he'd just come to town, and no one knew much about him—"

"Except that he'd been named Chief Counsel to the Senate Energy and Natural Resources Committee. And that he'd clerked for a Supreme Court Justice."

"Neither of which requires Senate confirmation. We knew he was well-connected. We didn't know how. His wealth and perfect manners blinded Mother, and she would brook no criticism of him. So Dad hired a small firm to investigate." Edwina pursed her lips. "Unfortunately, the Shamusnot Detection Agency came up to what we later learned were their usual standards. They uncovered his prior marriage, but only a few days before the wedding."

Claire sat frozen. Lincoln, the love of her life, the most honest person she'd ever known, the sweetest, kindest, sexiest man…a liar. *A bigamist.*

Her sister patted her awkwardly. "Sweetums, I'm so sorry. Turned out the first Mrs. Wilding was diagnosed with paranoid schizophrenia about six months into their marriage. She'd been institutionalized for ten years."

"What…what was her name?"

"Her name? Let me see…something exotic…that's it, Inez."

Claire pictured a slim, dark dancer with silky black hair that reached to her waist, her eyes deep pools of emotion, her lips as red as the rose she held between them. She rolled her hands into fists, willing her heart to slow. "How did they find her?"

"Our investigator had been intercepting Lincoln's email."

"What! That's…that's…"

"Illegal? Unethical? Maybe." Edwina gave a derisive snort. "Considering what he found out Linc

73

had no right to be outraged."

"And what did he find?"

"An alert from the hospital where Inez was incarcerated. It said Inez Wilding had taken ill and they didn't expect her to last more than a few days. The email identified her as Linc's sister, but the detective couldn't find any record of a sister. Three days before the wedding he unearthed a certificate of marriage between Lincoln Wilding and Inez Maria Felipe-Santiago, dated January 15, 2000, in Las Vegas, Nevada."

Claire's eyes clouded with both anger and unspent tears. "What…what did you do?"

"Dad and I confronted Lincoln with the information, but after some—how do I put this?—rather animated conversation, he convinced us that telling you would serve no purpose. Given the hospital's email, he assumed she'd be dead before the wedding day. In fairness, he believed himself a free man when he married you."

Claire stared at her sister. "Then he didn't lie."

Edwina touched Claire's cheek with a gentle hand. "He did, though. He never mentioned Inez to you, did he?"

Claire pushed her chair back and stood up. As she paced the kitchen she muttered, throwing her hands out. "He knew she was dying. He knew it was only a matter of time. He didn't want to hurt me unnecessarily. He—"

"That might be an excuse, if Inez had died before the wedding." Edwina bent down to give Toby another treat. This time the little dog hesitated a second before accepting it, as if such largesse usually meant a trip to the vet. Without looking at Claire, Edwina mumbled, "She survived for another month."

"A month?"

"She had slipped into a coma before your wedding day, but remained on life support. The hospital couldn't reach Lincoln while you were on your honeymoon, so he naturally assumed he had nothing to worry about."

"When did he learn she was still alive?"

"After you returned. Dad and I had no idea either, since we'd called the agency off the case. We thought we were out of danger and you and Mother need never find out. When Lincoln told us, we...we decided to wait a few days before we sprang the news on you, but she died before we could. She never came out of the coma."

A vein in Claire's neck throbbed, the only indication that she was alive. Acid burned her throat. She croaked, "I see."

Edwina touched Claire's hand, but her sister shook it off. The older woman's voice trembled. "Claire, we were between a rock and a hard place. They—Dad and Linc—thought it would be better to keep you in the dark. They didn't want to hurt you. I hated the lies, the obfuscation. They overruled me." She rubbed her eyes. "I blame Lincoln. Even under the circumstances, he still owed you the truth. You once asked me why I disliked him so, why I couldn't be in a room alone with him. Now you know."

The soft evening when Claire had set aside the golden vial of Lincoln's ashes came back to her. If only that peace would return. She looked at her sister's crumpled face and love poured back into the empty places. She rose and kissed her forehead. "I have to go."

A tear dropped onto Edwina's lap. "Do you forgive me, Claire?"

Claire hesitated. "It may take a while. I have to get used to new definitions for old feelings. My world has flipped."

Edwina's lips curved in a timid smile. "That one's an old world, long gone. You've got a new one here, and from the look on your face when you talk about Gideon, it holds promise."

****

Claire set her whiskey down and stared into the tiny fireplace. The last few days had been mercifully quiet. She'd spent the weekend gloomily reassessing her past with Lincoln, teasing out hints and clues that had escaped her in the throes of mad, passionate love. Her husband had disappeared for a few days following the honeymoon. When he returned he'd been very subdued. He would say only that it was a family matter and that everything had been resolved. When Claire tried to probe, he uncharacteristically lashed out at her. She'd bitten back the retort and stayed out of his way. Worse, her sister seemed to be in a similar mood.

Linc had gradually returned to his old self, and Claire soon forgot the dark period. She had left Capitol Hill and taken a public affairs job with the Bureau of Reclamation, the Department of the Interior's dam building agency. Even with Linc's demanding schedule as the chief legislative officer of a Senate committee, their life together bordered on perfect. They maintained a frenetic social schedule with influential people in Washington, in between business trips to areas under the committee's supervision. One jaunt took them to

Prudhoe Bay to see the base station for the 800-mile Alyeska oil pipeline. Another took them flying down the Colorado River from Glen Canyon to Parker and Davis Dams, returning finally to the massive Hoover Dam. Claire loved the colossal structures—as she told Lincoln, in them the intricate and fragile alliance between man and nature not only resulted in something useful, but exquisite.

She couldn't have been happier. Until that July day she'd found Linc slumped over on the floor. She'd been out buying fireworks—every Independence Day all the kids in the neighborhood were invited to see Linc's renowned pyrotechnic display. Instead, she took him to the emergency room. A month later he was dead. She remembered clearly the day before he died. She'd been sitting at his bedside and he'd grabbed her arm, his fingers pressing hard into her flesh. He'd whispered something about forgiveness. She wept and blubbered that nothing he'd ever done could spoil the purity of their love. He'd blinked twice and fallen back, exhausted, on the pillow.

For the first time Claire wondered if he had wanted to confess that day. *It doesn't really matter, does it? Not now.* She drained her glass. The telephone rang.

"Mrs. Wilding?"

"Yes?"

"This is Detective Angle…from the police?"

Claire thought of the face in the car window. *Why did he follow Gideon?* "What can I do for you?"

"Do you mind telling me how well you know Gideon Bliss?"

Gulp. Claire wondered wildly if Angle had been talking to her mother. As with parents and priests, she figured honesty was the best policy. Or a semblance thereof. "Not too well. We've...dated a couple of times."

"How long have you known him?"

He sounds almost angry. Claire thought back through the days that felt like years. "A couple of weeks, I guess."

"I see. And has he spoken to you about his work?"

"He's a senator. I know what that entails." *Where is this leading?*

"Sorry. I meant his research. He's a noted expert on George Washington. Amateur, but well-regarded."

That explains his presence in the museum. "I don't think he mentioned that."

"He co-authored a paper with Professor Frederick Nutley."

Claire wondered if she should gasp in awe. "Er...should I know him?"

"Nutley is an associate professor at Georgetown University. He was recently censured by the school for claiming to have found evidence that George Washington had a son."

"I beg your pardon?"

"Within a month three authoritative bodies discredited his findings. He continues to claim their legitimacy, but his reputation is shot."

"I'm sorry, detective, but what does this have to do with Gid—Senator Bliss?"

"He's been seen in the professor's company...at the temple. They recently attempted to enter the Memorial Library over the librarian's objections. They returned the next evening...after the memorial had closed."

Claire remembered the altercation on the sixth floor and the older man in tweeds. *That's right—Gideon called him Fred.* "Do you think they broke into the library? What for?"

Angle paused, then went on firmly. "An extremely valuable book has been stolen from the library. A significant and unique historical document."

Claire's confusion grew. "And?"

"Mrs. Wilding, according to Timothy Treadwater, it disappeared on the day you found the dead man in the temple."

Gideon's book? The cell phone fell from her twitching fingers. She could hear Angle's gruff voice calling. "Mrs. Wilding? Are you there?"

She picked it up. "How…how does he know when it was stolen? That was two weeks ago."

"Treadwater told me this morning. I gather he didn't think it had anything to do with the case. But in light of Senator Bliss's presence the day of the murder, and the recent dustup, we thought it worthwhile to follow up on it—see if there's any link."

"Is there something you want me to do?"

"As a matter of fact, I do. If you're seeing Bliss anytime soon, I want you to observe him—maybe even ask about his work. Report back to me if he seems worried or uncomfortable. Anything will help."

Spy on Gideon? I think not. "Do you believe he's mixed up in the murder of that man?"

Angle's tone stiffened. "We haven't established an official cause of death yet."

Oh, really? The bullet hole didn't give it away? "I see, but you are saying there might be a link between the dead man and the theft of the document."

"We have no idea whether the two are connected or not. We're pursuing all leads."

Might as well play along. "Yes, of course I'll help."

Angle paused. "I would consider it a favor. If you think of something—anything—you can call me anytime. My cell's 703-555-4423."

She wrote it down. "Well, goodbye." Her finger hovered over the off button. "Lieutenant Angle? Have you identified the corpse yet?"

"Not yet. We're pursuing all leads." He rang off.

****

"And that's why Masons wear aprons. Any more questions?"

"Yes, miss. I keep hearing about 'jewels.' Are they like the Crown Jewels or something? Are they *real* precious?" The young girl leaned forward, her eyes gleaming with avarice.

"No, Sally." *Sorry to disappoint you, you little mercenary.* "A 'jewel' is associated with each lodge officer. It's more like an object that symbolizes the duties and responsibilities of the title. For example, the jewel of the Worshipful Master is the square—"

"He's a square?" Snickers skipped across the group like a pebble over a pond.

Claire waited for the teacher to reestablish order. "The square is a stonemason's tool. Remember, I told you that the symbols and paraphernalia Masons use hearken back to their purported origins as real stonemasons? The mason uses the square"—she held up a sample and silently thanked Harry for suggesting the idea—"to ascertain the true and correct angle of the cut stone. In freemasonry it stands for virtue."

One young man who had already proved to be a challenge raised his hand. "So what does this *Worshipful* Master"—more titters—"do?"

Claire surreptitiously checked her watch. If she had to deal with one more high school group she'd quit. "He's in charge of everything, Jonah—every lodge member, every *jewel*, everything that happens under his watch."

The questioner looked around, shoulders hunched. "Is he…is he watching us now?"

She glanced over his head at the security camera and back to the boy. "Yes, Jonah, he is." The boy slunk away, trailed by jeers and catcalls. Claire managed to get through the rest of her explanation of offices and jewels before the teacher lost complete control. As she watched them trickle out the side entrance to the waiting school bus, Harry came up to her.

"Hey, Claire, I'm glad I caught you. Volume two of the *History of Freemasonry* came in this morning if you still want it."

"Oh, thanks, Harry. Yes, I do. It seems that the more I study freemasonry the more questions I have."

He chuckled. "Yeah, it can be hard to tell how much is consciously secret and how much is merely lost in the mists of time."

"You're not a Mason?"

"Nope. Just a man with a job. I'll set the book aside for you." Harry took a step but halted abruptly.

Claire swerved to avoid him. "Hey, see that guy?"

She followed his finger. A bland-faced man, his collar turned up and his hands in his pockets, shuffled out of the Shriners exhibit and pushed open the door to the men's room. "Uh huh. Why?"

"He's the guy who bought up all the books last week. Calls himself Joe Smith. Really. Like we figured, his name's as colorless as his face."

"I wonder what he's doing here today?"

Harry shrugged. "If he's interested in freemasonry, it makes sense he'd spend time here."

"Yeah, I guess. Then why hasn't he bought a ticket for the tour?"

"Dunno. At any rate, he can't do it today—yours was the last one."

"Thank God. I've had it with the Jonahs of the world."

Harry smiled. "You've been doing yeoman's work while Zoe Maguire's out sick. Do you want me to lock up for you?"

Claire shook her head. "Nigel said he'd check the exhibit floors for me tonight. Zoe will be back tomorrow, and we can start the full tour schedule again."

As Harry started toward the stairs, Claire paused, hoping to put her finger on what bothered her about the man Joe Smith. *There's something not quite kosher about his body language.* She waited. Sure enough, when the fellow came out of the restroom, he crossed the hall to the elevator instead of going to the exit door. Claire almost followed him but thought better of it. *He's probably just going to the main entrance.* She shook off her suspicions and headed to the parking lot. If she'd looked back she would have seen a tall blond man detach himself from one of the columns and amble after Joe Smith.

Chapter Six
The Italian Link

Gideon didn't show his face at the temple for another two days. Claire couldn't decide if his absence eased her mind or made her even more edgy. At least the freemasonry fan Harry had identified as Joe Smith took her mind off her romantic woes. Both omnipresent and nondescript, he sat for hours on the front steps reading the books he'd bought from the gift store, or wandered the public rooms from opening to closing time. On her way back from a break on Thursday she saw him. He had his back to her, facing a miniature reproduction of a Shriners parade. Bracing herself, she approached him. "Excuse me, Mr. Smith?"

The man did not twitch. In fact, he barely moved, merely rotating the upper half of his body to peer at her. Up close he was, if anything, blander than from afar. Pale gray eyes dissolved into a sallow, clean-shaven face. His thin, bloodless lips were clamped tightly together under an unremarkable nose. He stared at her for a long minute, then, in a sibilant voice, as though he were more used to whispering than talking, asked, "Can I help you?"

Claire took a step back. Nothing specific about him made her nervous, but frigid air seemed to drift from his vicinity. She shivered. "I'm the docent here, and I noticed you've been visiting the public rooms and…and

I wondered if you'd be interested in taking a guided tour of the rest of the building? That way you'll be able to see the tower levels." She stopped, out of breath.

His eyes narrowed. "All nine floors?"

"Well, not the library of course. That's on the sixth floor. It's only open by special appointment."

"Ah."

When nothing else seemed forthcoming, Claire tried again. "However, the observation deck is included in the price of admission. Our last tour starts in a few minutes if you'd care to join it."

Smith faced her, permitting a full-length view of his unexceptional attire. Claire recognized the suit he'd had on when Harry first pointed him out. Without the gray cap he usually wore, his dove-colored hair merged with his features, leaving the impression that he was actually bald. He spoke without moving his lips. "Yes, I would."

He reminded Claire of an actor in a black and white movie—Orson Welles in *The Third Man* perhaps. A colorless creature. A spook. "Very good. Would you come with me?"

The man followed her to the reception desk and bought a ticket. Claire led the way to a small clump of people assembled at the elevator and embarked on her spiel.

By the time they reached the Tall Cedars room she was exhausted. Smith asked endless, detailed questions in his indistinct voice, most of which she had no answer to—*I've got to finish that second volume ASAP.* Worse, he tried the patience of the entire group by dawdling on every floor. Yet his vague manner made it difficult to be angry with him—after all, how does one yell at a jellyfish?

Claire made sure he had left the building before she got her purse, said goodnight to Nigel, and walked out to the parking lot. She half expected to see the fellow hanging around, but caught sight of him crossing the lawn in the direction of the King Street metro. The streetlight clicked on as she searched for her keys.

"You're finishing up late."

She jumped at the familiar voice. "Oh Gideon, you startled me. How long have you been here?"

"Just drove up." He touched a button on his key and the flashy sports car parked in the Buses Only section beeped. "I came to meet you."

Did he? How did he know I'd be late? "So you're not here to work?"

He gave her a puzzled look. "Isn't the building closed?"

"Yes…yes, it is." *That didn't stop you before.* She unclenched her jaw and tried to stay calm. "Why are you here?"

"Like I said, I wanted to catch you before you left. Nigel—the tiler—told me you were still here."

"Are you two friends?" *Could Nigel have been the man who opened the door for Gideon that night?*

"Not likely." He scrunched his nose. "Something kind of icky about him, don't you think? No, I called the front desk and he answered." He nodded at the building. "Your last tour must have taken longer than usual."

The image of Smith poking into every corner of every room distracted her from the discovery that a scrunched-up nose could kindle remarkable heat in her loins. "Yes, it did. This one person—kind of an odd duck—held us up on every floor. He seemed almost morbidly interested in all the exhibits."

Gideon laughed. "Freemasonry will do that to you. There's so much mystery in the institution. How did it really start? Were the founders actual stonemasons or is that merely a symbol of the group's mission? Were the Knights Templar really associated with them or is the modern rite based solely on nostalgia for the Middle Ages and chivalry? You're always left wondering if they won't tell you because it's a secret or if they really don't know the answers."

Claire had only been half listening. *Nigel.* Gideon had been all in gray the night she saw him sneak into the temple—just like the faceless Joe Smith. What was Gideon's errand? Why was he so furtive? Had he stolen the book as Angle suspected? She closed her eyes, but when she opened them Gideon still stood there. Only this time her heart jerked at the sight of him. The wind in the open car had roughed up his rich brown hair, and his beryl eyes gleamed in the last flash of sunlight. The scent of his skin filled her nostrils. They must have flared, for Gideon bent toward her, his eyes anxious.

"Are you all right, Claire? You look a little strange."

Claire retrieved her libido and pocketed it. "Well, thanks a lot—nothing like a back-handed compliment to perk a girl up." At his crestfallen face she relented. "I guess I'm just tired."

"That's too bad. I had hoped to talk you into dinner with me. That's why I'm here. You weren't answering your cell phone, and Nigel said you were on your way back to the main floor. So I carpe'd the diem and drove over."

"Dinner?" Claire patted her head, retrieving a few rogue strands of copper hair and tucking them behind her ears. She licked her lips and took a quick gander at her frock. *How clever of me to wear the blue dress. Edwina says it brings out the azure in my eyes.* She bent her head back, the better to see Gideon's face that hovered a foot above hers and squeaked, "Okay."

"Great. Do you want to stop by your house and freshen up?"

Claire hated to succumb to self-doubt, but…"Maybe that would be a good idea. I have to take my car back anyway."

As she drove to Prince Street followed closely by the red sports car, Claire went frantically over her wardrobe possibilities. She left Gideon standing in the living room—"It's more comfortable than sitting," he said gallantly, ducking his head to miss the chandelier—and leapt up the steps to her bedroom. It only took a minute to realize that her current outfit was in fact the only nice bit of apparel still fresh and relatively unwrinkled. She redid her makeup, gave her hair a stiff brush-up, thanking God for the thick, easy-to-manage curls, and hurtled down the stairs.

"Geranio okay?"

"Perfect."

Claire loved the old-fashioned Italian restaurant, but when they reached the entrance, several couples waited outside. "Oh dear, it looks like they're full."

Gideon sailed past the queue, ignoring the pointed looks, and opened the door. "Let's just check, shall we?" He beckoned the maitre d', a tiny little man in evening kit. "Hi, Tony—any chance of a table?"

Tony tripped over the carpet, his expression a

mixture of titillation and terror. "Senator Bliss, of course, we'll find a table. Just give me a moment…" He scurried down a hall. Claire heard raised voices, Italian invective spewing like Mount Etna. A minute later a large, swarthy family of four marched out, muttering angrily, and headed down to the kitchen. Tony appeared, rubbing his hands. "Right this way, Senator, Signorina."

Gideon stopped him. "I hope you didn't evict those people to accommodate us."

Tony glanced toward the kitchen. "Them? Oh, no, sir! That's my family. They're used to making way for real customers. They were very happy to give up their table for a senator. They will be fine in the kitchen."

Claire wasn't so sure, but dutifully followed Tony.

****

Two hours later, replete with mussels à la marinière, the best veal piccata in town—no flour, lightly sautéed, brushed with lemon and sprinkled with large, sweet capers—and raspberry tart, they wandered the sidewalks of Old Town. Music blew out of a door and the sounds of clapping and cheers drew them toward a crowded bar. Gideon looked up at the sign over the bow window. "Tivoli Tavern? What is this place?"

"A real hidden gem in Alexandria. Do you like bluegrass?"

He looked dubiously at the chalkboard attached to the door, which listed the Blue Plate Special as cheese fries. "I'm from Connecticut, remember? We're a simple folk—washboards and dobros may be a little too sophisticated for the likes of us."

Claire danced a little jig in time to the music.

"Nevertheless. Shall we?"

They shouldered their way past a lineup of musicians sporting an assortment of outfits and instruments. A chubby waitress gave the laminate table a half-hearted swipe and stuffed her gum in her cheek. "What's your pleasure?"

"Do you have a wine list?" At the woman's blank face, Claire amended her request. "Do you have wine?"

"We got red, we got white."

"I'll have white, I guess."

Gideon ordered a beer and settled back to listen. The motley crew finished up the song and headed to the bar. A young girl and a man who could be her father took their places at the front. He popped a jew's harp on his lip, she placed a fiddle under her chin, and they began to play. A medley of toe-tapping Gospel tunes brought the crowd, including Gideon and Claire, to their feet. Claire couldn't resist. She shouted in Gideon's ear, "So what do you think of bluegrass now?"

But Gideon was too busy dancing to answer.

As the Christ Church bell chimed midnight, Claire stumbled up the steps of her house awash in laughter. Gideon followed, intoning in a perfect North Carolina twang, "We got raaad, we got whiiii."

"*Shhh*, the neighbors will think we're blotto."

Gideon kissed her. "We are. Now let me in."

Too late Claire remembered her plan to grill Gideon about the professor and their connection, if any, to the stolen book. What with him unbuttoning her dress and nibbling her neck, it somehow felt inappropriate to bring up any nefarious activities in which he might be involved. Also, she'd never been very good at multitasking and his lips were demanding all her attention. Also, her entire female apparatus had gone up in flames at his touch. *I guess it can wait.*

Gideon had managed to maneuver her to the stairs while removing most of her clothing. She hit the first riser and sat down abruptly. He took the opportunity to tear off his shirt and belt. She leaned forward, unzipped his khakis, and lifted out as handsome a piece of man flesh as she'd ever seen. He towered over her, staring hungrily up at the bedroom door. She held onto his cock, rubbing the tip with her thumb. "Going somewhere?"

"Uh, Claire, can we…uh, Claire. Claire, oh God, keep doing that." He threw his head back and pumped his penis in and out of her mouth. She held onto his ass and let her lips slide over the rough skin, tonguing the sensitive vee under the tip. It grew longer and hard as glass under her ministrations. Not much later he let out a huge sigh and warm, sticky liquid flowed into her mouth.

He bent down and lifted her under her shoulders. "Come on." He carried her up and dropped her on her back on the bed. She expected him to leap on top of her, but instead he knelt on the floor and spread her thighs wide. Clasping her knees, he pulled her to the edge of the bed. Cool air hit the sensitive flesh, raising goosebumps. When he gave a tentative lick, she shot up. He put a gentle hand on her chest and laid her back down. His tongue touched the top of her vagina, licked around the lips, and inserted itself deep inside. Juices gushed around his mouth and dribbled down his chin. He continued to suckle and tickle until the volcano erupted and she lost control, squeezing his head with her thighs and yelping, "More, more, harder, harder, ooooohhh yeessss!"

She collapsed back on the bed. Gideon laid his head on her inner thigh and smiled up at her. "Now we're even."

She longed to say, "Let's make it an even dozen," but thought that might be asking too much. Instead, she asked innocently, "What, no dessert topping?"

"Ah, babe, give me a minute, will you?"

As promised, he only took a minute. The topping took a bit longer. As they lay side by side contentedly stroking each other, Claire tried to ignore the words that spun round in her head. *Mrs. Wilding, an extremely valuable document has disappeared from the library.* She thought back to the day she'd met Gideon. The day she'd found the dead man. He—Gideon—had been in the museum. And he held a book tucked under his arm. A big, heavy, leather-bound book.

"Gideon?"

"Yes, love?"

"Why did you and the professor want to get into the library?"

She felt him stiffen beside her, but his tone remained casual. "Professor Nutley is an expert on George Washington, and he wanted to verify a source. I said I would help him. Why?"

"Oh, I just wondered. Why did he come to you? You're not a...Washington *buff*, are you?" Her stab at coquettish sounded flat even to her own ears.

He rose on one elbow. "Why are you bringing this up now, Claire? I told you before, I do happen to be a bit of a fanatic when it comes to the father of our country. Is that a crime?"

Better back off. "No, I guess not."

He rose and headed to the bathroom. "My mother's family is distantly related to Washington. In fact, the old homestead sits a few lots from his property in Stafford County. So I'm understandably interested in him. You know—blood thicker than water, that sort of thing." He disappeared.

Claire pulled the sheet up to her chin. His explanation didn't quite click on all cylinders. *He's keeping something back, I'm sure of it.* How to tease it out? She realized how little she knew her lover. She could recognize his private parts in a pitch-black wind tunnel, but his interests, talents—other than in the bedroom—and opinions remained as yet undiscovered. He opened the door and blew her a kiss and she forgot everything in the warmth of his smile.

"I've got to go. Let's hope the neighbors aren't looking in the windows—I think all my clothes are downstairs."

She let him go. *I have to think.*

****

"Will you accept a collect call from a Mrs. Letitia Canfield?"

"What? Yes, yes, certainly." Claire waited through the clicks until her mother's voice came on the line. "Mother? Why are you calling collect?"

"Oh, Claire, dear, I seem to have misplaced my cell phone. Monsieur Souris—the manager at the hotel here—kindly offered me the use of his office phone." She must have put her hand over the receiver, for Claire heard her muffled voice speaking in rapid French. "*Non, non, ça marche, monsieur. Très bien, merci, merci. Oui—à bientôt, Monsieur Souris…*Now, are you still there, Claire?"

Her daughter jumped at the abrupt rise in volume. "Yes, Mother. When are you coming home, Mother?"

"Soon, dear. I still haven't found that knob for your closet door. I know exactly what I want, but so far the item eludes me. Besides, I'm having too much fun with my new best friend."

"Mrs. Bliss?"

"Yes. She's a delightful lady, and we have so much in common. Except for the recalcitrant daughter-in-law of course."

"Like what?" Gideon's mother might prove more informative than her son.

"What do we have in common? First off, we're both widows, and both old Virginia stock. She's one of the Tidewater Millers—Malcolm Miller was attorney general back in the sixties. Their family estate sits right next to Ferry Farm—you remember, George Washington's boyhood home. Oh, and we both adore oysters."

Claire reflected that for her mother, good family and a taste for raw shellfish pretty much sealed the deal. "She's not from Connecticut? Her son's the senator from that state."

Her mother paused. "Yes, well. Andromeda explained about her moment of weakness."

"As in?"

"Marrying a Yankee. According to her, Ephraim Bliss swept into town on a magnificent stallion when she was sixteen and immediately broke every female heart within a five-mile radius."

"What was he doing in Virginia?"

"She says he wanted to buy land for a factory of

some sort."

Intriguing. "What kind of factory?"

"I've no idea. I gather he manufactured something…tools? Cars? *Hmm*, did Andromeda mention…" Her voice trailed off.

"Mother? You were saying Mr. Bliss swept into town?"

"Did I say that? Oh, my. Maybe not *swept*…although he did sweep her off her feet." Letitia paused to let her daughter savor the pun. "She says it took her family a decade to be reconciled to their marriage—and then only because Ephraim discovered that Jefferson Davis's niece was a distant cousin of his great great uncle."

Southerners, and Virginians in particular, as Claire well knew, were sticklers for kinship and hard to placate. If Gideon were any indication, his father must have been handsome and charming enough to overcome even the deepest prejudice.

Her mother continued. "She says her son is a devotee of George Washington—knows everything there is to know about him. In fact, he did a genealogical trace and found the two families are distantly related. Imagine. That's almost as impressive as our connection to Winston Churchill and Lady Di. Of course I didn't mention that to Andromeda. Not immediately anyway."

"Naturally." Claire tried to keep her voice steady.

"That's why I called. Andromeda told me Gideon thinks he's found something that belonged to Washington. She says he's very excited about it."

Aha. Thank you, patron saint of gossip. "Did he say what it was? A book maybe?"

"N...no, I don't think so. Oh, dear, I can't remember. That doesn't sound right, though." She clicked her teeth. "I'll ask his mother, shall I? Better yet, you could ask him directly. Edwina says you're seeing him."

"Edwina says..." *Damn.* "I've had a couple of dates with him, that's all, Mother. Look, I have to get to work. Let me know when you're coming home."

"I will. Oh, I see Andromeda out in the lobby. I'd better hang up. We're going to the Opera tonight—*Carmen.*" She sighed. "Remember, my love? That was your first opera. I never tire of telling the story—"

"Yes, Mother. Goodbye, Mother." Claire didn't need to relive the mortifying tale of her first visit to the grand old Opéra in Paris. She still ached from the polite laughter of the other guests in the Presidential box when her mother loudly announced that her thirteen-year-old daughter was wearing her first pair of stockings.

As she headed out the door her cell phone buzzed. "Mrs. Wilding? This is Lieutenant Angle. Are you busy?"

"I'm sorry. I'm on my way to the temple. I'm on duty this morning."

"Could you call me when you have a free moment?"

"I'll try."

Claire didn't get a chance to return his call until she finished her shift. As she was leading one tour—happy to be able to answer a few more questions about the Masons than she had before—she saw Mr. Treadwater scuttling through the great hall, and later noticed the library door stood open. It was so unusual that she mentioned it to Nigel.

The tiler folded his ever-present newspaper and shrugged. His small black eyes glittered. "Treadwater's been running around all day like Chicken Little. He found the book."

"The book?"

"Didn't you hear? He claimed someone stole a book from the library the day of the murder. I swear he almost had hysterics—had Comfrey and Quinn all aflutter over it."

Claire couldn't picture the most solemn worshipful master and his grave senior warden fluttering. Could this be the book she'd seen under Gideon's arm? "So he's found it?"

"Yup. Turned up in a glass case in the museum. Bugger probably put it there himself and forgot."

Claire's initial distaste for Nigel morphed into active dislike. She left him and walked outside to the main steps to dial Angle's number. As it rang, she gazed over the spires and chimneys of Alexandria. If she looked beyond the train tracks and raised highways in the foreground, she could detect the well-ordered grid in which the early settlers laid out the town. King Street ran in a straight line from the temple to the Potomac River. To the south lay Prince and Duke and to the north Cameron, Queen, and then Princess. The mystery of how Cameron had come to insert itself between a King and his Queen diverted her until Angle came on the line.

"Thanks for returning my call. I have some news to share. But first, did you get a chance to feel Mr. Bliss out?"

"Excuse me?" *My God, were the police spying on*

us?

"Did he let slip anything about a missing document?"

Whew. "I did ask him about the professor and the document—or rather, the book. He acted very reticent. I hear it's been found?"

"Yes, but not in its original location. We're pretty sure it was removed and returned, but we have no motive."

Claire thought about the professor. "Perhaps the thief merely wanted to check something in it."

"Then why not ask the librarian to see it?"

If Claire reminded Angle of the squabble in front of the library, it would only heap more suspicion on Gideon. "I don't know."

"Well, no matter. The big news is we've identified your corpse."

Claire put a hand to her throat. "And?"

"We had no leads here in the States and finally put the word out on Interpol. They got in touch this morning."

Pulse galloping, she finally sputtered, "Well?"

Angle shuffled some papers. "It's a complicated story. Why don't you come down to the office and we'll go over it. Or"—his voice took on a studied indifference that didn't fool Claire—"how about we meet for a spot of lunch? Say, Seagar's?"

Claire fought a silent war with her better judgment until one word triumphed—corpse. She had to find out what Angle knew. "Sure, when?"

"I can meet you there in fifteen minutes."

****

It turned out Lieutenant Angle belonged to that

species of lobster consumer classified as "thorough."
He reminded Claire of her cousin Ellie, who wouldn't
rest until she'd reamed out the last drop of juice from
the tiniest leg of the beast. She'd even been observed
gnawing the antennae. Claire waited patiently, sipping
her iced tea. At last Angle wiped his lips and sat back
with a satisfied pat to his stomach as if to say, *Job well
done*.

"Lieutenant Angle? You were going to explain
about the victim?"

He jerked upright. "Oh, er, please, call me Ernest.
Ernie if you prefer."

*Ernest Angle? What kind of mother would do that
to a child?* She made a determined effort to stifle the
stream of jokes that threatened to pour out of her
mouth. "Certainly. And by all means call me Claire."

"Claire it is." His shoulders relaxed as though a
major hurdle had been successfully cleared. He signaled
for more coffee. "As I told you, we contacted Interpol
after hitting a dead end here in the States."

"Because of his Peruvian suit?"

"What? No. Because of his shoes. They were made
in Italy. Handmade."

"Handmade? That sounds expensive. Why were the
rest of his clothes so threadbare?"

Ernest put his cup down. "I'll get to that. Stamped
inside the shoes we found the address of a cobbler in
Rome. Interpol sent photos of the shoes and the man to
the Italian police, who located the shoemaker.
Apparently the fellow remembers all his customers and
keeps their addresses in a finely-bound parchment
ledger. He provided them with the dead man's name."

"And? What was it?" prompted Claire.

Ernest checked his notebook. "Let's see if I can pronounce it properly. Ju...Giyou...Gasepp—"

"Giuseppe?"

"That's it. Giuseppe Cuomo. In the late 1970s Cuomo served as director of a bank used by the Vatican, the Banco Ambrosiano. He held a prominent position in Roman society until the bank collapsed in 1982 and he fled the country amid accusations of embezzlement. The Italian police finally tracked him down in Lima, Peru, in the nineties, where he lived under an alias, which was..." He checked his notes again. "Okay, this one's easier to pronounce at least. Gasparo Scordato." He looked for approval to his companion, who stared back at him blankly. Angle waited a minute, then continued. "Unfortunately, they couldn't prove his identity, so the Italians were unable to extradite him. Then, three years ago, he disappeared."

"So, this Scordato absconded with the bank funds and hared off to Peru. How did he end up in the States? On top of the Masonic Memorial?"

The detective stirred a third teaspoon of sugar into his coffee. "Would you like dessert? Anything?"

"No, thank you. About Mr. Scordato?" *Why is Ernest slow-walking this?*

"We could find no clue as to how he arrived in Virginia. In fact, I was about to close the file when we received an anonymous tip."

"Tip? From whom?"

"If we knew that, he wouldn't be anonymous, now would he?" To take the sting out of his remark, he patted her hand. "Interpol received an email yesterday and passed it along. The note advised them to look into something called P2."

"P2." Getting facts out of Ernest was harder than getting a hook out of a struggling bluefish. Could he be stringing her along in order to ask her out again? *Fine. Fine. Just spit it out.*

"I set one of our interns on the task of researching it. He handed in some preliminary background this morning. Turns out P2 stands for Propaganda Due. It was a notorious Masonic lodge, run by a fellow named Lazio Truffatore in the 1970s. Truffatore was implicated in the collapse of the Vatican's bank—"

"The dead man's bank?"

"The very same, but Truffatore's reputation for unsavory activity is far more extensive than Scordato's. He's been reported to have had dealings with everyone from Communists to the Mafia. Leftist groups accused him of collaborating with a right-wing group in a terrorist bomb plot in 1969."

"So he's been fingered for everything up to and including stealing candy from babies?" Claire snickered.

Angle gave her a severe look. "Yes. We're definitely not dealing with a model citizen. Apparently he ensnared many high-level politicians and businessmen in his schemes. A list he kept of members of P2 led to the fall of the Italian government in 1981."

"And this Truffatore and Scordato were partners?"

"Not exactly." He finished his coffee and signaled for the check. "Truffatore's the ultimate crook— persuasive, ruthless, power-mad. As master of P2, he pronounced himself the 'puppetmaster' of Italian freemasonry, which apparently irritated the hell out of the Masons. They erased his lodge in 1974, then reinstated it four months later—which constituted an enormous scandal in itself. Finally the powers-that-be expelled Truffatore from the Masons and shut down P2. Or so they thought."

"Wow. P2 doesn't sound like any Masonic lodge I've ever heard of."

"Both the Grand Lodges in the United Kingdom and the European Grand Orient disavowed him and his claims. I'm guessing Truffatore used Propaganda Due as a tool to further his illegal enterprises."

"And Scordato?" *Come* on, *Ernest.*

Her companion scrutinized the other patrons for the vacant expression that could indicate eavesdropping. Evidently what he saw concerned him, for he took her hand and led her outside. The sun already sat low in the sky. Claire checked her watch. Four o'clock. They'd been at lunch for more than two hours. Ernest swallowed a couple of times, an obvious prelude to an invitation, and Claire jumped in quickly. "You were saying? What do Truffatore and P2 have to do with our corpse?"

"Oh. Uh. We're not sure yet, other than that they were associates. The caller merely directed our attention to P2. Interpol is on it."

"They keep you informed though, right?"

Angle squared his shoulders. "I am still the lead investigator."

That's all she wanted to hear. Now when the inevitable request came she knew what her answer would be.

"Claire, do you…do you think you might…"

"I'd love to get together again. Perhaps for coffee? And thanks so much for lunch. I really have to get back to work." Wiggling her fingers at him, she scooted up the hill, tripping only once on a broken brick. When she got to the temple she found Harry in the bookstore.

"Oh, hi, Claire. I was just closing up."

"Harry, do you know anything about P2?"

The young man shook his head. "What is it?"

"It is…was…an Italian lodge. All mixed up in scandal thirty years ago."

"Italian, huh? That would be one of the Grand Orient lodges. You should ask Nigel Abernethy about it. I think he's been working on a paper on the European lodges for his Knights Templar application."

"Thanks. Is he still around?"

"I saw him at the front desk half an hour ago."

Claire walked down the hall to the front entrance. The tiler had his briefcase and umbrella in hand. "Nigel! Do you have a minute?"

He leered at her, no small feat with a bulbous nose that nearly eclipsed his sharp button eyes. "For you, Claire, of course. What can I do you for?"

Claire swallowed hard and managed to push the bile back down. "Can you tell me anything about P2?"

Nigel dropped his jaw, then his briefcase and umbrella on the floor. "No! I mean…er…" He bent down and grabbed his things and took a step away from her. "No, never heard of it. Never." He hopped down the hall and out the door in a remarkable imitation of the White Rabbit.

Chapter Seven
The Washington Link

Claire sat back and pushed her glasses up over her forehead. Her notes lay scattered on the desk before her—pages and pages of scribbles, squiggles, and arrows. Talk about convoluted! The Propaganda Due organization made playing chess with the Red Queen look easy. It did indeed exist, but even the Grand Orient d'Italia—which was itself considered irregular by the other lodges—had washed its hands of P2 in the 1970s. Still, it—or at least its master Lazio Truffatore—kept turning up like a frisky zombie. Truffatore considered P2 his personal piggy bank, using its illustrious members as shills for his innumerable scams and plots. As Ernest had said, he and his gang had been variously associated with skinheads, the Italian secret police, the Mafia, and even the KGB, with a few plain old crooks sprinkled in for good measure. Other reports linked him to a shadowy American black ops group thought to have been left behind to fight Communism after World War II. He had escaped arrest several times before the Italian authorities slapped him with a twelve-year prison sentence in 1998.

During one of his "absences," the police raided his villa and found two million dollars worth of gold ingots hidden in flowerpots. They also impounded a list of very prominent Italian leaders who were members of

P2. It was rumored he had stashed another fortune somewhere, but the treasure hunters who scoured his apartment in Cannes, and haunts or hiding places in Switzerland, Chile, and Argentina, never found anything.

Claire rubbed her eyes. She hadn't come across any reference to a Gasparo Scordato so far. *Oh yeah, Ernest said it was an alias—I know "Gasparo" means treasure-bearer. What about Scordato?* She clicked to her language dictionary website and keyed in the name. Up popped "Left behind, from the verb *scordare*, to forget." Ichabod meowed and she got up to feed him. *Maybe it's one of those gang nicknames, like Eddie One Hand or Carlos the Hamster.* The telephone rang.

"Claire? It's me, Gideon. Can you do me a favor?"

Anything, big boy. "What is it?"

"I want to look at something in the George Washington room at the temple. I understand as docent you have keys to the glass cases?"

"Yeeesss." Considering his recent nocturnal visit she decided to keep to herself the fact that the master keys hung in an unlocked janitor's closet on the main floor. "I have access to them."

"Great. Are you working today?"

"It's my day off. Zoe will be there. She'd be glad to help you."

Gideon paused. "I'd rather have you." Then he said hastily, "This isn't some pathetic excuse to wangle a date, Claire. It's just that…that I have something to share with you."

"Huh."

"It's about time I told you what I've been working on. Anyway, I need a cohort."

"You mean, an accomplice?" Claire thought of Ernest. "Are you asking me to do something illegal?"

"What? No! But it's a bit…delicate."

"All right. What's your plan?"

"Can you meet me at the side entrance at eleven?"

Only one way to find out what he's up to. "Okay. Sure."

Claire hung up and pulled Ichabod onto her lap. He submitted to her stroking with reluctance. *Probably senses my restlessness.* Should she call Ernest? Gideon claimed he was on the up and up, but it all seemed too pat. Gideon trying to sneak into the library with a professor who'd been censured for faking documents. Gideon with a leather book under his arm, spine carefully concealed. Gideon hanging around the George Washington museum. *The museum…wait, I forgot…he's an expert on Washington.*

After all, the Masonic Temple had been built not only as a lodge for the Alexandria Masons, but as a memorial to George Washington. It contained piles of important documents, paintings, and memorabilia related to the first president.

A slight breeze wafted through the window and lifted a scribbled note from the desk. She caught it in midair. It concerned a news item about a famous statue discovered in Lazio Truffatore's garden—a statue that had been stolen four years earlier. Could Gideon be like Truffatore—one of those obsessed collectors who didn't care how he came by his acquisitions? Did he have a mother lode of plundered items locked in a vault in his basement? He had yet to invite her to his house. Was it because he had something to hide?

One thing's for sure. I'm not letting him have the

keys. She pushed Ichabod off her lap and trudged up the stairs to change for her "date."

****

Gideon met Claire at the entrance to the museum and led her inside. "You know the stained glass portrait of Doctor Elisha Cullen Dick in the Memorial Hall?" Claire nodded. "Dr. Dick was the mayor of Alexandria and sponsored President Washington's admission to the first Alexandria lodge. He also attended the president at his death bed." He pointed at a glass case. "Here is the clock he stopped at the moment of Washington's death, and those are his dueling pistols. Now over here…" Gideon took Claire's hand and led her to the portrait of a balding man in cravat and coat. "…is Mr. Dick himself."

Claire nodded dutifully. She trailed after him while he moved from case to case expounding on the background of each item. Although she'd already studied the inventory of the museum, she had to admit he brought the bits and pieces of an illustrious life onto a much more animated stage. As he talked, the distant figure of our first president took on a human face. His personality filled out and breathed, clarifying both his finer and his less than stellar features. "Among his few faults, there's evidence that he and Jefferson indulged in a toke now and then…"

"Really? He smoked marijuana?" Claire stared at Gideon, who laughed.

"Hemp was grown for rope and cloth in colonial times. Taking a hit of the weed wasn't unusual. Now these papers are worth their weight in gold…"

He indicated several torn and creased letters, the florid handwriting faded. When Claire bent closer, she saw George Washington's signature at the bottom of each. She turned to ask Gideon about them and caught a fleeting expression on his face like the single-minded gaze of a wolf stalking his prey. It shook her. *Maybe there is something to the unscrupulous collector idea.*

She longed to ask him about the book that was lost and now found, but couldn't find a suitable opening. Finally she made a show of casting her eyes around as though searching for something.

It caught Gideon's attention. "Are you looking for anything in particular?"

"Yes. Mr. Quinn told me a book had disappeared from the library and that Mr. Treadwater discovered it in the museum. I was wondering where he found it."

Gideon stood still. "A book. Do you know which book?"

Shoot, why didn't I ask the title? "Um, I've forgotten the *exact* title—but I'm sure it had to do with George Washington."

He chuckled. "That should narrow it down."

This wasn't going well. "Er, I gather it was a large volume—leather-bound in black. Nearly priceless." She watched him closely.

He turned away from her. His voice floated over his shoulder like Isadora Duncan's scarf—graceful but deadly. "I'm sure Treadwater has already returned it to the library. He probably just misplaced it."

Okay, time to delve, Nancy Drew. "You're a Washington aficionado. What kind of book...or...or object would be so valuable that someone would want to steal it?"

He rounded on her, his eyes flashing. "Stealing any Washington artifact would be an unconscionable thing to do. These things are public property, part of our heritage, and should be available to all, not tucked away in some dungeon"—he glared at the locked cases—"for the sole entertainment of the inimitable Treadwater."

So much for the secret treasure chamber. Would Ernest's suspicions about Gideon's connection to Scordato have more traction? How to bring it into the conversation? Claire decided on an oblique approach. "Is that why you took the book? To ensure public access to it?"

"Me?" He took a step backward, hand to chest, an expression of righteous reproach on his mobile face. It was so effective that if Claire had trusted him she might have worried she'd gone too far. "I didn't steal it. I...uh..." Both his eyes and his hand dropped. He mumbled something.

"What did you say?"

"I borrowed it. Just for a few days."

"You *borrowed* the book? Why?"

"Because I needed to check...Shit. You tricked me, Claire." He ran his fingers through his hair and plunked down in Washington's chair, as oblivious as Mrs. Malloy had been to Claire's gasp. "I wanted to compare an entry in the book to...something. Another source. I wrote to Treadwater two weeks ago asking to use the library, citing Professor Nutley as a reference. I couldn't understand why he didn't respond until I brought Fred in. How was I to know about the bad blood between them? When Treadwater realized Nutley and I were working together, all my overtures went up in smoke. He no longer trusted me. When he refused access to the one book I needed, what could I do? I nipped into the library when he was out to lunch and…er…appropriated it." He gave her a weak "don't cut off my head" grin. "I did put it back."

"Not before Treadwater discovered it missing. He's on the hunt for the culprit. And he's enlisted the police."

"How do you know?'

"Because Ernest—I mean Lieutenant Angle— asked me to…observe you. He's curious because the book disappeared the day of the murder."

Rather than objecting to the implied accusation, Gideon zeroed in on her slip of the tongue. "Ernest?" His emerald eyes glittered.

Uh oh. Quick—deflect! Deflect! "Yes, Ernest. You remember the police detective in charge of the case, don't you? He's a very nice man." She threw in a perky smile for good measure.

"I see." He continued to contemplate her, his face inscrutable.

Okay, scratch insensitivity. How about moral indignation? "Don't change the subject. We're talking about you."

"Not anymore." Gideon bent his head and peered at her from under his thick, coffee-colored eyebrows. "Since when are you on a first-name basis with a policeman?"

"Since never you mind." Claire tossed her head. "What's so special about the book that you risked the wrath of the librarian, anyway?"

Gideon allowed his lingering stare to fade. "Maybe it's time I told you." He took a step toward the elevator but paused. "I almost forgot why I brought you here. Come."

She followed him to a glass case nearly hidden

behind a pillar, where he pointed out a small, worn volume. The book had been opened to reveal the yellowed pages of the Book of Genesis. "What is it?"

Emotion whipping across his face, Gideon breathed, "It's one of the Washington family Bibles."

Claire squinted at it, confused. "Isn't that the Washington family Bible over there?" She gestured at a large display case in the center of the room.

Gideon nodded. "Yes, that's the famous one. This, however"—he tapped the glass—"this could hold more significance. It belonged to a distant female cousin of Washington's, a woman named Eleanor Nutley. It may contain information that—were it to be made public— could possibly destroy Washington's image as a man of integrity."

"Oh my God." Claire gaped at him. "What kind of information?"

"Frederick Nutley believes we will find an entry that proves George Washington fathered a child by his cousin."

"In a *Bible?*"

"Why not? Before passports and birth certificates, people recorded births and deaths in their family Bibles. When my grandmother took her first trip overseas, she used the Bliss Bible to prove her birth date. Nutley suspects that a Magdalen Nutley is listed in this book as born on February 26, 1758, sired by one G. Washington."

"But why have we never heard of this Magdelen?"

"For one thing, he says she died four days after her birth. For another, there's been—so far at least—no evidence that George himself ever knew about her."

Clair, still skeptical, thought she'd found the flaw

in his theory. "If that's so, how would the professor know about the scandal?"

"He'd been researching his own family's genealogy over at Collingwood Library and came across a branch that was distantly related to Washington. Eleanor Nutley lived on a small plantation in southern Virginia. Among her papers he found a letter that makes a cryptic reference to George visiting their farm and leaving 'something' behind."

"That doesn't necessarily mean a baby. It could be a…a theodolite or something."

Gideon's eyebrows went up. "Theodolite?"

"I think that's the word—something a surveyor uses. Washington was a surveyor, wasn't he?"

"Yes, but that wasn't it." Gideon frowned. "Where was I?"

"Theodolite?"

"No. You're not helping, Claire."

She relented. "All right, something George left behind?"

"That's it. In another letter dated seven months after the first she speaks of the birth of a baby girl, quote, to Jane, unquote, on that date. Frederick is convinced it refers to Washington's child." He gestured at the case where the official Washington Bible lay. "When Washington's family donated that Bible, the librarian found half a page torn out, no one knows when or by whom. If Nutley is right, the missing piece listed the birth of an illegitimate daughter to George Washington. Since it's gone, this Bible"—he pointed at the crinkled page before them—"may possibly contain the only known evidence of his having any children. Nutley had to check this Bible to prove his theory, but he was thwarted at every turn."

"I know. Treadwater."

"They've been rivals and enemies for years."

"But what makes you think this Bible contains the information?"

"Nutley showed me the second letter. In it Eleanor mentioned the birth had been recorded in her Bible."

Claire tapped the glass case thoughtfully. "Does Mr. Treadwater know why Professor Nutley wants to look at it?"

"He does now."

Claire thought back. Hadn't someone said Nutley had been discredited? Understanding dawned. "Nutley published his findings without the Bible to back him up, didn't he?"

"Yes, the fool."

"And you wanted to help the professor regain his reputation by stealing it."

He started. "Nothing of the sort. I merely want to take a look at the Bible. Did you bring the keys?"

Claire made a show of checking her pockets. "Oops, I forgot."

He checked his watch. "We don't have time for you to go get them now. Damn—we're so close."

It's now or never. "Gideon, why did you steal the other book then? Why not steal this one?"

He glared at her. "The book I *borrowed* is a genealogy of Washington's extended family. It's the only copy of that particular genealogy in existence. I insisted to Nutley that we check the entries in it to ensure no other G. Washington could have done the dirty deed."

"What did you find?"

112

"Perhaps another piece to the puzzle. Perhaps not."

"Can't you be more specific?"

"Not yet. I'm waiting for one more bit of information."

Claire's head began to spin. "You have me totally muddled now. Gideon, why are you helping Professor Nutley anyway? What aren't you telling me?"

Gideon turned from the case and put a sinewy hand on each of her arms. Looking deep into her eyes, he lifted his chin as though he'd come to a decision. "We'll have to leave the Bible for now. It's time I let you in on the secret."

He led her out to his car and drove through the narrow streets, turning left on West and right on Cameron. They had almost reached the waterfront when he pulled into a driveway hidden under a thick wisteria vine and stopped next to a magnificent Federal style townhouse. The three-story-high brick walls were covered with ivy. Black-eyed susans, pink and yellow zinnias, and red nasturtiums ran riot in the backyard garden. In their midst a passionflower vine slithered up a weather-stained statue of Aphrodite to caress her breasts. Something sparkled in the dappled sun. She peered between the ancient boxwoods. "A swimming pool?"

"A small one—I love an evening dip, don't you?"

Claire remembered her beautiful pool in Potomac. "Yes, I do."

"Come." He circled her waist with his arm and nudged her gently to the front door. It opened on what could have been a Park Avenue gallery. The wide-planked yellow pine floor had been waxed to a high gloss, setting off the colorful kilims scattered here and there. To her left lay a drawing room that held, besides the John-Richard designer chairs and coffee table, a baby grand piano and a Brazilian cherry bar. On her right, a glass-topped table ran the length of the dining room. Raspberry speckled oriental lilies—heavy with perfume—tumbled carelessly from the tall Dale Tiffany crystal vase in the center.

Gideon led her on down the hall. Through a door she glimpsed a gleaming stainless steel kitchen with all the latest appliances. Taking up the back half of the house was an octagonal room. Large windows unencumbered by curtains opened onto the gardens. Graceful wingback chairs upholstered in white leather set off the brilliant Carl Hunter abstracts. Enchanted, Claire exclaimed, "It's a beautiful house!" A second later a wave of embarrassment washed over her. *Gideon must have felt so squashed in my little Prince Street place.*

"It is rather nice, isn't it? Funny, for all her faults, Dorcas has fabulous taste. You don't think it's too outré for Old Town?"

"I admit I expected a dark haven crowded with Washingtoniana and overstuffed club chairs. Clay tavern pipes on the walls, that sort of thing."

Gideon let out a guffaw with a hint of chagrin. "You're too close by half. If I'd had my druthers it *would* look like that. But since Dorcas and I had only been married a few weeks I still wanted to please her. We bought the house from some Oklahoma tycoon who'd furnished it with all kinds of hideous antiques. Dorcas forced him to remove them all. They had a real row over it—this guy insisting the stuff was all top-drawer, and he ought to know, he'd paid an arm and a leg for them. He threw out the name of the biggest decorator in Old Town to prove his point."

"Sounds like he met his match in your wife." Claire hated the sound of that word. It reminded her to bury the lascivious thoughts zigzagging through her body.

"Oh, he did. Let me see, what was the fellow's name? Oh, yes, Mr. Remington Doyle. Chuck to his friends. He owns a chain of the biggest box stores in the country—More for Less—you know them?" His eyes crinkled with glee. "With all his millions even he couldn't stand in the way of a bitch in her lair. Not that he didn't hire an army of lawyers to try. When he lost anyway, the poor guy had a hissy fit right here." Gideon surveyed the room, a reminiscent smile playing across his lips.

Claire rolled her eyes. "He hardly sounds the gentleman—but then, nor do you for amusing yourself at his expense."

"The guy was a creep, Claire. I hope he learned his lesson."

Against the back wall of the living room a wrought iron staircase wound up to the second floor, transforming into a balcony. Gideon raised his eyes to it, his arm across Claire's shoulders. "The study, a guest room, and the master bedroom are up there." The scent of bay and lime enveloped her, and the warmth rising from his skin filled her consciousness. She wanted him so badly she could have jumped him then and there. She put a hand out, but at that moment he walked away. "You hungry?"

Yes, but I don't think it's on the menu. She wasted some time trying to remember what movie the line came from and finally gave up and followed him to the kitchen. He had set out a bottle of wine, a couple of plates and two glasses. As he busied himself in the SubZero refrigerator she checked the label. A 2008 Olivier Leflaive Puligny Montrachet. *A very, very good year.*

On one side of the sparkling white quartz island he set down a long board covered with a round of ripe Vacherin Mont d'Or, a crispy baguette, and slices of red Anjou pear, glistening with juice. In the center he placed a *salade niçoise* arranged in a complex spiral pattern on a deep green glass platter that reflected his eyes. Lost in admiration, she pulled a stool out and sat down. He poured her a glass. "Sköl!" When she didn't respond he seemed puzzled. "Aren't you going to say something?"

She started to say "Chin chin," but instead blurted, "Did you plan this or are you always so…so organized?"

A slight wash of red bloomed on his cheeks. "I confess, I hoped I could talk you into coming home with me."

And I thought I'd *kept my raging libido under wraps.* Claire sipped her wine and allowed Gideon to fill her plate. "It looks delicious."

"I hope you don't mind eating the entrée and cheese course at the same time." She didn't bother to answer and they ate in companionable silence for a while. The level in the wine bottle seemed to be going down rather rapidly, and he brought out another and opened it.

Claire popped a slice of pear into her mouth.

Gideon leaned toward her. The edges of his face

were slightly blurry—*where did I put my reading glasses anyway?* He seemed to be talking. She concentrated.

"I want to show you something."

I'll show you mine if you show me yours. She raised a hand to her mouth to stop the giggle and missed.

He rose. "Let's go before you fall asleep." He went to a small door hidden under the stairs. "This leads to the cellar."

In Claire's befuddled state she failed to ask the obvious question. She cast a longing glance toward the wrought iron stairs but kept her lips firmly sealed. Gideon pulled a string. A bare bulb swung slowly back and forth, its weak light illuminating an unfinished cellar. A cold, damp smell rose from the depths. She wanted to turn back to the light and air, but he held her hand and guided her carefully down the rickety wooden stairs.

Just as Claire began to wonder how this part of the house had escaped the attentions of the new bride, Gideon spoke. "We were still arguing about what to do with the basement when Dorcas ran off with another man."

Oh. When they reached the bottom, an acrid odor filled Claire's nostrils. She sniffed. "I smell burning…burnt wood."

Gideon nodded. "My house is built on the foundations of a building that burned down almost a hundred and forty years ago."

Claire surveyed the blackened walls. "Did fires happen often in those days?"

"Yes. In the nineteenth century, Virginia houses

were built mainly of wood. Alexandria suffered major events in 1827 and 1871. In 1871 the Market House, which contained the city offices and the first Alexandria Masonic lodge, burned down. Land records show fire destroyed this house a few years later, in 1875."

Claire wrinkled her nose in the bitter air. "What does any of this have to do with George Washington's child?"

"I'm getting to that."

Gideon's words echoed in the gloomy chamber, and Claire shivered. He turned on a flashlight and pointed it at a corner. She followed the beam of light. A piece of plaster hung precariously from a splintered stud darkened with soot. Gideon pulled the sheetrock down, revealing a box sitting on a crossbeam. Its corners were singed, but the brass lock and hinges shone brightly.

"I started to polish it, then realized I shouldn't touch it, let alone clean it. But I couldn't resist opening it." He lifted the lid.

In the tiny light of the flash Claire saw a pile of crumbling papers. She reached out a hand but Gideon grabbed her wrist. "They're very fragile."

"What are they?"

"At least one is a letter from George Washington. I could tell they were quite old so I took the top one out—very carefully, with gloves on. I could make out the salutation and the signature. It said 'Dear Elisha,' and was signed 'G. Washington.' The rest was in very bad shape, although in the second paragraph the name 'Eleanor' is legible. At that point the letter began to disintegrate, so I sent it to a conservator for stabilization. He's examining it as we speak. If he

118

agrees with me I'll send him the entire box of letters. They could have inordinate historical value."

"They must be priceless."

Gideon dropped her wrist. "That's not important."

She recoiled at his frigid tone. "It could be important to *someone*."

He took her hand and kissed the palm. "Sorry. Of course, you're right. If word gets out about this cache too soon, it could be vulnerable. That's why I haven't told anyone about it yet."

"Not even Treadwater?"

"Certainly not. The man's a buffoon. He'd lock them in a vault and only let Worshipful Masters holding the highest levels of both Scottish and York Rites see them. A criminal waste of a critical primary source."

"I take it you're not a Mason."

"No, but every other male member of my family, living and dead, is. I have no grievance against the Masons—but I want these documents available to anyone for study, which Treadwater would be unlikely to agree to."

Claire pointed at the box. "These papers are probably the property of the federal government. You may not have any right to set terms."

Gideon shook his head. "According to the law, materials found on my property—private property— belong to me. This is my house."

His house? "Gideon, does...does Dorcas have her name on the title?"

He bent down and tied an imaginary shoelace, mumbling something.

"What did you say?"

He straightened. "Yes, Dorcas is still joint owner.

That's why I need Mother to get her signature on all the papers, and fast. One reason anyway." He faced her, his eyes softening. Her whole body leaned toward him, wanting to be enfolded, wanting to shut out the grim surroundings, the chill and the charred timbers.

Not here. "So how did these letters end up in your house?"

Gideon closed the box with his elbow and hung the plaster up again, hiding it from view. "As I'm sure you know, the first lodge met on an upper floor of the commercial building on Cameron Street until the 1871 fire. While they were rebuilding, the Masons found temporary space nearby."

"I hadn't heard that." Claire wondered if the interim site were one of those secrets a non-Mason shouldn't be privy to. "Mr. Quinn told me they used the Market Square site until 1944 or so, when they moved to the present Temple."

"He may not be aware of it—I only found two references to the Masons' use of this house in obscure city documents."

"Wait a minute." Claire stared at him. "You're saying the temporary headquarters were here in your house?"

"I think so. Yes."

"So why would anyone hide letters by George Washington? And why here rather than the temple? Or at least the new Market Square lodge?"

"Good question. The 1871 fire destroyed a lot of the material bequeathed by Washington's family, but the lodge brothers did manage to save some items— which are now in the museum. I think the box also survived, but someone hid it behind a wall and it remained here."

"Where it endured a second conflagration." Claire sat down on an overturned keg. A fruity scent wafted from it. *Cider?* "What do you think the letters will say?"

"I haven't found any other Eleanor associated with Washington, so I'm guessing the letter refers to our Eleanor Nutley and, with any luck, the child. According to the genealogy, Magdalen Nutley was sired by G. Washington. No name is given for the mother. These letters may tell us who she was and if the president was involved."

"Have you told Professor Nutley about them?"

"No." Gideon turned to the stairs. "I don't want to bring him in until I hear from Allen Greystone, the conservator. Now, come on."

Claire took his hand and they climbed the stairs to the hall.

"What are you going to do now?"

Gideon closed the little door behind her and took her face in his hands. "I am going to make love to you."

One would have thought this would take Claire by surprise, but since she had managed to keep her own desire on the back burner only by dint of fingernails jammed painfully into her palms, she didn't quibble. "Take me upstairs."

Claire assumed the king-sized bed filling the center of the room was there by necessity, given Gideon's six-foot-three frame. *Thank God there's no ceiling mirror.* Light filtered in through the wooden Roman shades, revealing a room with few feminine touches. She hoped that meant Dorcas hadn't spent much time here. The bureau had a small mirror, a brush, and a bowl of coins.

Clothes were dumped unceremoniously near, but not on, hooks.

It didn't take them long to add to the pile. As they stood amid the detritus Gideon bent down to kiss the top of her head. She took a forefinger and pushed him slowly but irresistibly onto his back on the bed, noting with satisfaction the flicker of trepidation that licked his features. The hours leading up to this moment only made her hungrier for him. Setting one knee on each side of his hips, she slowly inched up his body, gliding over the erect penis with only a casual rub. He grabbed her thighs and drew her to him. His tongue lodged itself in her vagina, sucking and tickling. She rolled the aching flesh over his mouth and opened her thighs wide. The orgasm rose just before she wanted it to, but when she heard him mumble, "Come on, come on, baby, come," she let go.

She arched over him, shaking and yelping, before collapsing on his chest. He held her arms and moved her off his body. "My turn," he whispered.

When he'd finished, not a skin cell on her body remained unfondled. His penis lay inside her pumping its last ounce of love, and his lips were fastened on one ear lobe, nibbling the soft flesh.

She awoke to find the sun that slipped through the shades glistening red and checked her watch. Six o'clock! "Oh dear, my mother was supposed to call. She'll wonder why I didn't pick up." She scrabbled about on the floor for her purse and sat back on the bed, stumped.

"You left it downstairs." Gideon stretched and let a hand fall on her breast. He tickled the nipple till it stood up. "Just tell her you were indisposed."

She brushed the hand away. "I have to go, Gideon. I can't believe what we did."

"It's called 'Afternoon Delight.' Delightful. Come here."

"Really, no." She found her light cotton shift under the bed and pulled it on, then ran a comb through her hair. "You haven't told me what you're going to do with the box."

Gideon sighed and pulled on his jeans. "I need a little more time. If Nutley's theory is correct, the letters could be explosive, but I'd really like to be sure of their authenticity before the news gets out."

"When will you know?"

But he didn't have a chance to answer her. Loud pounding came from the front door. Gideon didn't bother to button his shirt before running out to the balcony. From the front windows Claire saw strobe lights flashing in the street. *Police cars?*

As her lover leapt down the stairs they heard a deep voice trumpet, "Mr. Bliss? Open up. This is the police."

Claire began to descend the stairs but stopped when she heard Gideon's voice. "Yes, officer. Yes, I'm alone…Certainly, just let me get my wallet and phone, and I'll be right with you." She crouched behind the railing and waited until she heard the door slam. As the flashing lights faded away, she crept down the stairs, picked up her purse, and slipped out the garden door. Too late she remembered that she had never gotten around to bringing up Scordato. *Is it out of my hands now?*

Chapter Eight
A Key Link

Claire didn't want Ernest to think she knew about Gideon's arrest before it hit the papers, so she decided to wait until Monday to call the police station. She spent Sunday awash in worry. Her brain a mass of darting thoughts, she paced her living room for an hour, and when that didn't relieve the tension—mainly because she could only go two steps before smacking into a wall—she walked the streets of Old Town. Gravitating reflexively to the waterfront, she sat down on the bench where she and Gideon had snuggled on their first date.

She tried to focus on the long-lost letters and their potential historical value, but instead kept returning to the day before and an afternoon of lovemaking. She'd never thought she'd find someone who fit her so perfectly, who mirrored her movements, her desires, even her moods. Lincoln had been an imaginative lover, skilled with accessories and schooled in erotic positions, but only now did she recognize the constant distance he maintained between them, as though he couldn't give himself wholly. *Did he ever really love me? Did his heart always belong to Inez?* For some reason, the thought did not devastate her. She closed her eyes. The spicy scent of lime filled her nostrils and she felt again the warmth of an embrace filled with love. When she opened them a policeman stood before her.

"Ma'am? Are you all right?"

She jumped up, straightening her skirt. "Yes, officer, I'm fine. I'll just be toddling off now. Yes, I will. Thank you so much for your concern. Yes...yes, right." *God, just what I need—a suspicious policeman.* It reminded her that more than one obstacle to a happy ending lay before them.

****

A fitful night's sleep later, she called the station on Mill Road. "Ernest, I heard on the news that you arrested Senator Bliss. What is he charged with?"

"I can't tell you much, Claire. At this point we're still sorting out the various accusations. Mr. Treadwater is not a very helpful witness. He's in a stew over Professor Nutley and demands that we haul him in too."

"What for?"

"He's convinced Nutley is the ringleader of a gang that plans to loot the Masonic Memorial of artifacts, starting with the document from the library he claims Bliss stole."

"I heard Mr. Treadwater found that book." *Albeit where Gideon left it.*

"He did indeed. He's still bringing charges, however. Plus, during his search he discovered another missing item."

"What?"

"A key."

"Key?"

"A gold-plated key. Evidently it had come in a large trunk full of stuff donated by Washington's descendants. Neither Treadwater nor anyone else could discover what it went to, so Comfrey suggested they put it in the exhibit with—get this—a card saying 'Key to the Jewels.' "

"Funny." Claire's laugh stuck in her throat. "And you think the senator stole it?"

"He's the only unsupervised non-staff person who's been alone in the museum in the last two weeks."

"But why would he steal a key to nowhere?"

"We're not sure yet, Claire. The key lay in the case where Treadwater found the book—a case that was forced open. Ipso facto."

"And what does all this have to do with Professor Nutley?"

She could almost hear Angle shake his head in bafflement. "This is the crazy part. Treadwater insists they're in it together. He keeps saying 'Bliss is an honorable man'—like he's Brutus to Nutley's Cassius or something."

Claire tried to listen with an open mind. She didn't really know Gideon that well after all. He'd made no secret of his fascination with George Washington. *Wait a minute...key...box. Hmm.* "Ernest? Can I..." Claire paused. It wouldn't do to have Ernest think he had a rival. Or worse, that she was knee deep in the business. If she could keep the detective's romantic hopes alive she could both distract him and stay in the loop. At least for a little longer. She stifled the guilt and cooed, "Ernest?"

"Yes?"

"I...er...wondered if you...um...wanted to meet for coffee today? I'm free at eleven."

She heard a quick intake of breath. "That sounds wonderful, but I'm afraid I'm bogged down with paperwork—you know, thirty seconds of action and thirty hours of documentation. How about dinner tonight instead?"

Gulp. But...Gideon. She stared at her reflection in the mirror. *Gideon's married. Gideon may be a crook.* She heard her sister's voice. "You've got to get out more—do man tastings. Don't fall for the first hunk who walks past your door with a Russian wolfhound and Italian leather gloves."

"Claire?"

It could be the only way to get some answers. "Sure."

"I'll pick you up at seven then. How does the Chart House sound?"

She started to object but caught herself. *Just because Gideon took me there doesn't mean it's off limits.* "No, I mean yes, that would be...lovely."

****

Try as she might she couldn't get Ernest to focus on his case. He continually sought her hand, gazed soulfully into her eyes, and spoke softly and poetically about music and art. He ordered oysters with enthusiasm and urged the chocolate molten lava cake on her with arch allusions to her thin figure. In short, the perfect date. For some other time. Or someone else. Someone who didn't have a pressing need to learn the truth about the man who kept her awake at night, whose voice echoed in her brain at the most inappropriate moments, whose touch raised the tiny hairs on her arms and fizzled her nerve endings. She had to know if Gideon were guilty. Even more important, she had to know if he'd told her the truth. *That he isn't another Lincoln.*

"Coffee?"

"No, thanks. It *is* a school night—I'd better be getting home."

Ernest's face sagged, but when they walked out into a balmy night he perked up. "Shall we walk? It's only a few blocks to your place."

Actually it's about ten, but this might be my chance to ferret some information out of him. "Why not?"

They strolled through the alley behind the old munitions factory now known as the Torpedo Factory Art Center, passing two jugglers and a wine glass musician, and crossed Union Street at Cameron. Angle started to turn left down Union, but Claire took his arm and pressed on until they passed Gideon's house. Darkened and lifeless, it depressed her to think it might stay that way. She pointed it out. "That's Senator Bliss's house, isn't it? How long will you keep him in jail?"

"What do you mean? He's not in jail."

"But…how? When?"

"He got out on bail this afternoon. The judge didn't think theft and trespassing charges were serious enough to make him a flight risk."

"Do you know who posted bail?"

"His mother." Ernest's gray eyes twinkled. "My desk sergeant is still wagging his head. Apparently she's a real piece of work. Gave Bliss a tongue-lashing they could hear three blocks away. Most of it in French, so it's probably a blessing Sarge didn't understand a word. They say French curses are very racy."

From what she knew of Mrs. Bliss, Claire figured she understood a tirade in English could end up in the tabloids and jeopardize her son's budding congressional career. "Then why is the house closed up?"

"We've roped it off until we finish the investigation."

She regarded the yellow police tape strung across the front stoop. "What are you looking for?"

"The golden key, for one thing. Plus, given Bliss's presence in the memorial on the day of the murder, not to mention his association with shady characters—"

"Professor Nutley?"

"—among others, we want to eliminate any possibility that he was involved in that crime."

"But that's absurd." Claire's voice rose despite her best intentions. "Why would Gideon kill Scordato? He didn't even know him. And besides, he was in the George Washington museum at the time. He couldn't have made it to the observation deck without my group seeing him. And I assure you we would have noticed him shooting someone."

Ernest shielded his chest in mock terror. "I hope that's just an instinctive female defense of the accused and nothing more." He reddened, evidently embarrassed by his burst of jealousy. Turning away, he muttered, "Besides, we don't know whether he knew Gasparo Scordato or not. Or if he has any connection to the Propaganda Due bunch. As I said, the investigation is ongoing."

Claire wrote on her mental to-do list—growing at warp speed—to ask Gideon what, if anything, he knew about P2. "Ah, here we are." They stopped in front of her door, and she pulled out her house key.

Ernest made a gurgling sound she assumed meant he wanted to be invited in. She ignored it. "Thank you so much for a lovely evening. I find it so pleasant to speak of things other than crime now and then, don't you?" She smiled brightly both for Ernest and God—who she suspected would judge her lie more harshly—stepped inside, and softly closed the door on him.

"Consorting with the enemy?"

Claire wasn't given to shrieking, so she confined herself to a piercing squeak. "Gideon!"

He attempted to enfold her in his strong, manly arms, but met only empty air. When he tried again, she ducked under his elbow and marched to the kitchen, head high. "Claire! Aren't you going to ask me what I'm doing here?"

She pulled out one glass, filled it with ice, and poured a hefty measure of bourbon into it. When she returned to the living room he still stood by the door. She sat down in the middle of the loveseat and indicated the packing crate. "What are you doing here?"

He lowered himself carefully onto the box, his eyes locked with thirsty attention on her glass. "I take it from your shocking lack of hospitality that you are angry with me."

She considered an eloquent *Duh*, but felt that would constitute too great a courtesy. "*Hmph*."

"So much for standing by your man."

"You're not my man."

"Apparently not. Yet." He waggled his eyebrows and gave her a come-hither look.

She almost fell for it, almost laughed. Instead she gritted her teeth and said, "I don't date jailbirds."

"Ah, now we get to the crux. You think I'm a criminal just because I was arrested."

Claire shook her head to clear it. "Where did I go wrong in this analysis?"

"I'm not guilty. At least, not of anything more than borrowing a book because a nasty little librarian wouldn't let me look at it. And my motive, as you well know, is unassailable."

"No, I don't know. Enlighten me."

"I want to prove or disprove the rumor that George Washington fathered a child out of wedlock. I found no reference to Magdalen in the book, so I went on to check George Washington's family tree to see if there were other 'G's and what, if any, the link to the woman named Jane could be. I found Eleanor, but no Jane. My theory is that Jane was a slave in the household, and Eleanor used her pregnancy to further her own pecuniary designs on the father of our country."

"*Hmm.* And they say life was so much simpler then."

Gideon rose abruptly, went into the tiny kitchen, and fixed himself a bourbon. When he came back, he held up the glass and glared at her. "I'll reimburse you, all right?" He plopped down on the packing crate, which whined slightly as though in pain.

"So, how do you plan to prove this theory?"

"First, with the letter from the box in the cellar. Allen—the expert—is hard at work deciphering it. I enlisted Frederick Nutley because he had done so much preliminary research. And because his name is dirt in academic circles."

"I don't follow."

"He wants to debunk the allegation that he fabricated the story of Washington's bastard child." He sipped his drink. "What's ironic is that the initial results from the conservator indicate that Nutley is wrong. However, he's a serious academic. I'm sure he'll want to find the truth no matter what."

"He thinks he'll be reinstated if your document is legitimate?"

"Yes. So do I."

"But you just said the letter refutes his thesis. Is he okay with that?"

"I haven't told him of Greystone's results yet. But I'm sure he won't mind because this is a bigger bombshell than George Washington siring an illegitimate daughter."

"I see."

"You will. The letter is from George to his friend Dr. Dick—and stop giggling. I hate that."

"Sorry."

"Allen has managed to transcribe the last paragraph. Washington wrote that 'Eleanor' had rescinded her claims to have borne a child. He thanked Dick for uncovering her shady background and earlier attempts at blackmailing prominent men. He prayed that the matter would never be made public and hinted that 'G' had been suitably chastened by the affair."

" 'G'—who's 'G' if not George?"

"George's brother, John Augustine."

"You think his brother was the culprit?"

Gideon hesitated only a second. "Yes, I do. I knew John was familiarly known as Gus, but I wanted to check the dates in the genealogy I borrowed. In 1758—when the child was born—he would have been twenty-two, and by some accounts a randy fellow. At the time, George was courting Martha Dandridge Custis, and it's unlikely he would have engaged in an illicit affair with so much at stake. Gus, on the other hand, had a less savory reputation. Plus, a year later, in 1759, John

Augustine moved with his wife from Mount Vernon to her father's estate in Westmoreland County. To get away from the scandal? You be the judge."

Claire put her drink down. "Let me get this straight. You're postulating, based on a cryptic paragraph in a letter and a vaguely worded note written by a distant cousin of George Washington's—"

"And the entry in the Nutley Bible—"

"Which you haven't yet seen. You're asserting that George Washington's brother had an affair with their cousin—"

"Actually, it would have been with Eleanor's slave."

"—after which her mistress tried to hit George with a paternity suit, correct?"

Gideon nodded. "That's the gist. No one would have been concerned about a slave, but a lady…"

"Poppycock."

Gideon tossed off his drink and a lock of glistening sable hair and stood. His emerald green eyes sparked with annoyance. "I'm going to ignore your rude remark in the interests of science. We have, after all, established one fact, one that will roil all the Washington experts and conspiracy theorists. Not to mention a cottage industry in claimants to Washington ancestry."

Claire contemplated the man before her. "So this bombshell, this dramatic discovery, this earth-shattering revelation, is that George Washington *didn't* have an illegitimate child?"

"Yes! Isn't it fantastic?" His radiant expression almost swayed her. Almost.

"Big whoop."

Gideon's face fell, and yet still, Claire thought, he could give Hugh Jackman a run for his money. "You don't understand. This refutes forever the urban legend that Washington had direct offspring. Plus it's…it's really historic."

At his expression, simultaneously entreating and frustrated, Claire's heart made a belly flop. *Goddammit. The man's too cute.* She opened her mouth to ask a question, but found herself crooning, "Shut up and kiss me."

He obliged. The rest played out elsewhere in a very satisfactory manner for both man and woman.

****

"I understand your mother bailed you out."

Gideon groaned. "You would bring that up."

"I hear your mother is one formidable lady."

"That she is."

"Are you going to tell me what happened?"

"Do I have to go over such painful ground while it's still smoking?"

"It might help ease the sting."

He flipped over on his back and wrapped a muscled arm around Claire's neck. "Why can't you let me wallow in the pleasure of recent activities?"

She sighed. "I should, since it's not going to happen again."

"Why not?"

"Gideon, you need to resolve the Dorcas issue before we go any further."

He removed his arm and turned to face her, anger and misery warring in his voice. "You don't think I'm working every angle I can to do just that?"

She couldn't deny it. "Still…" She pushed his lips

away. "Besides that, you're also awaiting trial for theft. I'm not one of those women who are attracted to convicts."

"That's what Mother said. I swear you're as bad as she is."

"I hope that's a compliment."

"You are free to decide when you meet her."

"I've heard no rumblings concerning such an event. Are you by any chance embarrassed to introduce me?"

"Not you. Her."

Claire raised her head and cocked an eyebrow. "Surely you're not ashamed of your own mother."

Gideon put a finger under Claire's chin and gazed at her fondly. "No, I'm very proud of her. In fact, I think you two will get along famously. Not good news for the boy child."

"I like her already."

"You'll meet her day after tomorrow. She asked me to invite you to tea."

"Wednesday!" Claire's hand went automatically to her hair. She blinked. "Will you be there?"

"No, it's just the two of you. She wants to get to know her new friend's daughter. At least that's her story."

"Urp."

Gideon stared at her. "Oh, this is too precious. You're nervous!"

"Am not. Now hand me my bathrobe."

"Claire is ascared to meet her boyfriend's mother. Nyah nyah."

Head held high, she strutted to the bathroom, groping madly for a comeback. *Ha*. She spun around and thrust. "Not as scared as you'll be to meet *my* mother."

He grinned. "On the contrary, I look forward to it." He called after her retreating back, "From what I've heard they're a congenial and dangerous pair."

****

"So you are Letitia's daughter."

Claire wasn't sure how to respond to the statement. She finally chose to feint. "Mother has told me so much about you, Mrs. Bliss. Is she well?"

"As well as can be expected, considering she's in Paris."

"She does love it there. Has she bought enough yet?"

"I don't think so. I did my best to introduce her to the art and music scene, but she persisted in dragging me to antique stores and fashion shows. Most disagreeable." She smiled happily and folded her delicate hands in her lap.

Claire studied Gideon's mother. *Andromeda Miller Bliss—you don't hear names like that anymore. Or meet a lady who fits the description so perfectly.* Ramrod straight, her hair silver white and wound in an elegant chignon, she wore a Chanel suit with the requisite string of pearls—pearls that in this case shone with the translucent glow found only in those gathered from the turquoise depths of the South Pacific. She sat so still and composed that the room appeared to have been built around her.

A waiter approached. "More tea, madame?"

"Thank you. The young lady would like a slice of that lovely angel food cake." Claire started to protest, but quickly saw the futility of it. "Oh, and let's have another plate of cucumber sandwiches." She bestowed a gentle smile on Claire. "The Morrison House has the only proper high tea in Alexandria, don't you agree?"

"It is certainly...um...bountiful." Mrs. Bliss had so far said little beyond pleasantries and Claire's anxiety deepened. *When is she going to strike?*

"Your mother tells me you and my son have been...er...dating." She made the idea sound slightly Bohemian.

"Yes—no, I mean, we're just friends." *Oh great, my first test and I fold like a wet napkin.* "We've met a couple of times at the Masonic Memorial. I'm a docent there." *Not bad, but will it suffice?*

The old lady gave her a hard stare, but apparently decided not to cross-examine just yet. "Ah, the Washington memorial. Gideon has been doing some research there before Congress goes back into session after the August recess." She beamed at Claire. "Did he mention he's just been elected to the Senate?"

"Yes, he did."

"He will be representing the state of Connecticut. Nevertheless, the family is quite proud of him." She took a sip of tea from the delicate Limoges cup. "As a respite from the arduous duties of office I have encouraged him to maintain his hobby—the study of our first president. I'm not sure why, but he's been fascinated by George Washington since he was a little boy. At eight years old he decided we must be distantly related and has been pursuing that idea ever since."

"Is he wrong?"

"I doubt it—he's rarely wrong."

I guess she doesn't feel it necessary to add that he takes after his mother.

Andromeda picked up the last sandwich and took a dainty bite. Claire noted that her plate, as well as the sandwich platter, remained free of the tiniest crumb. "I just don't see the point. Our family tree is distinguished enough—what would we do with a connection to a fourth-generation man whose great-grandfather didn't arrive until 1656?"

Claire opted to gulp down her tea rather than reply. A few minutes later Mrs. Bliss rose. "It has been a most enjoyable afternoon, Mrs. Wilding. I do hope we see more of you."

Claire knew the rules. "Oh, please, Mrs. Bliss, do call me Claire."

She smiled with regal satisfaction and replied formally, "And you of course must address me as Mrs. Bliss." She laughed—a silvery tinkle—at Claire's expression, and fluted, "I'm not without a sense of humor, my dear. You may call me Andromeda. Now, I promised my son he could escort me to the theatre tonight, so I must take my leave of you."

She preceded Claire out to the lobby and graciously allowed the bellhop to press the elevator button for her. Claire walked home.

****

"Glenfiddich, please. Make it a double." Gideon let the waiter take Claire's order, and when they were alone, growled, "Bad news."

Claire smirked. "Other than your mother's taking a fancy to me?"

He shook his head. "Much worse. Dorcas is here."

A ten-pound weight dragged Claire's heart down to her knees. "Oh."

"I told you my mother has been engaged in the

ticklish task of wringing her signature out of her. Well, Mother believed she had sufficiently softened her up and was ready to clinch the deal when she got the call."

"The call?"

"From the police. Stating that her beloved son needed bailing out. She rushed home in a dither—"

"I doubt that."

"—well, perhaps a better phrase would be 'high dudgeon.' Anyway, she left Dorcas dangling. As it were." He paused and Claire took a moment to savor the image, adding a noose around her neck for good measure. "So my beloved wife"—he scowled—"never one to be ignored, commandeered the next plane and arrived here this morning. Hopping mad."

"What does she want?"

Gideon finished his scotch and savagely ripped a piece of bread in half, scattering bits all over the table. Before he could answer, a disembodied voice spoke from the shadows. "Steak and kidney pie?"

The waiter hovered, balancing large crockery plates in each hand. As he bent down, the fire lit his face with a demonic glow.

"Here, thanks, and I'll take a pint of Guinness. Claire? Another drink?"

Claire considered her order, a rather wilted Caesar salad. O'Connells apparently didn't approve of vegetables that weren't boiled to death. Or any dish that didn't include potatoes. "A glass of the South African dry Riesling, please."

At least the ambience fit their mood. They sat at a high oak table by an unnecessary fire, overshadowed by dark wood choir stalls stolen from an Irish monastery and next to a heavily varnished organ façade stolen from an Irish church. A tea light made a heroic effort to pierce the obscurity. To Claire, it all served to heighten the sense of approaching doom.

"You were saying?" she prompted.

"Why is Dorcas here? Simple. She wants to make my life miserable. According to Mother, the man she left me for dumped her unceremoniously. I imagine her plan is to take it out on me."

"Was the man with her in Paris?"

"Yes, but Dorcas told Mother he went back to Argentina. That's where she originally met him. When she arrived here, she learned that he left Buenos Aires for the States a month ago and is somewhere in the District. She claims if she finds him she'll give me my freedom."

"That sounds promising."

"Not if he doesn't want to be found. This could go on forever." He touched her hand. "I hate putting you through this."

"Me?" Claire ignored the throbbing of a quickened pulse and did her best to assume an indifferent air. "What does it have to do with me?"

His emerald eyes bored into her blue ones. "I shouldn't have to spell it out, should I?"

Claire blinked and took a large swallow of wine, coughing only some of it up. "I told you—I have renounced disporting with both jailbirds and married men."

"Disport? Will you gambol with me then? Cavort?"

"The answer to any synonym you come up with is still no."

The waiter skipped up and set a second Guinness down before Gideon with a flourish. "Compliments of the lady." He gestured toward the long mahogany bar, sparkling with polished brass and crystal glasses.

Gideon followed the waiter's pointing finger, and Claire followed his gaze. A woman sat alone facing away from them. She wore a burgundy Donna Karan suit and three-inch stiletto heels. The matching broad-brimmed hat hid her hair and most of her face. Claire checked the mirror behind the bar and dropped her fork when she saw what she would later describe to her sister as Audrey Hepburn's doppelganger. A few tendrils of glistening black hair curled out from under the hat. High, aristocratic cheekbones flanked a flawlessly proportioned nose over ruby-kissed lips. The woman swiveled on her stool to face them, and Claire nearly fell off her own. Dorcas—for it could only be Dorcas—would indeed easily pass as the twin of the late exquisite actress. Her huge, liquid, brown eyes locked on Claire.

If Gideon hadn't stood up and stepped between them, Claire wouldn't have been able to break the spell. She slumped, breathing heavily. "I feel like a trapped mouse."

"Dorcas does that to people." Gideon tossed the words over his shoulder. After a tense minute's staring match he swung around to Claire. "Come on, let's go." She didn't argue. He dropped some bills on the table and stalked after her.

She had reached the door before she realized Gideon was no longer behind her. She turned to see him nose to nose with Dorcas, their lips moving rapidly, showing off very white teeth. Claire could have sworn Dorcas's canines were unusually long and sharp. She waited.

A minute later Gideon swept past her out the door. He didn't speak as he drove Claire home, unless one counts foam bubbling from his mouth and an occasional snort. He left her at the door. She trudged up the steps. As she fit the key in the lock, she heard ringing. *That's the landline.* Who would use that? She ran in and picked up the receiver. "Hello?"

"Claire? This is Ernest. I have news."

Chapter Nine
The Argentine Link

"Thanks for coming down." Angle indicated the chair across from his desk. "I thought you'd like to know we had a call from Interpol. They've dredged up quite a bit more about Scordato and his connection to the Propaganda Due lodge."

Claire took a tentative sip from the plastic cup filled with coffee. The sleeve kept slipping, threatening to spill the contents in her lap. Luckily the drink was only tepid. And not actually brown enough to stain anything. "What did they learn?"

"Evidently Scordato was a very close associate of Lazio Truffatore, the self-proclaimed puppet master of P2. Due to frequent run-ins with Italian law, Truffatore spent quite a few years in South America." Ernest opened a notebook. "This is from the Interpol report. He claimed to have founded a P2 cell in Argentina in 1973 and inducted Juan Perón himself, as well as other members of his military junta, into the Masons. After the Vatican bank collapse in 1982, Truffatore fled to South America again, this time to Chile, and Scordato went with him. Truffatore returned to Switzerland in 1987, but Scordato remained behind, making his way to Peru and eventually back to Argentina. That same year someone broke into Perón's tomb and cut off his hands."

Claire spilled the coffee. "Did you say his hands? You mean Perón's hands? Why would anyone cut off a person's hands?"

Ernest nodded. "Yeah, it seemed too bizarre to be true so I looked it up. Argentinians believe that Perón's power resided in his hands and if they were destroyed, Perónism would cease to exist. Even though he'd been dead thirteen years, he still held incredible sway over his people and the loss of the hands shocked the nation."

"And you think—"

"Not me—I'm only repeating Interpol's theory."

"Okay, *they* think"—she took the paper towels Ernest handed her and mopped at the wet spot on her skirt—"that Scordato committed the crime?"

"No, not at all. You're getting ahead of me. The Argentine government refused to pay the ransom demanded for their return, and the hands were never recovered. Then a month or so ago an enterprising Italian journalist claimed he had evidence that Truffatore—through Scordato—had acquired them and sold them to the highest bidder."

"What kind of evidence?"

Angle poured more coffee into Claire's cup before she could stop him. "He followed a money-laundering trail that led from Buenos Aires to a bank in Milan—the very same bank Scordato had embezzled from in 1982. In 1987, the year Perón's hands disappeared, a large sum of money had been deposited in its successor bank, the Nuovo Banco Ambrosiano. Now, everyone assumed after Perón died that his lodge had dissolved, but the reporter says it hadn't. Scordato kept it going with help from a mysterious reserve of funds, which he used to underwrite assorted schemes and political comeback attempts in both Italy and Argentina. The reporter believed those funds came from Milan."

"Why didn't the Argentine police arrest him?"

"Well, primarily because they wrote off the reporter's findings as typical Italian sensationalism. Scordato had been operating behind the scenes, much like Truffatore did. The authorities couldn't pin anything on him. Then last year, an investigator tracking Nazi war criminals for the Simon Wiesenthal Foundation came across Scordato. He notified Interpol."

"Why would a Nazi tracker be interested in an Italian scam artist?"

"Ah, that's where all this starts to get complicated."

"Really? Only now?"

"Very funny. Propaganda Due has been linked to nearly every shady group in existence—right, left, or just plain crooked. Truffatore and his colleagues, including Scordato, had their mitts in the activities of the Mafia, Italian secret police, Communists, terrorist groups, and Perónistas. Why not the Nazis as well?"

Wow. This outpaced even a Tom Clancy novel. If only she could tell Edwina. *It would probably be her best Christmas present ever.* "So the Nazi hunter saw a chance for another notch in his belt."

"Yup. By all accounts, he thought he was looking at a hefty bonus. Up till then Interpol had assumed Scordato's money came from underground Perónistas still hiding in the interstices of Argentine society. They began to rethink the whole scenario after hearing the Nazi hunter's story."

Claire put the cup down, untasted. "Did Interpol know about the reporter's story? You know, the dirty hands money?"

Angle cackled. "Dirty hands? Cute. You should write headlines. Yes, they did. That, and pressure from the Wiesenthal people cleared the way for Interpol to issue an arrest warrant, but at the last minute the mission was aborted."

"How come?"

Angle leaned across the desk and spoke in a conspiratorial whisper. "Officially they blamed it on budget cuts. Unofficially? Some high muckety-mucks in the Italian government called it off. Truffatore amassed quite a pile during his heyday by using prominent Italian politicians as shills. My guess is they didn't want any more headlines reminding the Italian public of their earlier peccadilloes."

"Didn't you tell me Truffatore had fled Italy for Chile in 1982? You're thinking he managed to get his…his filthy lucre out of the country?"

"Some of it, yes, but when the Italians brought him back in 1987 he claimed he was destitute."

Claire frowned, trying to remember what she'd read online. "I did a little research, Ernest. Wasn't he extradited from France in 1998?"

"Yes. Evidently Truffatore spent quite a bit of time fleeing this or that country, only to be collared and returned a few years later." Ernest made a wry face. "The day he was due at an Italian prison to start an eight-year sentence he disappeared. He turned up later in Cannes."

"From which lovely city he was extradited yet again. I remember."

"At that point the Italians could no longer suppress the reporter's investigation. They traced some of Truffatore's money to a bank in Argentina. And to Scordato."

"Why didn't they bring Scordato back to Italy to face charges?"

Angle snapped his fingers. "Seems the Americans told them to back off."

"Americans? What does any of this have to do with Americans?" Claire no longer even attempted to keep all the threads in her head.

Angle rose and held out his hand. "Walk with me."

Where have I heard that before? Oh, yeah. That's what the Mafia boss says to his victim in every James Cagney movie.

The heat smacked into them as they walked out of the police station into an empty parking lot. Washington had finally clawed its way out of August, but September looked to be more of the same—hot enough to grip your diaphragm and shake it, and humid enough to forestall dehydration. Claire wiped a drop of perspiration from the tip of her nose. "I feel like I'm slogging through a bathtub full of water."

Ernest pointed to a high-rise office building in the distance. "Since they built the new station on landfill nobody wanted, we'll have to hike a few blocks to get to the commercial district." They strolled up Eisenhower Avenue, trying not to breathe in the aromas of melting deodorant and sunscreen from passing bodies, until they came to a coffee shop. "Let's get something cold to drink."

Claire's mouth watered at the prospect of iced tea. Ernest found a table for two by the picture window and went to the counter while Claire watched a Lincoln Navigator and a Mini Cooper duke it out for the last parking spot.

When he returned with two large glasses, he carefully surveyed the restaurant. The place was empty except for a booth on the other side of the room. He sat down and said in a low voice, "Have you ever heard of Operation Gladio?"

Claire dipped the napkin in the tea and dabbed at the back of her neck. "No."

"According to military historians—and a lot of conspiracy theorists—the CIA and NATO set up a secret organization at the end of World War II to disrupt any attempts to establish Communist governments in western Europe."

"Oh, yes, I did read about that—black something…"

"Black ops—short for operations. Until yesterday I would have shaken my head in regretful disbelief at the idea. We've got one guy at the station who does nothing but monitor wacko websites. You wouldn't believe—"

"You're saying it exists?" The coffee, a pint of water, and now iced tea, were taking their toll on Claire's bladder. She thought she could manage another ten minutes of literary foreplay, but that was it.

"Yes. I have a contact at the Pentagon—he sometimes feeds me information through non-official channels. He told me Operation Gladio is still very much alive, and they were the ones who told the Italians to back off. My man told me Truffatore had been linked to Operation Gladio after World War II, and he thinks they're on Scordato's trail. One agent has been after him for over ten years."

"Do you suppose he's looking for the lost treasure?"

"Lost treasure? Oh, Truffatore's stash? Nah—these are government types, not treasure hunters. It must have something to do with P2 and its dealings with the KGB. Or the Mafia. Or the Perónistas. Or…" He took a long pull on his iced tea. "At any rate, a couple of months ago, the Gladio agent intercepted a message from Truffatore's daughter to Scordato. Whatever it said, it sent Scordato into a tizzy."

"What do you mean, 'whatever it said'? If the black ops guy intercepted it, why couldn't he read it?"

"According to my source, it was in code—a new one. When he couldn't decipher it, he got the wind up. The last his superiors heard from him he had hopped a plane to Washington, in hot pursuit of Scordato."

"Has he turned up?"

"Not that we know of—but then we wouldn't. My friend said all communication from the Gladio people abruptly shut off a month ago. He has no clue what's going on."

Her body indicating in no uncertain terms that she would embarrass herself if she didn't find a ladies' room immediately, Claire stood. Ernest rose, an anxious smile on his face. "Was it something I said?"

"No, no, I'll be right back." As she wended her way through the empty tables toward the restrooms, she approached the one occupied booth. A hat of indigo straw bobbed just above the tall seat back. She heard furious whispering. As she passed the booth she slowed and a woman looked up and straight at Claire. *Dorcas.* She turned hastily away, but not before Claire saw a reddened nose and flushed cheeks that clashed harshly with enormous chocolate eyes filled with tears.

Puzzled, she went on to the ladies' room. Dorcas didn't seem the type to cry at all, much less in a public place. She had dried her hands and patted her curls back into place before it occurred to Claire that she should have checked out Dorcas's companion. Gideon's wife in tears had so thrown her she hadn't given him a glance. She had a brief impression of…nothing. Sort of a hazy, gray figure—gray clothes, gray hair. *Now why does that sound familiar?* Gideon sneaking into the Temple, dressed all in gray. *Or…I wonder…* She picked up her purse and pushed open the door.

The booth was empty. Ignoring Ernest, she ran to the front and through the revolving door. *There, on the corner.* The man had flagged down a taxi. As Dorcas bent down to get in, he kissed her cheek. She gave him a wavering smile and closed the door. The taxi drove off and he began to walk down the street away from the coffee shop. After two steps, he turned as though he'd forgotten something, but when he caught sight of Claire he jumped into a second cab. The vehicle left the curb with a squeal of brakes while she stood frozen. She had just seen the man who'd been haunting the Masonic Memorial for the last few weeks, the man who took her tour and asked an inordinate amount of questions, the man she had seen slip back into the Temple after closing. *Could he be Dorcas's Argentine lover?*

She managed to ditch Ernest with a vague reference to a doctor's appointment. He went off mumbling and shaking his head. Claire wondered why he'd told her so much about the case—it seemed a bit odd for a policeman to be so forthcoming. *Could it be that he merely enjoys my company? Or does he have an ulterior motive?* Hand to her mouth, she stopped short on the sidewalk. *Does he still suspect Gideon's involved somehow? Does he want to pry incriminating information out of me?* An approaching couple split to pass on either side of her as though she were only a shoal in the river of their life, both glued to their respective smart phones. She walked on, her synapses whirling in Brownian motion. *Ernest wouldn't use me to get to Gideon unless he knew we were...together. And he doesn't.* She thought of Ernest's earnest gray eyes—*yikes*—melting as they looked at her. *He trusts me, that's all. He needs a sounding board. All the same, I'd better lighten up on the flirting. Just in case.*

She crossed King and headed toward Prince Street and her house. *Maybe if I empty my mind of all the minor details, a pattern will emerge.* Five minutes later she was back to listing bad guys. *Nazis, bastard children, Perónistas, embezzlers, rogue Masons...Damn! There's got to be a link. But where?*

She walked through the house and went to sit in her garden. Ichabod wound his tail in and out of her legs, now and then catching it in his teeth. She noticed a small pile of red feathers by the birdfeeder. "Oh, Ichabod, not the cardinal!" He gave her a hurt look and moved off to clean his paws by the back door.

Okay. One thing at a time. Let's focus on Dorcas and her fellow. She wracked her brain for the gray man's name—how could she forget it? She remembered only that it was as unmemorable as the man himself. Finally she gave up and drove down to the Temple. She found Harry in the bookshop.

"Harry, do you remember the name of the guy who

bought my second volume?"

Luckily Harry had the gift of unraveling a twisted knot of illogic without wasting time on idle questions. "You mean of the history of freemasonry?"

"Yes. He bought a bunch of other stuff, too, didn't he?"

"Cleaned me out. I don't recall his name now, but I should have a record of the sale." He checked his computer. "Here it is—he used an American Express card...no name. Sorry."

Claire tamped down her impatience. "You told it to me though, remember? You pointed him out. He's a very bland person."

"You're right. He'd be right in your face one moment, clear as a bell, and the next he kinda went out of focus. Strange feeling." He closed his eyes, then opened them and shook his head. "If I think of it, I'll let you know."

"Thanks, Harry." Claire walked slowly toward the main hall. Nigel sat at the desk as usual. She wondered idly if he had a real job. His position as tiler was ceremonial and unremunerated, although the senior warden of a lodge ritually "paid" the lodge members with mark pennies—a relic of the early days as a guild. Visitors often asked her about the wide variety of coins displayed on the fifth floor and how much they were worth. Mr. Quinn had said some were quite valuable. She made a mental note to ask him to point those out.

Nigel saw her and ducked his head, busying himself with something on the desk. As she approached, he bent even lower, his nose nearly touching the surface. *He seems nervous. I wonder what I said that spooked him?*

She heard a door open behind her and Harry's voice. "Hey, Claire, I was tossing out a bunch of old requests and found one from that guy you were asking about. No wonder I couldn't remember his name. It's Joe Smith."

Claire waved at him and turned to find Nigel's rear end disappearing out the side door. He'd left his briefcase lying open and his paper half-folded. She shrugged and left by the main door, resolving to use the puzzle as dinner entertainment.

****

"I understand you had tea at the Morrison House. A delightful place."

"Yes, Mother. Mrs. Bliss was very gracious."

"Ah. Yes. About that. Did she ask you about her son?"

Gulp. "Yes."

"You didn't tell her you were involved, did you?"

"I'm not involved, Mother. We're just friends."

"Yes, well, I understand the wife is in Washington. I do not approve of threesomes, especially not with felons."

Claire didn't bother to ask how Letitia knew all this. "Threesomes? What on earth are you talking about?"

"I mean it's not done in our family, Claire. If anyone we know saw you with this Dorcas and Senator Bliss, imbibing and…and consorting, well—"

It felt so good to laugh. "No, Mother—we weren't consorting. You're right though, Dorcas is definitely a harridan."

"I told you so. Still, when you see Gideon tomorrow I'd like you to convey my feelings on the

153

subject."

How does she do that? "Mother, how did you know—"

Her mother replied airily, "Oh, a mother likes to keep tabs on her children." Claire heard the snap of a pocket watch. "Now will you look at the time? I have to hunt down Monsieur Souris. I'll talk to you soon, dear."

The line went dead.

****

"More ribs?"

"Yes, thanks. You'd better get back in here—the game's about to start."

Gideon sat down next to Claire and handed her a plate and a roll of paper towels. "Mother doesn't think she can make it to my court appearance next Tuesday."

"Is she upset with you?" Claire tore the last whisker of meat off the bone and chewed lustily. Gideon leaned toward her and gently wiped the sauce from her mouth. They took a minute to gaze happily into each other's eyes.

"Well, a bit. After all, no Bliss has ever been accused of theft. Dueling, yes. Womanizing. Gambling. But not theft. I'm afraid she thinks I'm guilty."

"How? I mean, why?"

"Maybe because I won't confide in her. At this point only three other people know of the Washington letter—Allen Greystone, the conservator, you, and Frederick Nutley."

"I thought you hadn't told Professor Nutley?"

Gideon took a swallow of beer. "Fred came to see me after my arrest. I had to tell him."

"So why hasn't he shown up to support you?"

"I don't know. I imagine he thinks he would only

make it worse, considering his reputation."

The first quarter started and the two were drawn into the inglorious battle between her favorite team and his. Claire leapt to her feet, scattering potato chips on the floor. "Did you see that catch? Ellis is amazing, isn't he?" she crowed. "The Redskins might as well give up now and head for the locker room."

Gideon sniffed. "We've got three more quarters to go. The Vikings are notorious for blowing it in the fourth."

"Never. Vikings never give up. Why, when Fran Tarkenton—"

"Spare me, m'dear. That was thirty years ago. The Purple People Eaters have been on a slow slide to oblivion since then."

He caught her arm in midair, turned her palm toward him, curled her fingers over it, and kissed them. "Kiss a fist for peace."

"I'll show you a fist. I'll—"

Her pummeling had no effect, at least on Gideon's chest. When he pinioned her arms and held her close she could feel the erection grinding into her thigh. He let her arms go and circled her waist, pulling her to him. He groaned, "Claire."

The noise of gridiron battle faded and she heard nothing but the steady thrumming of her vulva and the rhythmic thumping of his cock against her. "Gideon. Gideon? Remember what I said. Remember I…We shouldn't…"

"You're right, not here." He lifted her, tossed her over his shoulder, and took the narrow steps to her bedroom two at a time.

After a short mental struggle, Claire accepted the

inevitable. *How to turn defeat into victory?* "You just don't want to watch your Redskins lose, do you?" When he didn't answer, she took the opportunity to undo his belt and pull the zipper down. He fell backward on the bed, allowing her to free his cock and fasten her lips around it. She shifted around to face away from him and shimmied backward. He took a mouthful of quivering red flesh and sucked. She gasped with pleasure, then bent to her task. It didn't take long to reach the tipping point…literally. At the moment of impact, Claire fell off the bed. Ichabod screeched and bolted out from under them.

Claire waited for her breath to come back. "Vikings will win. Mark my words."

****

Gideon guided Claire to a pew and sat down next to her. "Uncle Andrew says this won't take long. The court's so backed up the prosecutor will probably ask for a continuance."

"You don't have to be in the dock?"

"What? No, this is a preliminary hearing. The judge will hear the evidence and Uncle Andrew will ask that all charges be dropped. The DA will concur and my troubles will be over. At least that's what Uncle Andrew says will happen."

Claire examined the stout man in a discreetly pinstriped suit to whom Gideon referred. With his magnificent mane of white hair and flowing mustache—not to mention the florid complexion—she could imagine him better in seersucker, iced mint julep at his elbow. "And Andrew is?"

"Andrew Miller. My lawyer. Second cousin on my mother's side. That's the side that looks down its cobwebbed nose at George Washington's lineage."

Claire remembered Mrs. Bliss's withering comments. "But is he good?"

"The best. He'll take care of it."

Just then the judge arrived and the bailiff called for all to rise for His Honor Judge Weebly of the Alexandria General District Court. The Commonwealth's Attorney stepped up to the bench. Andrew jerked his head up, then threw his papers down and followed him. Much whispering ensued, rising at times to an angry hiss from Andrew. Finally, he returned to his desk. The prosecutor smiled a superior smile and announced loudly, "Your Honor, I call as a witness Professor Frederick Nutley."

They heard a rustling behind them and Nutley shuffled down the aisle, wearing the same frayed tweed jacket and baggy corduroy pants as when Claire first saw him. Gideon sputtered, "Nutley! What's he doing here?"

The bailiff proceeded to swear the professor in. For his part, Nutley kept his eyes on his shoes and only answered in monosyllables. The prosecutor asked him if he knew the accused and to point him out. Nutley bobbed his head and wiggled a fleshy thumb in Gideon's general direction.

"Professor Nutley, according to your deposition, you saw the defendant steal a book from the library located on the sixth floor of the George Washington Masonic National Memorial. On that basis, a search warrant was sworn out and Senator Gideon Bliss was arrested for theft. Do you affirm that statement?"

"I do."

"Please tell the Court the circumstances under

which you saw the accused steal said book."

Nutley paused to inspect his coat buttons. "I was conducting research on documents related to George Washington in the library. I saw Senator Bliss enter the room, take the book, and hide it in his briefcase."

A shrill voice rang out from the rear of the courtroom. "Not true! Not true! He's lying! I would never allow that man in my library!"

All eyes turned to the door, where a red-faced Treadwater pointed a trembling finger at the professor. Claire almost expected him to shriek, "*J'accuse! J'accuse!*"

The judge glanced at the bailiff and raised his eyebrows. The latter marched down the aisle and crooked a finger at the librarian. "Will you come with me please?"

Treadwater goggled at him. "I…uh." He backed away and began to skip toward the exit.

The bailiff grabbed his arm, but when Treadwater staggered, hand to his heart, he gave him a reassuring grin. "It's all right, sir. The judge would like to hear your testimony. This is not a trial. We're simply gathering evidence."

Treadwater meekly followed the burly officer up to the bench while the professor shot daggers at the librarian. The judge surveyed the two men and said gravely, "You may step down, Mr. Nutley." For a brief moment the audience beheld the struggle in Nutley's mind as clearly as if it were the battle of Princeton. Finally he pushed himself to a stand and, without a backward glance, walked unsteadily to a pew.

Judge Weebly removed his reading glasses and addressed Treadwater. "Now, sir, please give your name to the bailiff, who will administer the oath."

Treadwater did as he was told and then sat down in the witness chair. He still panted heavily and rage distorted his features. The judge spoke again. "Mr. Treadwater, you are the person who reported the theft to the police?"

"Yes, but—"

The judge interrupted him. "Please make your statement to the Court."

"Your honor, it's true that I *thought* someone stole a very precious registry of South American lodges. It's the only copy in existence and it is irreplaceable." Pride diluted the ire and his face returned to a more normal color. "But that...that man—Nutley—could not have seen anyone steal it. He has never been in my library. I would *never* allow him in my library. He has no right to accuse Senator Bliss."

As the librarian spoke, Gideon half rose in his seat, an astonished look on his face.

"You 'thought.' Are you saying that the book in question was not stolen?"

If it were possible to see into his body, Claire would have sworn the little man's lungs collapsed in fright. "Yes...yes."

"To clarify, the library book which you reported missing, was not in fact purloined?"

His voice a little firmer, Treadwater cast a stealthy glance at Gideon. "Yes, I mean no. No one stole it. I merely misplaced it. We found it in another part of the building. I...I'm afraid I may have been careless."

The judge put his glasses back on and checked the paperwork before him. "According to the record, you also reported a missing key. Have you found that as well?"

Treadwater looked puzzled for a minute, then his face cleared. "Oh that. No, we haven't found it, but it's not important—not like the directory. We didn't even know what it went to."

"I see. So, do you request that all charges against Mr. Bliss be dropped?"

"Yes, yes." He made as if to stand and the bailiff laid a friendly but heavy hand on his shoulder.

"All right then." The judge banged his gavel. "Case dismissed." He glared at the librarian. "However, Mr. Treadwater, you should have reported any change in the case immediately to the police. If you had done so the Court's time would not have been wasted." He pushed his chair back and disappeared behind a curtain.

Gideon leapt forward to shake the librarian's hand. "Treadwater, you're a godsend. I can't thank you enough."

Treadwater narrowed his eyes at the professor, who was attempting to leave by a side door. "How dare that man claim to have access to my library. I couldn't let him get away with it."

"I see." Gideon drew him aside and spoke in a low voice. Claire sidled closer in order to hear. "I didn't want to interrupt your testimony, but I think there's been some misunderstanding. I did in fact borrow a book, but it had nothing to do with South America."

The librarian stared at him. "What do you mean?"

"I took a book on the genealogy of George Washington's family. Since you wouldn't let me back into the library, David Comfrey helped me return it. I'm so sorry—I was desperate and given your hostility toward Fred—"

Treadwater's shoulders relaxed and he looked up with a glad smile. "Senator, I only called the police because I thought Nutley was responsible. In view of your reputation as an expert—amateur though you may be—on our Charter Master, I would gladly have lent you any document you needed if you had only asked me directly."

Gideon shot Claire a wry smile. "I guess my mother was right, huh? Honesty always pays." Claire took his hand and together they walked out of the courthouse. The sun rode high in the sky and the sidewalk steamed. "Shall we find a dark, cool bar and celebrate?"

"Okay, but first you should catch Professor Nutley. I think he has some 'splainin' to do, don't you?" She indicated a figure retreating down Jamieson Avenue, back hunched over, soft hat smashed on his head. Gideon blew Claire a kiss and strode after him.

She watched him catch up to Nutley at the corner. The professor cringed before the flailing arms of his adversary. Gideon's mouth opened wide and his eyes flashed as he yelled at the old man. Nutley said nothing, and eventually Gideon slowed and finally stopped. At that point the professor began to speak. Claire still couldn't hear them, but she could tell he spoke softly and quickly. And obviously persuasively, because Gideon began to nod. The old man stood stock still, his hands at his sides, but his eyes never left Gideon and his lips moved continuously. Gideon's head bent lower and lower as though he were yielding to a superior argument. Just as Claire decided to head for her car, he patted Nutley on the shoulder and began to walk back to her. She waited.

"What did he say?"

"I need a drink. Let's go over to Ted's Montana Grill. It should be empty this time of day."

They walked the few blocks to a strip mall on Eisenhower Avenue. Gideon ordered a Pouilly-Fuissé for Claire and vodka for himself and sat staring at his hands until Claire couldn't stand it anymore. "He must have had a hell of an excuse. You didn't deck him."

"I can see why his classes are always filled and he's been voted the most popular professor at Georgetown, despite his reputation as a shameless plagiarist and spinner of tales. He could win a propaganda contest with Goebbels with his mouth wired shut." He slugged down his drink and signaled for another.

Claire pressed her lips together, holding the anger at bay. "Are you saying he fed you a line and you ate it?"

"I had no choice. He apologized profusely for his deception. He blamed his insatiable hunger to reestablish his reputation. He thought if only he could claim the discovery of the letter all past sins would be forgiven. He hatched this ridiculous plot to finger me. Then, with his rival safely incarcerated, he could announce his discovery and receive the adulation of an adoring academic world."

"The man is a monster. How dare he?" Claire had to wait for her hands to stop shaking to put the glass to her lips. "There is no excuse for such behavior."

"No, none. Except that I did in fact nick a book. If it weren't for Treadwater, the avenging angel, Nutley's plan would have succeeded."

"About that—did I hear him say the stolen book

was about South America?"

"Indeed you did. Apparently two different books went missing in the last few weeks. Treadwater only knew about one—he was unaware of my little transgression until I told him. Come to think of it, didn't you say he discovered the theft on the day of the murder? I didn't take the genealogy until a week later. And I returned it to the library, not the museum."

Claire remembered a gray form slipping into the side entrance of the Temple. "You returned it the night of the fourteenth, didn't you?"

Gideon's mouth dropped open. "How did you know?"

"I saw you. So did Ernest."

Gideon growled, "Again with the Ernest. What were you doing with him?"

"I saw him in the parking lot." Claire set her chin. "For your information, I don't make a habit of hanging out with policemen when they're staking out suspects. Who let you in, by the way?"

"David Comfrey. He thought it would be easier than dealing with Treadwater and I agreed. He opened the library for me." Gideon pursed his lips. "I can't believe you saw me. I've got to learn to be sneakier." He finished his second drink. As he started to signal the bartender, Claire handed him the bowl of peanuts. "Oh, yeah, you're right. Better stay alert."

Claire sipped her wine, reflecting on his words. "Sneakier. You know what this means, don't you? There's another thief wandering around."

"Nutley?"

"What would he want with a history of South American lodges?"

"Who the hell knows? The guy's a little off his rocker."

Claire scrutinized her lover. "You forgave him, didn't you?"

Gideon didn't look at her. "Um."

"You did."

"Look, the poor old geezer has lost everything. I, on the other hand, do not lack for blessings." He touched her cheek and smiled. "Nor do I require exclusive credit for this incredible find. Yes, I forgave him."

"And you're going to let him share the credit."

"Yes. To be fair, he did pony up substantial research that helped speed the process immeasurably."

Claire thought a minute. "Does he know where the letter is? Does he know where the box is?"

"No. That much I won't share with him."

"Good. Now, are you going to feed me or were you hoping to get me tipsy and have your way with me?"

He saluted. "Both."

****

"Oh. My. God."

Gideon put down his coffee cup. "What is it?"

Claire folded the *Examiner* and handed it to him. "There."

Gideon tossed a cursory look at the headline, bent his head, and read the article through, his mouth working. "That bastard. After I let him off the hook, he went and called a press conference. He's claiming full credit for the Washington letters!"

This didn't seem the appropriate time for an "I told you so," so Claire sat quietly.

Gideon stood up, poured more coffee, and sat

down. He stared at the paper for a minute, then picked it up again and reread the article. "It's funny. Yes, Nutley claims to have made an earth-shattering discovery of great historical importance, but he doesn't actually specify what it is."

"Could it be because he doesn't really know what's in the letters? The conservator hasn't finished deciphering the first one yet, has he?"

"He's almost done, but I haven't told Fred what he's found so far." He stared at the newspaper. "What does Nutley think he'll get by announcing now? If any reporter asks him for specifics, he won't have an answer."

"I doubt he cares, so long as he gets first dibs on the fame and fortune."

Gideon slammed the paper down. "Not if I have anything to do with it. I'll give the letters to Treadwater before I help Nutley to any more of my pie."

Claire took their plates to her tiny sink and rinsed them off. Too bad a dishwasher would take up so much space—like all of it—in the kitchen. When she returned he still sat brooding. She kissed the top of his head. "You know, that's not such a bad idea."

"What?"

"Giving—or rather donating—the letters to the Masonic Memorial. You'd be able to kill at least three birds with one stone."

Gideon cocked his head. "How's that?"

"First, it would cut Nutley out of the limelight entirely. Second, it would give Treadwater and you a perfect revenge on the professor. And three—"

"And three, the document would be protected and conserved properly in Washington's own lodge."

Gideon whistled. "I like it. Just so long as Treadwater agrees to have it on public display."

"Besides, you wouldn't have to sneak around like Light-Fingered Louie anymore—you'd have the entire Grand Lodge at your back."

He rose and went to the telephone. It rang before he had a chance to pick it up. "Claire? Just a moment." He handed the receiver over with a scowl. "It's your boyfriend."

She raised her eyebrows and he mouthed, "Angle."

Oh shit. "Hello? Ernest?" She listened for a minute, her cheeks reddening. "Not that it's any of your business, but Senator Bliss dropped by on his morning walk." She listened a little longer. The blush faded, to be replaced by chalk white skin. "Yes, I'll ask him. I'm sure we can both come down. In an hour? Okay." She put the phone down and turned to Gideon. Her hand at her throat, her sapphire eyes wide with shock, she stared at him.

"What is it?"

The words came out in a frightened croak. "It's the professor. He's...he's dead."

Chapter Ten
Broken Links

Edwina dropped her purse on the floor and sat down on the loveseat. "Oh my dear, people seem to be dropping like flies around you! Are you all right?"

Claire let the easy reassurance her sister always conveyed envelop her. "I'm fine. Just shocked. I didn't really know Nutley at all. Gideon worked with him—"

Edwina held up a hand. "Gideon? This is becoming serious, isn't it? Mother told me you had tea with his mother." She sat back, as though that settled the matter.

"Only because she came bearing gifts for me. Mother has been buying porcelain puppies again." Both women laughed tolerantly. Their parent wouldn't allow a real animal in her house, but her mantels and tables overflowed with depressingly cunning china livestock.

Edwina caught her breath. "Tell me, is her name really Andromeda?"

Claire nodded. "Gideon told me his grandfather was an avid amateur astronomer."

"As usual, the child bears the brunt of the sire's idiosyncrasies." Edwina picked up her phone and checked her messages. "Mother said she'd call today. She's worried about you getting involved with Senator Bliss. She says even considering Mrs. Bliss's distinguished Virginia ancestry, a politician in the family could constitute an obstacle to their friendship."

"Especially a politician from Connecticut."

"Even though the felony charges were dropped."

Claire reflected that she and her sister understood their mother very well. "Those two have become fast friends, it seems."

"I'm not surprised—they have so much in common. They're terrible snobs, enthusiastic shoppers, and constant travelers. Plus, their children are in love."

"Don't be absurd, Edwina. Now, do you want to know about the murder?"

Edwina pulled a South Beach cereal bar out of her pocket, unwrapped it, and took a hefty bite. "The latest one? Yes."

"Ernest says—"

"Ernest? Is there another swain on the scene?"

Claire stuck out her tongue. "*Detective* Angle says they found the body in his house."

"The body? You mean the professor?"

"Who else?"

"In whose house?"

"The professor's, of course." Claire frowned at her sister. "He'd been strangled—they think with a thin piece of material, like a scarf."

"How did they know that?"

"The medical examiner found a few black silk threads embedded in his neck."

Edwina finished off her granola bar and pulled a second one from her purse. "Black silk…what does that remind me of? Ooh, ooh, I've got it! Giselda is studying ancient Indian cults in school. It's part of some segment on world religions, although I don't know why they have time for these obscure foreign customs and can't get around to teaching American history. Why—"

Claire put out a hand and gently covered her sister's mouth. "Edwina? Did you have a point?"

"Of course." Edwina set down the half-eaten bar and took a sip of iced tea. "Every day this week she's come home with pictures of dancing elephants or gods with hundreds of arms. Yesterday she showed me this garish purple portrait of a goddess holding a bloody head and wearing a skirt of human skulls. Hindu goddess of death, according to Giselda. Name of Kali. Anyway, her adherents were called Thuggee—that's where our word 'thug' comes from. Isn't it fascinating how—"

"Edwina."

"Okay, okay." She grinned. "I promised Mother I'd channel her inclination to digress while she was away. Anyway, these thugs waylaid travelers and killed them with a quick yank of their ritual scarf."

Claire temporarily waived her objections to fifth graders learning about murderous Asian gangs to ask, "And they did this why?"

"Why? Um…" Edwina took a bite of her bar and chewed, her nose pinched in distaste. "What I wouldn't give for a nice fudgy brownie."

"The thugs, Eddie?"

"I don't remem—oh, that's it. They would present the victims to Kali as a sacrifice. Nasty piece of work, that Kali, from what Giselda says."

"I see. Assuming we're not dealing with the last surviving member of a fanatical sect driven by lack of suitable victims in India to come here to America—"

"No, no, listen. I'm getting to my point. I took Giselda to the dentist after school and while I waited for her I picked up a copy of *Popular Mechanics*. It happened to have an article about methods of assassination so I skimmed it to see if it mentioned the thuggee. Guess what? It said the garrote is still in use by clandestine groups—you know, mercenaries, black ops, spies." She warmed to her subject. "Shadowy figures proficient in all the tactics of guerilla warfare who sell their expertise to the highest bidder—"

"Eddie!"

Edwina smirked. "All right, I'll stop, but you might have your friend Ernest look into a possible connection to the CIA or MI6 or something. The victim—this was the guy who claimed to have seen Senator Bliss steal a book, correct?"

"Yes. He'd been booted from academic circles by an earlier spurious claim to...er...to some historical discovery or other, and we think he wanted to appropriate Gideon's find in order to restore his reputation."

"And what is Gideon's find?"

Claire stopped, aghast. She'd almost given it away. Gideon had sworn her to secrecy until he'd authenticated the documents and could make a formal donation to the Masons. "I...I'm not sure. Some document or other." She waved a dismissive hand. "Only of interest to single-minded George Washington addicts."

"And is Gideon one of those?"

Claire tried not to preen. "He's a very well-regarded amateur expert."

Edwina sniggered. "Oh yeah? So how is he in bed?"

Her sister bestowed a virtuous smile on the hapless Edwina, knowing her husband Ray spent more time asleep on the couch than awake in the bedroom. "*Fabulous*."

That shut her up. After a minute, she asked meekly, "So did *Ernest* have any more tidbits on the murder?"

"Not much. The police found no evidence of forced entry, but his house was in shambles—drawers pulled out and closets emptied. Every box opened and its contents tossed on the floor. The killer must have been looking for something."

"Gideon's document?"

"Couldn't be. Nutley didn't have it, and he had no idea where Gideon kept it or where it came from."

"Didn't you say he'd been quoted in the newspaper stating he'd found something super important?"

"Ye-ess."

"Well, that must have been what the killer was after. He wouldn't know anything about Gideon's...*find*'—here Edwina cast a suspicious eye on her sister—"and only wanted whatever he thought Nutley had."

"Maybe." Claire cupped her chin. "It's funny. The professor never actually talked about a document. The interview quoted him as saying he'd discovered something of enormous historical value. He implied it would rock the world and would be worth millions to a collector. He even used the word 'priceless.' "

"If it wasn't Gideon's thing, what could it have been?"

"I have no idea. He's been working with Gideon. He wanted his reputation back after a bit of scandal and Gideon needed his expertise. Maybe he ran across something while he researched Washington's bro...urm..." She ended lamely.

Edwina peered at her sister. "I can tell you're not at liberty to tell me. Don't worry, I won't pry. But"—her eyes flickered—"I think we should assume for now he was talking about Gideon's document. No one else knows that in fact Gideon has it and not the professor, right?"

Claire nodded.

"Good. Otherwise, he could be in danger as well."

So this is what it feels like to have your insides cave in. "I…uh…"

Edwina didn't seem to have noticed her sister's ashen face. "You said the professor's place was trashed. Perhaps the killer didn't actually know what he was looking for. Maybe he had kind of a *I'll know it when I see it* MO."

Claire grabbed at the straw. "Yes, that makes sense. If he doesn't know what it is, he may still think it's hidden somewhere at the professor's."

"And therefore he'll return to the scene of the crime. I assume the police still have the place under surveillance?"

Claire had no idea. "Of course, Ernest will have thought of everything we've thought of."

"*Hmph.*" Edwina finished her second cereal bar and rose. "Keep me posted. I've got to get home—the kids will be out of school by now. Oh, by the way"—Edwina's casual tone raised the gossamer hairs on Claire's arms—"Mother's back."

****

"What'll I tell them then?"

"Tell them anything—tell them I'm sick."

"It's only luncheon with our mothers. I'm the one who should be nervous—I haven't even met yours yet.

Besides, they can't misbehave in a restaurant."

"You underestimate them."

Gideon touched Claire's arm, concern clouding his rich, brown eyes. "Is it Dorcas? I'm sure she won't be there, if that's what's bothering you."

It did, but not half as much as facing two formidable matriarchs at the same table. She'd have to bring along a portable oxygen tank. "Not really, but regardless, Dorcas is still your wife. I don't feel comfortable walking into a public place on a married man's arm."

Gideon made a wry face. "I'm not really married you know."

"There's no such thing as being *halfway* married." It had to be said. They were getting too close. She had to force him to act or she feared their relationship would be in limbo forever.

"I know. You're right." Gideon slammed the newspaper down. "Damn the professor! His tomfoolery cost me more than a night in jail. Mother says Dorcas has her back up now—I'll get the divorce papers only over her dead body."

Claire couldn't help it. "Could we use any dead body? We've got a few handy."

"Ha ha. If I have to enlist the maters, I will."

Claire raised her hands in mock horror. "Be careful what you wish for."

"I'll try anything. And now that Dorcas is here in Washington, maybe a full frontal assault with all the troops will break her down." While Claire tried to erase the image of a platoon of little old ladies whapping their parasols at the knees of a statuesque, armor-clad goddess, Gideon knotted his tie. "Are you coming or not? They're expecting us at Vermilion in twenty minutes."

Well, if Dorcas isn't there..."All right. Just let me fix my face."

"Good, it's a bit crooked."

By the time Claire had straightened her face to Gideon's satisfaction, they were late and had to drive the five blocks to the restaurant rather than the planned leisurely stroll. Claire's already frayed nerves split into a million filaments of tension. To make it worse, the restaurant was empty except for the table in the front window, where their hostesses held court. The maitre d' escorted them across the echoing room and presented them as though they were visiting royalty. Claire started to curtsy, but Gideon pulled her up in time.

With equally gracious manners and equally large hats, the parents greeted their progeny, reeling them seamlessly into their conversation. Both Letitia and Andromeda, it seemed, were skilled at treating controversial topics with a light and amusing touch, and the discussion moved at a lively pace. Claire began to relax.

"I hope you two don't mind that we took the liberty of ordering for you," said Andromeda. The waiter set down a basket of assorted rolls and a crystal bowl filled with ice and shaved butter balls.

Claire wondered why he didn't take the fifth place setting away. Her mother saw her looking. "Yes, we have another guest."

At that moment Claire caught a whiff of Shalimar. A slim figure in a white Balenciaga suit took the chair next to hers. In the artificial light Dorcas's ebony hair shimmered like the opalescent feathers of a glossy ibis.

Her exquisitely carved face, framed by delicate netting attached to a white pillbox hat, turned a fraction of an inch toward her neighbor. She arched one disdainful eyebrow and said in a brittle voice, "You must be Claire." Without waiting for acknowledgement, she pivoted gracefully toward the two older women. "I do apologize for being late. Rogers hasn't quite mastered the maze of Old Town streets yet." She bestowed a dazzling smile on Gideon. "I expect he will ere long."

Claire wasn't sure how she survived the next hour. Dorcas—*big surprise*—had a good ten inches on her, making her feel puny and dispensable. Every so often her mother would catch her eye and lift her palm up, and Claire would realize that she'd slumped so far down her chin almost rested on the table. Dorcas held the floor during most of the meal, relating clever stories in her lilting mezzo-soprano, a slight exotic accent adding a touch of red to the black and white ensemble. Gideon barely spoke.

Finally the hostesses called for the check and argued amiably over it. Letitia leaned toward Dorcas and held out a limp hand. "So nice of you to join us, Dorcas. Andromeda has spoken of you often. Such a shame you'll be returning to Paris soon. But then there's no reason to stay here when you can be in Paris, is there?" She gazed around the table with an inane smile on her face. No one said anything after Dorcas's slight gasp, but Claire noted the malicious gleam in her mother's eye.

The injured wife quickly recovered her wits and stood with a soft rustle of silk. She planted an air kiss in the vicinity of her mother-in-law's cheek. "Thank you so much for lunch, Mother Bliss. As always, lovely to see you."

Andromeda's lips set in a thin line. "Yes, indeed. Oh, by the way, my lawyer has drawn up an extra copy of the…papers. In case you neglected to bring them with you. It will be so much more convenient to sign them here and avoid all that international postage, don't you think?"

Dorcas was equal to the onslaught. "How thoughtful of you. However, I will not be going back to Paris any time soon. In fact"—she glanced at Gideon—"I shall be so busy over the next few weeks, I fear I'll be unable to find the time to sign anything." She swept out the door, pirouetting neatly around a group of tourists.

Claire watched her go, partly due to the grace of her stride and partly because she wanted to be sure she'd actually gone. So it was that she saw a man get up from the bar and follow her out. The gray man she'd seen in the coffee shop. The man who made Dorcas cry. *Joe Smith.*

She didn't get a chance to tell Gideon as the mothers carried him off, Letitia demanding a tour of his senate office. "Since they're still in recess, perhaps you can take us onto the Senate floor as well. That would be so exciting." Considering Letitia had been one of the first women named to the professional staff of a Senate committee, Claire took that as evidence that her mother had taken a shine to Gideon.

****

She heard not a peep from Gideon for the next three days, a welcome respite because it gave her time to think. The meddling of the mothers aside, the issue lay between Dorcas and Gideon. It didn't matter that

Dorcas had left Gideon—Claire still felt like the other woman, and it didn't sit well with her Southern upbringing. Another skirmish with Wonder Woman would be the death of her. By the time Gideon called, she'd made up her mind.

"Hi, sorry I haven't been in touch. I—"

"I understand. You're dealing with…family matters."

"No," he said slowly. "Actually, the Senate will be back from recess this week. They had a pro forma session Friday and being the lowest life form on the seniority pole, I had to preside." He paused. "I sent the papers to Dorcas. She hasn't responded."

Claire didn't want to get sucked into the soap opera. *Bite the bullet. Take the bull by the horns. The horns of a dilemma? No, that's not right. Take my medicine—take* his *medicine. Oh dear, I wish I were better at these idioms.* "Gideon, I…I think you should clear this matter up before we see each other again."

The phone went dead. *Hmm, he took that surprisingly well.* She resisted the urge to cry and went into the kitchen. When she came out carrying a glass filled with ice and a bottle of vodka, she found Gideon sitting on the packing crate. His eyebrows bristled. Claire didn't think she'd ever seen eyebrows actually bristle. It made him look like an angry centipede.

"Claire, you can't dump me over the phone. I forbid it."

She poured a large tot into her glass. "I see."

He stood and paced, not an easy thing to do in a room the size of a refrigerator box. Watching him, it occurred to Claire that she should decorate her house in the Shaker style—have all the furniture hang on pegs, up and out of the way of large trampling feet. She forced herself to focus on the words spilling out of the side of his mouth. "I never hid my predicament from you. It's unfair to let me fall head over heels for you and then suddenly go all ethical on me." He stopped and peered down at her. His face drooped. "Claire, I need you to help me through this."

Her heart tried to claw its way out of her body and rush to him. She deliberately folded her arms across her chest. To muster her resolve, she pictured herself burning at the stake, the crowd chanting, "The other woman must die." When she finally spoke, her tone was hard. "You're a grown man, Gideon Bliss. You have to clean up your own messes. I begin to wonder if your mother may have spoiled you just a teensy bit."

His cheekbones went rigid and his eyes narrowed, firing bullets of angry red light at her. "That was unnecessary, Claire. And unjust. But you're right—this is my mess." And with that he twirled, bumped his shin hard on the hall stool, and charged out the front door, leaving it open.

That went even better than the phone call. This time she did not resist the urge, and burst into tears.

Chapter Eleven
The Operative Link

After two days of non-stop moping, Claire decided to concentrate on the murder mystery. This entailed schmoozing with the local constabulary, which had other advantages. Ernest's admiring gaze, his dove-colored eyes alight with pleasure, pumped her mood up considerably. He made her feel special, not like…

"I'm so glad you were free, Claire. I…I had begun to think that…that—"

"That I was avoiding you?" Claire gave him the full force of her best smile. "Not at all. I expect you've been busy with all the murders." She simulated sober sympathy. "Plus, my mother has returned from Paris and requires a great deal of my time. You know mothers." She took a stab at a girlish giggle. *I should be auditioning for a reality show.*

"Not really."

It took Claire a minute to realize Ernest wasn't joking. "What do you mean?"

The detective handed the cashier a bill and accepted two cups of iced coffee. He gave one to Claire and they walked out of the food court onto the waterfront. The sun sparkled on both the mushy gray water in the marina and the silver-painted mime standing inert by the door to the Torpedo Factory. Ernest didn't speak until they had reached the end of the pier. Gazing out at the wide Potomac, dotted here and there with floating logs and lumps of unidentifiable flotsam, he whispered, "My mother disappeared when I was six months old. My father raised me by himself. No siblings…and I haven't married—at least so far. So, no, I'm not familiar with mothers."

Claire was at a loss for words. Her posturing and simpering seemed so cruel in light of Ernest's disclosure. She looked at the detective, sensing a depth of feeling in him she hadn't felt before. "I…I'm sorry, Ernest." She touched his elbow.

He swung around so fast his coffee shot out of the cup, splattering the deck and her new suede flats—the ones it had taken three months to find because they had to match her pink skirt, and cost an arm and a leg to boot. "Damn! Here, let me…" He went down on his knees, pulled out a large handkerchief, and started mopping.

Why don't I just crack a whip over him? "Ernest, it's okay. Please don't. I'm fine." She raised him to his feet. Before she could stop him, he grabbed her shoulders and gave her an impassioned kiss. When he let her go, she backed away, hand to mouth.

He stood, arms dangling at his sides, the coffee cup forgotten on the ground. "Oh God. I'm…so…sorry. I just—"

She couldn't look at him. Only one name filled her brain—*Gideon.*

Ernest stammered, "I shouldn't have done that. I don't know what you're thinking, Claire, and I'm not going to ask."

A family of four came up behind them, chattering in French. The mother was telling them the next stop on their itinerary would be the Masonic Memorial. Momentarily distracted by their conversation, Claire suddenly realized Ernest had his hand stretched toward her. Without thinking she gave it a hearty shake. He looked at his fingers, and pain washed over his features. "Maybe it would be best if we talk tomorrow."

"Yes. All right." She watched him stride down to his squad car. *Oh dear, I screwed that up badly, didn't I? So, how to smooth things over so Ernest keeps feeding me information?* Ignoring the pang of guilt at her callousness, she found her car and drove home.

Ernest called the next day. When Claire started to apologize he brushed her words aside. "Water under the bridge. My fault. Too much, too soon, right? Anyway, it was very unprofessional of me to let emotions get in the way of an investigation."

Stifling a sigh of relief, Claire said casually, "So tell me, how is it going? The investigation, I mean?"

"We're pretty much at an impasse with the first murder. I told you about Scordato's P2 connection?"

"Yes, Propaganda Due. The Italian lodge."

"It's more like a mob than a lodge. When Interpol went after Scordato, the folks at Operation Gladio told them to back off."

"That's the undercover American group, right? "

"Yup—black ops, it's called. Well, they didn't have any jurisdiction here so we were merrily conducting our murder investigation when Chief Martingale got the word from Interpol that we were to cease and desist."

"Can they do that?"

"They can if my police chief says they can. Apparently they're working another angle and don't want us in the way."

"But the murder happened here, on American soil. How can they dictate the course of the investigation?"

Ernest didn't answer for a minute. Then he said in a low voice, "Look, I can't talk here. Where are you?"

"I'm at the Torpedo Factory. I'm supposed to meet my sister in fifteen minutes."

"Can you put her off?"

"Is it important?"

"Only if you're interested in what we've uncovered."

"I'll call her right now."

Ernest met her by the Factory's waterfront door. He checked over each shoulder, took Claire's hand, and guided her past the building and around the Old Dominion Boat Club to a bench facing the river. He waited until the thin, sandy-haired man who'd been occupying the bench got the hint and strolled off, leaving only a trace of cologne. Claire sniffed the air. She loved that scent—it reminded her of her grandmother. *Clean, fresh, lemony. What the heck is it?*

They sat in a tiny vortex, the cries and laughter of belated Labor Day revelers rolling past them down the Strand to Waterfront Park and up King Street. Ernest bent his head close to hers. The masculine aroma of Old Spice rose from his wrinkled cotton shirt, overpowering the last vestiges of her grandmother's perfume. "I don't think Interpol is calling the shots. I think Operation Gladio is. They've pursued Truffatore for decades—"

"Decades? You told me Truffatore was active in the seventies and eighties. He's got to be dead by now!"

"Not by a long shot. He's past ninety and in jail in Italy, peddling his life story and writing poetry. I believe he was nominated for a Nobel Prize in literature."

Claire goggled at him. "You're kidding."

Ernest shook his head, grinning. "You can't make this stuff up. Besides dabbling in composition, we think he's also running a global cabal. Scordato was his man in Buenos Aires. The Gladio people trailed Truffatore to Argentina, Chile, Switzerland, and Cannes. Everywhere he went, they left an agent in place, even after he left. My guess is they're looking for more than just the man."

Argentina. Argentina—someone else has ties to Argentina. Now who? It was no use. The link had sailed off with the river breeze.

A sleek yacht floated by, its crew furling sail as they eased into their moorings. Clouds rushing in from the water passed overhead, dampening the noise of the crowd. In the muggy quiet Ernest's voice rang loud. "Before we were shut down, I'd sent a team to Argentina to check on Scordato's movements there. They found a witness who knew Scordato and had seen him talking to a man in the Buenos Aires airport before he flew here. He said the two were arguing about something. He only overheard a few words, but they included 'jewels' and 'papers' and something about a 'mark.' "

"Isn't a 'mark' the fellow you target in a scam?"

"Or assassination. Yes."

"Do you suppose Scordato came here to kill someone?"

"No—everything we have on him points to his being mainly an accountant for P2. Remember he was originally a banker. He may have been a charlatan and a crook, but he wasn't a murderer. He left that to his cronies in the Mafia. One of his partners, a man named Calvi, tried to abscond with some of the money embezzled from the Ambrosiano Bank. They found him hanging from Blackfriars Bridge in London."

Claire swallowed. "Oh."

"The man at the airport might be the key to Scordato's death. We need to identify him, but we've been told to halt any attempt to find him."

"By whom?"

"I think by the wonderful folks at Operation Gladio."

"Are they here? In Alexandria?"

"Possibly. A man came to see Chief Martingale today. CIA by the looks of him." Ernest let an arm drop casually across Claire's shoulders. When she didn't move, he relaxed. "If Gladio is here, we can leave it to them to bring the killer to justice."

"Black ops are what? Mercenaries? Spies? Special Forces? Are they military types or intelligence types?"

"Both. They're originally military, but now in deep cover. They're allowed to use whatever means necessary to accomplish their mission."

"Like a bunch of James Bond clones?"

"That's about it."

Claire had an image of a gray suit, gray hair, limpid pale eyes. "I wonder…"

"What?"

"If the man in the airport was black ops, he may have followed Scordato here."

"That seems obvious."

"And if his mission is to find some *thing*, not someone, he'd still be doing that even after Scordato's death."

"Makes sense."

"So he'd still be here."

"Yeah, so?"

"So I think I know who he is."

Ernest stared at her. "You do? Who? And how?"

Claire told him about Joe Smith, about how he'd cleaned out the bookshop and spent hours in every room of the temple. She mentioned she'd seen him in public as well, but not that he was with Dorcas. Bringing Gideon and the divorce issue into this would only complicate matters. Ernest would no doubt decide Gideon was linked to the murder and it would be ages before they straightened that out. She had absolute faith in Gideon's innocence. *He's too...he's too...well, lovable to be a murderer.*

Angle jumped up and grabbed her arm. "Let's go to the station. I'd like to take down your statement formally."

"My statement? It's just a guess." As Claire reluctantly rose to follow him, the blond man reappeared and recaptured his bench with a bored sidelong glance at the usurpers. "Whatever could you do with it?"

Ernest helped her into his squad car. "Hopefully I can convince Chief Martingale that the police should stay involved. He won't like these clandestine types sneaking around on his turf."

Her companion's excitement was infectious, and by the time they reached the station Claire pressed an imaginary accelerator with as much fervor as Ernest did with the real one. The detective left Claire with a sergeant while he made his way to the office of the chief of police. "Send her along to us with her statement when you're finished, Pete."

All the blinds in the glass-enclosed office were down when she approached. Voices murmured inside. She knocked.

"Ah, there you are, Mrs. Wilding. I'm Chief Martingale. Won't you come in?" A well-stuffed man in a spiffy uniform teeming with braid rose from behind the desk, extending a beefy hand to her. Claire hoped his ill-starred attempt to cover the gray in his hair was usually hidden under his police chief cap. He exuded the kind of confidence so well defined by Murphy's Law. As one local wag put it, 'Who needs competence when you have a glib tongue, no shame, and lots of subordinates?'

Lieutenant Angle stood leaning against the wall, his face closed. Claire could make out bits of anger and frustration hiding in the corners of his eyes. She turned back toward the chief and froze. The last person she expected to see lounged calmly and somehow half transparently in the one guest chair. Joe Smith.

Smith stood and offered her the chair while Chief Martingale made the introductions. "You know Lieutenant Angle of course, and this is Anton White. Is that your statement?" He took the paper from Claire and handed it to the stranger. "Angle tells us you had some ideas about the murder you witnessed. We'd like to have you reiterate them here." He bestowed a benevolent smile upon her. "Mr. White is quite interested."

Claire, trying to gather her shaken wits, let him continue. When he took a breath, she broke in. "I have met Mr. White before. Or is it *Mr. Smith*?"

The man looked puzzled. "Smith? No. My name is Anton White. I don't think I've had the pleasure."

"But…" Claire stopped. Now that she had a moment to study the man she realized that his resemblance to her theoretical black ops agent was only superficial. Sure, they both had the ability to blend into the décor and to apply facial expressions like theatrical makeup, but this man had a slight air of authority missing in Joe Smith. "Perhaps you're right," she ended lamely.

Chief Martingale decided to retrieve the floor. "Mr. White is with the government."

The man produced a mirthless smile. "Yes, I'm from the government, and I'm here to help you."

Martingale paused, clearly uncertain whether he should laugh or not. When no one else did, he went on. "He has a letter from Inspector Marchand of the Interpol and one from"—he checked a form letter on his desk—"the Bureau of Syndicate Operations. That's in the Defense Department, right?"

White conveyed agreement without actually moving his lips.

The chief continued. "He's been tracking our murder victim from Argentina. Anton, will you do the honors?" Martingale blushed. Claire wondered if he felt entirely comfortable addressing a government agent by his first name.

"Certainly. One of the missions of the BSO is to monitor groups both here and abroad who may intend to do harm to United States' interests."

"Isn't that what the CIA does?"

"There are several organizations who are responsible for surveillance," White said smoothly.

"You're familiar with the theory of multiple layers of security?" He didn't wait for an answer. "Your chief has informed me that you are aware the victim, Mr. Gasparo Scordato, belonged to a rogue Masonic sect called P2. You may also be aware that he was a colleague of a man named Lazio Truffatore, currently in jail for an exceedingly long list of crimes. Truffatore and his cohorts used P2 as a cover for their illegal activities, which included financial transgressions, bribery, and possibly murder."

Angle interrupted. "Yes, we know all about P2. And that Scordato came here from Argentina. What we don't know is why he ended up dead on the observation platform of the Masonic Temple, and who put him there."

White allowed himself another cold smile. "Welcome to the club, Detective. I only learned of his demise upon my arrival. Our operative followed Scordato to Washington a month ago, but then his dispatches stopped. We've had no word since then and we are concerned. I'm here as much to find him as to solve the mystery of Scordato's death."

The chief shuffled some papers. "I haven't received any reports of a missing person or an unidentified body turning up here. You're sure your man left Buenos Aires?"

"Yes."

Angle looked at Claire expectantly. When she continued mute, he said, "Claire? Can you tell the Chief and Mr. White what you told me?"

Claire broke her gaze from the steady, almost mesmerizing, stare of the agent. "I may have seen your man. He's visited the Washington Masonic Memorial several times. He bought several books on freemasonry, and he took my tour of the temple."

"Your tour?"

Ernest raised a hand. "Mrs. Wilding is a docent at the temple. She's the one who discovered Scordato's body."

"What makes you suspect the man you've seen is an agent?"

How to explain without insulting White? "I…I'm not sure. He's just kind of…shifty."

"Definitive." The man raised the corner of his mouth a millimeter to show he appreciated the joke before his face flattened out again. "What name did he give?"

"Joe Smith."

"Ah. You thought he and I were the same man?"

"No, no." She had to say it. "But…you *do* look alike."

"Shifty?"

Claire blushed.

White let her suffer a few minutes before continuing. "The agent I'm looking for is Simon Peel."

Claire gaped at him. *Simon Peel?* Could there be a third gray man? *Is there a whole army of them?*

Chief Martingale, his eyes blinking rapidly, stammered, "Could…uh…Joe Smith be an alias…Anton?"

White picked up Claire's statement and scanned it quickly. His pale eyes fixed on Claire, the words seeped through his lips like oil over water. "I think we can assume Peel and Smith are one and the same. Those were the only times you've seen him?"

Don't tell him about Dorcas if you can help it.

Claire thought feverishly. "Yes. No. I forgot—I saw him sneaking into the temple once as we closed."

"Can you give us dates for your sightings?"

Claire tried to think. "I'm not sure. Harry's accounts will show the date of his purchases. That's the first time he appeared at the memorial that I know of. We conduct tours every day. Since we don't take names of tour participants it would be hard to pinpoint the date he took it."

"How about the last time?"

"I'll have to think about that. At least a week or so."

White leaned forward, his expression grave. "Can you be more specific?"

Claire squirmed on the hard seat. "I…uh…saw him in a coffee shop. With a woman."

The muscle in his cheek stopped twitching. "Ah. What did this woman look like?"

Claire could honestly say, "Beautiful. Stunning. She and Audrey Hepburn could be twins."

"Dark hair and eyes?"

"Yes."

He nodded. "We know about her. Peel took up with her in Argentina. We didn't know she was in Washington. She checked out."

That's it! That's the other connection to Argentina. Claire gave White a speculative stare and wondered what "checked out" involved.

He took out a tablet and swished a finger across it. "I understand you're dealing with a second murder." He studied the screen. "A Frederick Nutley, professor of history and a specialist on the subject of George Washington. He was recently overheard in the temple, having some sort of argument with the librarian. Have you any evidence the two murders are related?"

"None so far. The professor was killed the day after he announced he'd made a significant historical discovery. The perpetrator broke into his house, ransacked it, and killed Nutley there."

"Really? What kind of discovery?"

"He didn't say. In his press conference he said he'd be coming out with more details at a later date."

White made a note. "Probably serendipity."

Claire watched the agent. Even his eyes remained blank as he wrote on the tablet's tiny screen. She found it hard to trust him. The Washington letter might well shed some light on the affair, but something kept her from mentioning it. *He's not all he appears to be.* She studied his hands. Could they hold a thin black scarf around a man's neck and kill with one quick stroke?

White finished writing and closed the tablet. "Now back to Scordato. Tell me, do you think on the day of his death he was leaving the temple or arriving at it?"

Dead silence greeted this question.

Chapter Twelve
Hyperlinks

"Mother, I don't want to talk about it."

"I know, but—"

"No."

Letitia Canfield carefully laid her lavender and petal pink fascinator down on the kitchen counter and patted her hair. "I can't believe you'd let that…that hussy hold sway over your love life."

Claire poured her mother a glass of iced tea from a crystal pitcher. "Let's go out to the patio." She unfolded two plastic chairs and a plastic table and set the pitcher on it. In the tiny open space their knees almost touched, but the profusion of roses, purple ageratum, and coreopsis the color of lemon sherbet surrounding them made up for the cramped quarters. She clinked her mother's glass. "Hussy or not, she's also Gideon's wife. Until that's resolved I do not want to see him. I will not see him."

"He's beside himself."

Claire couldn't imagine the tall, broad-shouldered man she might possibly love "beside himself." "I doubt that."

"Well, his mother is, anyway. She's fit to be tied. Dorcas hasn't answered any of her calls. They sent her the papers, but there's been no response from either Dorcas or her lawyers."

"Has Gideon tried to get in touch with his…his wife since our luncheon?"

"I don't know. The Senate went back into session this week, and I'm sure he has his hands full. He's left it to us to get this thing resolved."

"Mother!" Claire spilled her tea. "Say it ain't so."

Her mother's indignation was genuine. "Don't give me that look, child. Someone's got to take action. You young people always think you have plenty of time, that nature will take its natural course and lead you to the Promised Land without your lifting a finger to help it along. Well, Andromeda and I both know sometimes destiny needs a little goose. And don't use 'ain't,' even in a quote."

"Yes, Mother."

Her mother acknowledged the apology with a benevolent nod and sipped her tea. "You don't have any of those scrumptious deviled eggs you make so well, do you?" She looked around vaguely.

"Sorry. I have some raspberries."

"That would be nice."

The small box of scarlet berries took up most of one shelf in the mini refrigerator. When Claire returned with a bowl and napkins, Letitia took up arms again. "Andy believes—and I agree—that if we keep up the pressure on Dorcas she'll have to cave. What woman wants a mother-in-law who hounds her constantly?"

Claire took a raspberry and nibbled on it. The tart sweetness burst on her tongue. "What do you think she wants anyway?"

"Dorcas? I'm not sure. After all, her lover has apparently been in touch with her."

Claire stared open-mouthed at her mother. "How

did you know?"

Letitia's half-smile would have put Mona Lisa out of sorts. "You are always staggered by my powers of observation, aren't you, my dear? I know because I saw him."

"That day we were in Vermilion?"

"Of course." The old lady ate another berry. "Andy says he's the man she left Gideon for."

"Andy?"

"Andromeda. We've been indulging in a little sleuthing since our luncheon."

Nuts. Just what we need—two Miss Marples on the case.

"They met in Argentina."

"Argentina?"

"Dorcas comes from a distinguished and well-to-do Spanish family. They own a large ranch in the pampas a few hundred miles from Buenos Aires and breed racehorses. Andy says she spends several months a year there."

The words of Lieutenant Angle came back to Claire. "Everyone assumed that the lodge dissolved after Perón fell, but it didn't. Scordato kept it going with help from a mysterious reserve of funds." They'd theorized that Scordato had used the money from the sale of Perón's hands, but could those funds have come from Dorcas instead? Could she be mixed up with P2? Could her lover have drawn her into the gang? *Or the other way around?* White said the BSO had lost touch with their man Peel. She conjured up the exquisite, shatterproof face of Gideon's wife. *The face that launched a thousand ships.* Yes, she could see Dorcas as the ring leader. Claire decided to pump her mother for as much information as possible.

"How did Mrs. Bliss know what Dorcas' lover looked like?"

Letitia stopped with the raspberry halfway to her lips. "What? Oh, you seemed lost in reverie for a minute there—I do hope you weren't daydreaming about Gideon."

"No, Mother. You were saying?"

She popped the raspberry in her mouth and, with a reproving look, went on. "When Andromeda first arrived in Paris, she went to the embassy for help in locating her daughter-in-law. She says the ambassador was most kind and offered the services of his first secretary."

Claire kept the facetious remark to herself. Her mother's obvious gratification at the deferential treatment of her friend couldn't have been more endearing.

Letitia continued, "As she was leaving the secretary's office, she saw Dorcas in the hall. He was with her."

Let's just see how much our lady sleuths know. "Did she learn his name? His profession?"

"He goes by Simon Peel, but we think that's an alias. He's definitely too bland to be anything other than a spy. And anyway, Dorcas wouldn't find him attractive otherwise."

"He couldn't be a reclusive billionaire?" *Or a P2 confederate?*

"Dorcas wouldn't care about money. She's extremely wealthy in her own right. No, according to Andy, she craves danger and sex, preferably in combination."

"Er…are you talking about dominance? Sado-masochism?"

Letitia's faded blue eyes opened wide, feigning shock. "My heavens, Claire. You certainly didn't learn about such things from your parents!" She plucked the last raspberry from the bowl and swallowed it. "However, Andromeda confided to me that she suspected Dorcas's…inclinations…lay along those lines. If our current theory is correct, a spy with latent violent tendencies would be just her cup of tea." As if to underscore her point Letitia held out her glass. "Speaking of…"

Claire poured while digesting her mother's news. A clearer picture of the perfidious Dorcas had begun to emerge, and it was not a pretty one. How much had Gideon participated in this danger/sex thing? She remembered the first time she and Gideon made love— he had used savage words about strangling and stabbing. They had frightened her at first, but he meant them as a metaphor for his attraction to her, not as an invitation. He never touched her with cruel intent, but always with gentle adoration. Had he declined Dorcas's proposals? Is that why she left him?

Her mother took a sip of tea. "Yes, I'm sure that's why she left Gideon."

Claire gave her a wry smile. "I hate it when you read my mind."

Her mother smiled. "I *am* good, aren't I? At any rate, Andy thinks if Dorcas hadn't walked out, Gideon probably would have done so. She perceived an increasingly pronounced distaste for the lady on the part of her husband. The execrable Dorcas should, therefore, be no impediment to your happiness. So…" She gazed expectantly at her daughter.

"What, Mother?"

"Will you see him?"

"No."

"No?"

"Mother, nothing has changed. Dorcas still refuses to agree to the divorce. Gideon and Dorcas are still married. I have no say in the matter."

"I see." Letitia rose. "Now, where did I put my hat?"

"Mother." Claire's tone was menacing. "Do not get involved. I repeat—"

"You don't have to tell me twice, dear," said her mother primly. "I do have a life of my own, you know."

****

"Thanks for coming in, Claire. Zoe took the one-thirty tour, but we need someone to man the front desk."

"No problem, Mr. Quinn. Where's Nigel?"

The senior warden shook his head. "He didn't show up today."

"He didn't call?"

"No. It's very troubling. As a master mason and our tiler, his duty is to be constantly on guard to ensure the safety of our members and our lodge. That's why he carries the sword as his jewel of office."

Jewels. Who recently mentioned jewels? Claire shook it off. "He has a real sword?"

"Yes, he does. It's of course quite dull," Quinn said hastily. "Not dangerous at all."

"But the manual you gave me said a jewel is just the Masonic term for symbol of office, correct?"

"Yes. Each chair is associated with a jewel."

"I remember, but why are they called jewels? One tourist asked me that last week, and I had no answer. He thought Masons had some sort of crown jewels that they keep buried in the basement."

Apparently Quinn's sense of humor was not up to the challenge. He said soberly, "Not by any means. They are called jewels because the everyday tools a stonemason used contained an inherent moral force that makes them jewels of inestimable value. They have come to symbolize the standards of behavior expected of a Mason."

"I see." *No, I don't.*

Quinn seemed to sense her confusion. "For example, my jewel as senior warden is the level. It reminds us that all Masons meet on the same level without regard to social, political, or religious status or beliefs. The plumb—a tool for ascertaining the alignment of a vertical surface—is held by the junior warden, and symbolizes upright behavior."

"And the tiler's jewel is the sword because he protects the doors?"

"During our meetings, yes. The sword has no scabbard, to indicate that he is always ready to defend the lodge."

"So," Claire spoke slowly, "when the tiler isn't here, you're—at least symbolically—unprotected?"

Mr. Quinn didn't seem to like the direction of the discussion and abruptly turned away. "Only symbolically, you understand. We no longer need to protect our members or our lodge with force. Now, if you would kindly take over at reception, I am sure Nigel will resume his duties in due time."

Claire settled at the desk and watched the senior

warden's retreating back. She thought about the dead man on the observation deck. *"We no longer need to protect our lodge with force." Can he be so sure?*

****

Claire dragged herself up the steps to her door. Night had fallen. All the school groups seemed to be front-loading their field trips in the first week of school, and she'd been run ragged by wayward children, searches for lost notebooks, and demands for attention—not always from the teachers. She hadn't realized till now how taxing Nigel's job was. Whenever she'd seen him he was wrapped up in his newspaper or doodling on his pad. She wiped a damp forehead. Indian summer had hit Washington hard this year. Cool weather couldn't come soon enough.

She checked her refrigerator. Letitia had eaten all the raspberries and finished off the iced tea. Apparently the tub of margarine and jar of peanut butter didn't appeal, so she had generously left them for Claire. Nothing for it but a trip to Tivoli Tavern for a burger and beer.

Claire sidled past the lineup of inharmoniously-costumed musicians playing a listless version of "Rocky Top," her eye barely escaping the tip of the fiddler's bow. She stopped, ready to give a piece of her mind to the rather gaunt, hatchet-faced blond, but he kept his eyes on the crowd and increased the speed of his bowing. She glared at him just long enough to make her point and also to realize that, while he reminded her of someone, she'd never, ever figure out who it was. She remembered her mother's perennially irritating advice about picking one's battles, and found an empty table. The music grew slightly livelier.

A waitress with implausibly yellow hair and a perfectly square figure wiped her table with an elbow and pulled the cigarette out of her mouth long enough to ask, "What'll it be, hon?"

Claire started to ask for wine but thought better of it. She checked the woman's name tag. "Um, Wanda? What kind of beer do you have?" The waitress rattled off a list of some twenty-five beers. Claire latched on to the only brand she recognized. "Pilsner Urquell, please. And a cheeseburger."

"Fries?"

"Sure…and could I have extra lettuce?"

"On the fries?"

Claire started to correct her when she saw the twinkle in her eye. "Yup. Thanks."

The fiddler took center stage for an underwhelming rendition of "The Devil Went Down to Georgia." When it ended, the group disbanded and reassembled at the bar. A hairy young man with more tattoos than skin plugged his battered Fender guitar into an enormous amplifier and proceeded to blow away his audience with splendid abandon. He'd set the bass frequency so high Claire couldn't make out any melody. Wanda brought her order and shouted, "Back room'll be quieter."

Claire took her advice. One lone couple huddled in the far corner and she sat down with her back to them, facing the bar. Halfway through her meal the guitarist took a break, and in the sudden silence Claire heard a woman's voice, its rich alto flecked with a Spanish accent, from behind her. A familiar voice. *Dorcas.*

"Of course Father belonged to the highest orders in the Masons, but he never mentioned any treasure."

Her companion said something in a low, urgent voice.

"No, the jewels are merely symbols of office. I don't think they're actually valuable. I wouldn't know about any secret cache. What did Gasparo tell you?"

The man spoke again.

Claire decided to risk it and twisted her head to look.

Dorcas's voice took on a skeptical edge. "That's all he said? 'A box in the lodge?' I told you he didn't trust you. His loyalty lay only with Truffatore. He used you to get to the States." Dorcas jerked back at his next words as though she'd been slapped. Her face hardened and she spat out, "Well, he's no longer alive to guide you, is he?"

The man shot out a hand and wrapped it around her neck, pulling her to him. He kissed her savagely, then, in a perversely affectionate gesture, touched her chin with his finger. Both voices dropped to a low rumble. Claire longed to get within earshot. The hall to the ladies room lay to their right. *If I just stroll past them maybe I can hear more of the conversation without drawing their attention.* She pushed her plate aside and grabbed her purse.

Just then Dorcas raised her voice. Irritation slurred her words. "Well, if he had no idea what he was supposed to retrieve, why are we here? What good is the key?" When he didn't respond, her tone softened. She coaxed, "Can't we just go back to Paris, Simon? This whole thing seems like a wild goose chase. We were so happy there."

Simon. Simon Peel. Mother was right.

The man grew more strident, yet Claire still

couldn't make out any words.

Dorcas stifled a small scream. "Anton White? Why? Does he know about…"

More whispering. Claire dropped her purse and any pretense and turned to watch. Dorcas held a hand to her mouth. "You think he suspects you? How? You've had no contact…He doesn't know about me, does he?"

She made as if to stand. Peel grabbed her arm, spitting his words out like machine gun fire. "…can't back out now. You're in it to the end, Dorcas."

His companion wrenched herself free and strode past Claire toward the bar. Claire dropped down to her seat and hunched over her glass, only peeking out when she heard a crash. The tattooed youth watched in horror as Dorcas kicked the remains of his amplifier out of her way and stormed out of the tavern. Claire wondered if she should follow her, but the mob of outraged musicians at the front door persuaded her to wait until the uproar died down. As she took a long pull on her beer, she felt a presence beside her. Joe Smith—or rather, Simon Peel—gazed down at her speculatively. "I've seen you somewhere before."

His calm voice didn't convey any menace. But then, the man never seemed to display emotion of any kind. Claire tried to breathe slowly. *The truth is easier to remember than a lie.* As long as she told it in a roundabout sort of way. "You took my tour of the Masonic Temple a few weeks ago."

His blank eyes seemed to suck her words in, then lay them out on a kind of mental platform to ponder before spewing them into the void. She wondered if spies were trained to receive, absorb, and then quickly erase from their memory potentially dangerous information. "Oh, yes." He smiled thinly. "You were very patient with my endless questions."

"Not a problem—that's my job after all." Claire picked up her glass with a trembling hand, hoping she could get the beer to her lips without spilling it. When she looked up again, Peel was gone.

She walked home slowly, careful to stay with the crowds, stepping into every doorway to check if she were being followed. *This is absurd, Claire. If Peel wants to kill you you'll never see it—or him—coming.*

No light shone in the house. She must have forgotten to put the porch light on when she left. Or had she? *No I didn't. Forget, I mean.* She swung around and sprinted back down the block, found her car, and sped the ten miles to Edwina's house.

Her sister took one look at Claire's face and called up to the second floor. "Ray, I won't be up for a while." She shut off the television, and, motioning for Claire to follow, crossed the hall to the kitchen. As she pulled out the gallon-sized bottle of whiskey, a falsetto voice trickled down. "Mummy, aren't you going to kiss us good night?"

"*Oops.* You pour. You know what I want. I'll be back in a jiffy." Edwina took the stairs two at a time. Claire heard the sounds of children using any and all powers at their disposal to hold their mother hostage. She had no doubt Edwina would be up to the task. She poured a stiff drink for herself, cut a piece of cake for her sister, and carried them into the living room. Two minutes later Edwina flopped on the couch. She took a bite of chocolate cake and put the plate down. "Okay, out with it."

Claire told her sister everything—from the hellish

luncheon with the mothers, to black ops agent Anton White's appearance, to the conversation between Peel and Dorcas.

When she'd finished, Edwina poured her more bourbon. "The Vermilion encounter must have been…what's the word I'm looking for? Awkward?"

"You'd need a thesaurus to find the most apt description. Anyway, playing the rival to the ravishing Dorcas is the least of my problems."

"Good, then you've concluded that refusing to see Gideon until the divorce is final is a tactical error, right?"

"What? Why?"

Edwina blinked. "It's obvious, isn't it? All reports indicate that said Dorcas is gorgeous, a delight to the eyes, a dazzler to rival Helen of Troy—"

"And your point?" Her sister's soaring adjectives were doing little to cheer Claire up.

"Also a harridan and a hussy. Nevertheless, a person of considerable attraction to any male. Do you really want Gideon to spend any more time with her? At least without someone equally charming to compare her to?"

Her last words did not create the sought-after mellowing effect. Claire frowned. "Hanging preposition? Really, sis? I'm telling Mother." She swallowed the last of her drink. "Edwina, focus. I think a man wants to kill me."

Edwina stretched her legs out, dropping her feet onto Claire's knees. "You're overreacting. People don't just run through crowds slicing and dicing whoever's in their path. Besides, you don't know that he's killed anyone at all."

"But…Scordato?"

"Dorcas merely said he wasn't around to help anymore."

"True." Her anxiety began to dissipate. Then another thought struck her. "What about the professor?"

"Do you have any evidence of a link between Peel and Nutley?"

"N…no." Claire scratched her head. "But I did get the impression from the conversation that Peel doesn't know what he's looking for. Perhaps when he read Nutley's announcement, he thought it was the treasure he'd come in search of."

"For which he'd been searching. Ha, now we're even." Edwina took another bite of cake with a preoccupied air. "There may be something to that, but if Simon Peel is a good guy—black ops are supposed to be on the side of justice, truth, and the American way, right?—then he wouldn't kill people."

"Number one, these guys are authorized to use any force necessary. If what they seek is vital to our national interest, they'd stop at nothing."

"Whoa, you sound like Eliot Ness. Or that guy in *24*. What's number two?"

"Two? Oh, the other agent—Anton White. He's come looking for Peel. He said Peel hadn't reported to the…er…agency in weeks. Yet Peel's alive and well, so—"

"So he probably intends to keep whatever this treasure is for himself."

"And Dorcas."

"And Dorcas. Say, wouldn't that get Gideon off the hook?"

Claire brightened, then deflated. "No, not if she

and Peel disappear. She's unlikely to sign any papers while basking on the beach of an island without an extradition treaty."

"Damn." Edwina rolled the last crumbs around on the plate, mashed them together, and popped the little ball in her mouth. Suddenly, she put the plate down and gazed at her sister with new concern. "I think this Peel fellow may be a bad penny. You know what? I—"

At that moment the lights went out.

Chapter Thirteen
The Missing Link

"Did that one do it, honey?" A disembodied voice from the cellar reached the living room where the two women sat hugging each other.

"No, Ray. Read the labels, Ray."

"Funny. I was sure that was it. There's only one tab left and—" The two women heard a thump and muffled cursing. Suddenly the house flooded with light.

"That's it, sweetie. Thanks!"

Edwina's husband trudged up the cellar steps rubbing his elbow. "Damn these old houses. Whacked my arm on that broken beam."

"I *told* you...no, never mind." Edwina smiled fondly at him.

"I didn't expect sympathy," sniffed Ray. He patted Claire's clenched shoulder. "Sorry about the delay. Turns out each circuit works on only a few outlets in every room. Number one connects to Giselda's overhead light and the living room sockets, number two is the washing machine and the garage door opener, number—"

"We get it, dear. It's an old house with jury-rigged wiring. I know." Edwina detached herself from Claire's clutching hands and gave her husband a peck on the cheek. "But we love it, don't we?"

Claire made a concerted effort to stop shaking.

Thank God she hadn't called 9-1-1 the minute they lost power. She and Edwina had been holding each other and gibbering when Ray leapt down the stairs and headed for the circuit breaker. Now, with every bulb in the house blazing, she felt better. "What do you think triggered it, Ray?"

"No idea."

"Wait a minute." Husband and wife stared at each other, comprehension dawning on their faces. Ray yelled, "Samuel Fortescue Gillespie, get down here."

A boy of nine tiptoed down the stairs, guilt oozing from every pore. His Green Bay Packers pajamas and strawberry blond cowlick would have melted the heart of any woman, so Ray took his son by the scruff of his collar and led him out to the kitchen. Claire turned to Edwina. "How did you know?"

Edwina growled, "I warned Ray not to let him have a computer in his room, that our electric panel can't handle the power demand. Sammy's been getting up in the middle of the night to play video games on his computer. This isn't the first time he's blown the circuit." She kissed Claire's cheek. "The timing couldn't have been worse, though, huh?"

"It's not funny, Eddie. Black ops isn't known for playing nice."

Edwina yawned. "Well, you're safe here. Your room's all made up. I'm going to bed. Do you want me to go to the police with you tomorrow?"

Claire thought of Ernest. Edwina's sharp eyes were sure to pick up on his attraction to her sister. The last thing she needed was more harping on her pathetic love life. Or more censure. "I'll be fine." She managed half a titter. "They know me there now. 'Night Eddie."

"Sleep tight. Ray can take the first watch." Edwina's tinkling laughter followed Claire as she climbed the stairs.

****

The morning sun filtered through the dirty blinds in Chief Martingale's office. Dust motes glittered in the weak light. The two men in the room paid close attention to Claire's story of the tavern encounter.

Ernest turned to Martingale. "We'd better get hold of White."

"You're right. Now where is that card he gave me?" The chief scrabbled around in his desk drawer and came up with a business card. He held it up. "This must be it." Claire could make out a number printed in white letters on black stock. Martingale pushed his glasses up his nose and read, "800-555-4343. *Hmm.* Let's put it on speaker phone." He dialed.

They heard a ding and a metallic voice said, "Please leave a phone number at the tone."

Ernest clucked his tongue. "Talk about not giving anything away. I sure hope that's the right number."

"If it is, he'll call back." The chief turned to Claire. "In the meantime, Mrs. Wilding, let's go over your evidence again."

Claire repeated the conversation between Peel and Dorcas for the third time.

Ernest rubbed his chin, thoughtfully picking at the stubble of a twelve-hour beard. "Of course, you didn't actually hear Peel say anything damning. You say he asked Mrs. Bliss about jewels? Do you suppose he believes this hidden treasure consists of gemstones?"

Claire shook her head. "If he's expecting a cache of Masonic jewels, he'll be disappointed. They're simply badges of office."

The chief mumbled something.

"What did you say?"

"I said"—his face flushed—"the jewels of office are precious indeed to a Master Mason. So are other emblems or tokens we…er…they receive during the course of our…their journey through the levels."

Angle gave his chief a sharp look. "Such as?"

Martingale's jaw relaxed when he realized they weren't going to force him to confess. "Mark pennies for one. When a Fellow Craftsman becomes a Master Mason his lodge presents him with a mark penny or token."

"And he places his own unique mark on the penny to identify it and him," said Claire. "We have a whole room of them on display at the Memorial. Mr. Quinn says some are quite valuable."

Angle asked the chief, "Could the pennies be the treasure he's looking for?"

Martingale shrugged. "I doubt if any of the tokens would be worth enough for the needs of a man like Truffatore."

"But Truffatore is a Mason—Peel isn't. Remember, he asked Mrs. Bliss about the jewels—he may not have a clue what's valuable and what's not." Angle studied his notes. "He could have been colluding with Scordato, but then again, he could have been playing along in order to wangle information out of him."

"Then why kill him?"

The chief jumped in. "We have no evidence that Peel killed Scordato. If he had, Mrs. Bliss would have said so. She merely said he wasn't around to help."

Claire hated to cut Dorcas any slack, but she had to keep up her side of the speculation. "Dorcas may not know whether or not he killed Scordato. It's not clear how deeply she's involved in the operation."

"If you heard Peel correctly, she's in pretty deep," said Ernest slowly.

Exasperation roughened her voice. "But what is she involved *in*? A criminal enterprise or a rescue operation? For all we know, they could both be working for Operation Gladio and White is the bad guy trying to horn in."

Ernest threw up his hands. "But…but…"

Claire indicated the card on Martingale's desk. "After all, White shows up here, his only identification a card you can have printed up at any Staples."

"He brought the letters of introduction." Martingale indicated his inbox.

"They could easily have been forged. After all, did *you* ever hear of the Bureau of Syndicate Operations before? And what did we get when we dialed the phone number? A recording. No name given, no indication that he would return the call. Think about it—do you really know who Anton White is? Ernest, did you check with your Pentagon source?"

Both men hesitated. Ernest finally said, "You're suggesting that White is after the treasure too?"

"Or maybe he's the only one who is. Look, we can trace Peel's movements pretty well—Argentina, Paris, Argentina, here. We could probably obtain verification of his identity from Interpol. But where did White come from?"

The chief stood up. "This is getting us nowhere. The bottom line is we don't have enough evidence to make an arrest, even if we could find any of them."

Claire opened her mouth to protest, but Ernest jumped in. "You're right, Chief. We might as well wait until White gets back to us."

"Good. I've got some other lines of inquiry out as well. We'll solve this case one way or another. Now why don't you run along, Mrs. Wilding? We'll keep you posted."

Ernest walked her out. In the parking lot he touched her hand shyly. "If you're up to it, why not let me take you out to dinner?"

Exhaustion clogged every pore, making it difficult to think. "Not tonight, Ernest. I never sleep well at my sister's. I'm dog tired."

"Maybe if you go home and take a nap you'll feel better later?" His eyes pleaded with her.

She had to smile at his persistence. "Perhaps."

"Tell you what, I'll escort you home. That way I can check your place out for you."

"That would be nice."

The house appeared to be both undefiled and clear of squatters. Claire checked the porch light. "Bulb's out." *That's one mystery solved.* She went through the kitchen and opened the back door. The garden offered up only the scent of flowers and a hungry cat. She returned to the living room as Ernest came down the stairs. "All clear." Claire thought it best to ignore his slight blush. "You should be quite safe here, Claire. Neither Simon Peel nor Dorcas know where you live. Since you've only recently moved, your address won't be on any lists. Besides, you didn't actually get as far as the front door on your walk from the tavern, so even if Peel had followed you, he wouldn't know which house was yours. There's no reason to believe he thinks you're a danger to him—whichever side he's on." He shuffled his feet. If he had a forelock he would have tugged at it. Claire waited. "If you're still uncomfortable, you could always…er…stay with me?"

Oh dear. Claire hastily searched for the words to let him down easy, but the thought occurred that she didn't really have to. At this rate the whole nightmare would never end and Gideon would never be single. *I might as well move on.* "Thank you, I'll think about it." She gave him what she hoped was a dazzling smile and closed the door after him.

Coffee would taste so good right now. Instead, she flopped on the loveseat. Mulling over the morning's events, she pulled Ichabod onto her lap and scratched the top of his head. His purring helped her think. She lined up the players. Gideon. Professor Nutley. Simon Peel. Dorcas Bliss. Anton White. Gasparo Scordato. *Is there a pattern that makes sense?* White good, Peel bad. Dorcas good, Peel good, White bad. White good, Peel good, Dorcas…irrelevant. Gideon, bad. Gideon good, Nutley bad. Scordato? Definitely bad. And dead. *As is Nutley.*

She sat up suddenly, leaving Ichabod to slide unceremoniously off her lap, and spoke to the ceiling. "Scordato was murdered. Nutley was murdered. If the two acts are related, and Peel didn't do it, who did? Who else of our cast of characters knew both men?" *Not a one.* "Were any of them present at both events?" *No.* "Is there any possible connection between a long-lost George Washington letter and a purported cache of Italian treasure?" *Not that I can think of.* Claire rapped her knees, both perplexed and annoyed. Not a single suspect could be connected to both victims. She stood up and headed toward the kitchen. Presented with yet another obstacle to her comfort—the empty larder—she went off to the grocery store.

****

Claire dumped the bag of groceries on the folding table and lunged for the land line. "Hello?"

"Claire? Mr. Quinn here. Do you mind coming in this afternoon again? Zoe is here, but Nigel has yet to show his face."

"That's two days he's been gone. Has he called?"

"No, and believe you me, there will be serious discussion at our next lodge meeting about removing him from his post. It's very unmason-like behavior." He clearly considered Nigel's truancy worse than treason or even than selling lemonade without a permit.

"Let me get something to eat and I'll be there."

She had a nice cheese omelet browning and tomatoes sliced when her cell phone rang. *Can't a girl get a moment's peace—or at least a bite?* "Wilding here."

"Wilding? Is that how you always answer your phone? Sounds like a television cop. 'Sergeant Friday here. Just the facts, ma'am.' "

How can he joke about police when... "What do you want, Gideon?"

"Can you come up to the Temple?" Behind the bravado Claire detected real agitation. "ASAP?"

"As a matter of fact, Mr. Quinn asked me to come and fill in for Nigel. I'll be there *after* lunch."

The emphasis on "after" blew right past Gideon. "Nigel? Is he the one who mans the reception desk? The prematurely balding fellow with the stash of

Penthouses?"

So I was right. "Yes. He's been missing for two days."

"Probably went home to Mama. Anyhoo, get here as soon as you can. Treadwater and I have uncovered a new mystery."

The news did not thrill Claire. She'd had enough of real or imagined threats for a while. *Still.* She changed into a rose-colored linen blouse, with a matching skirt that set off her shapely legs, checked her makeup, and drove up to Shuter's Hill—after she finished the omelet.

Gideon met her at the side door. "Come on, Treadwater's waiting for us."

"What about Mr. Quinn?"

"Bill Overbrook is filling in at the desk. I told Peter we needed you more." He pulled her down the hall without giving her a chance to comment on his Dolce & Gabbana suit and Ermenegildo Zegna tie—she knew high-end men's designer lines well, since Lincoln had never worn anything that cost less than a car. They took the elevator to the fourth floor.

The doors opened to reveal the librarian, today sporting a crimson bow tie and an anguished expression. He crooked his finger at Claire and led the way into the museum with quick, mincing steps. They stopped before a glass case. "This exhibit contains items donated in 1966 by Washington's descendants Anne Madison and Patty Willis Washington. They include Washington's inkwell and a small chest containing his combs and brushes. Someone has pried open the case and both containers—see how the inkwell latch has been scratched?" Claire dutifully examined it.

"And they're not the only ones." Moving to another case, and then another, his stricken face said it all.

Gideon put it into words. "The locks on all these cases and some objects inside have been jimmied."

"Was anything stolen?"

Treadwater shook his head. "I think the professor must not have found what he was looking for."

"Why the professor?"

The librarian stared at her. "Who else could it have been?"

Claire examined a lock. "It looks like the perpetrator used a sharp, pointed object—maybe even a key. Did you ask the senior deacon? Isn't he in charge of closing up?"

"He's out of town. Nigel volunteered to lock up, but he hasn't been seen for two days."

"Could Nigel have tried to open them and then lost his nerve and run away?"

Gideon interrupted. "That's what I suggested, but Treadwater says the cases were fine when he checked them Thursday. It must have happened yesterday or this morning."

"Well, in that case, the professor is out."

"Why? Oh."

Gideon nodded. "Frederick was already dead. He wasn't in a position to do anything, legal or illegal."

"So we're left with an unidentified vandal or vandals."

Treadwater mumbled, "The master set of keys is still on the hook. Whoever did this couldn't have used it."

"Or maybe he—or she—put them back when he was finished." Claire paused. *Keys. Key.*

Gideon shook his head. "If he had the master set, he would have been able to open the cases. There wouldn't be any damage."

An idea flicked on. Claire turned to Treadwater. "Didn't you report a stolen key to the police? When you…when you…" She stopped, remembering too late that Treadwater had accused Gideon of its theft. Gideon turned to the little librarian.

"That's right. Did you ever find it?"

Treadwater's entire head turned a rich burgundy color and he began to stutter. "No. No. I…uh…assumed you…you…"

"That I had it? Is that it?" Both Treadwater and Claire expected Gideon to explode with anger, but instead he tapped his fingers on a case, his eyes meditative. "I took…er…borrowed the Washington book from the library and returned it there. The fellow who stole the other book must have taken the key."

"Aha!" Claire thanked her lucky stars Treadwater stopped short of shouting "Eureka!" "All the cases should have been locked at that time. That means the thief—I mean the key thief, not the book thief"—he blushed again—"must have used the master keys to open the case."

"And put them back on the hook afterward."

All three sighed happily. Gideon broke the contented silence. "Wait a minute. If the person who stole the key and the one who fiddled with these cases are one and the same, he would have had access to the building keys and wouldn't have needed to jimmy the locks. Unless…unless two different people broke in here? And if so, why?"

"What are you talking about? You mean one

burglar knew about the master keys and one didn't? But that makes no sense!" Treadwater scowled.

Claire held her head to keep it from spinning. "I don't think we can find the answers here. Maybe we should call the police. They can at least take fingerprints." She opened her eyes. "Why were you two here in the first place?"

Gideon beamed and Treadwater's lower lip wobbled. "Senator Bliss has…has offered to make an extremely significant donation to our collection. We were scouting out an appropriate spot for the display."

"I see. So you told him of your discovery?"

Gideon put a finger to his lips. "In the strictest confidence. When I received Greystone's report I brought the box here. We decided to send the letter out for a second evaluation. That way we'll be able to present incontrovertible proof of the document's authenticity. We should be hearing any day now."

Treadwater rubbed his hands together. "What a coup! What a glorious coup! Old Farragut at Mount Vernon will have a thumping great fit when he learns we have the letters. Not that they don't belong here," he added hastily.

Gideon patted his shoulder. "Timothy has agreed that the letters will remain here, available to the public, and not kept in the library. Right, Timothy?"

Assorted emotions washed over the little man's face, but resignation won out. "Yes, of course."

Claire moved to the door. "At any rate, you should call the police about this—it could be mere vandalism."

"They're on their way. We asked you to come in case you noticed anything yesterday."

Gideon gave her a meaningful look. "I wanted to

ask you *personally*. Seems to me you've spent quite enough time with the *police*."

Claire raised her chin. "I can spend time with whomever I want, Gideon Bliss."

He took her arm. "Then you'll want to spend it with me." He piloted her out the door. Treadwater called after them. "Senator, we haven't decided on the exhibit location yet!"

Gideon gave Claire a glance and winked. "I'll be back shortly, Timothy. I'm just seeing the lady out."

As they took the steps to the parking lot, Claire shook his hand off. "Gideon, nothing has changed between us. Dorcas is still your wife. I meant what I said."

"But…"

She touched his lips. "But in this case, there's something I want to tell you. It has to do with her. And maybe all this."

His jaw dropped. She gently pushed it back into place. "Your place or mine?"

Chapter Fourteen
The Weakest Link

"So, you're telling me that Dorcas—my Dorcas—is mixed up in this—what did you call it?—P2 caper, along with the man she ran off to Paris with?" Gideon rose and paced the room. After he'd knocked into Claire's knees the third time she pushed him down on the chair, reflecting that even in his own spacious house he bumbled around like a clumsy ox. "It seems awfully far-fetched for her to be drawn into this Truffatore's web. You have identified her...her lover?"

Claire paused. Anton White had declared Joe Smith and Simon Peel to be one and the same, and he should know. "Yes. So has your mother—she saw him with Dorcas in Paris, and both our mothers saw him here in Washington."

"What does he look like?"

Claire studied Gideon's face—was there a trace of jealousy in his eyes? Could he still have feelings for his wife? A little voice in the back of her head moaned, *Please let the answer be no*. She shook it off. "I know this sounds weird, but he's quite difficult to describe. His features all run together in a wishy-washy mish-mash. I couldn't tell you what color his eyes are. Even his voice is kind of insubstantial—almost as though he throws it."

"Like a ventriloquist?"

Claire nodded. "And Anton White—the black ops agent who's come looking for him—could be his twin. In fact, when I first met him, I thought they were the same man. White told me his name is Peel. Simon Peel."

Gideon picked up a manila envelope and absent-mindedly set it back down.

"What's that?"

"It's the letter from the box in the basement. I told you we sent it to a second expert for confirmation. Treadwater has the box at the temple for safe keeping. If Connors confirms Greystone's conclusions about the first letter, we'll send all the documents out for examination."

"Does that mean you have to postpone the big event?"

"No, no. Treadwater—and for that matter David Comfrey—can't wait. They want me to make a formal presentation of the letter…with details to follow." Gideon tapped the package, his face a bit melancholy. "It's rather a shame that Professor Nutley won't be present at the ceremony."

"Why?"

"Well, it was his field, and he did help me in the initial research. The publication of the papers might have restored his reputation and revived his career."

Gideon's sympathy puzzled Claire. "Maybe so, but he also tried to frame you and then take credit for the discovery. Gideon, he was a bad man."

"Nobody deserves to be murdered."

Claire wasn't so sure.

"Say…" He stood up. "You don't think Nutley's murder may be connected to the P2 stuff?"

"I don't see how. Nutley had nothing to do with the Masons. Peel is looking for something in the temple—something precious to the P2 lodge. He'd have no reason to suspect Nutley had it. An obscure letter from George Washington doesn't really fit the bill."

"Didn't Dorcas imply that he had no clue what or where this treasure is? Perhaps when Nutley made the announcement about the letter Peel thought he meant the treasure."

"That's what Edwina guessed."

"Edwina?"

"My sister. After I left the tavern I went to her house."

Gideon sat down again. "Why?"

"I…I…panicked, I guess. Peel recognized me from the temple. I was afraid of…I don't know what."

He moved closer to Claire and put his arms around her. "Very sensible. Who knows what a guy like that is capable of?" He began to nuzzle her hair.

"If Ernest is right, he's capable of anything."

Gideon dropped his arms. "Ernest again."

The way he spit out the words reminded Claire of her ultimatum. She pushed him away. "Stop it. Nothing has changed between you and me."

"You mean you still like me better?"

She stifled the laugh. "It has nothing to do with that."

He frowned. "This isn't fair. We've just established that Dorcas is involved not only with another man, but with one looking at a possible life sentence."

"We only know he's after something."

"Yes, something illicit, something he might have killed for. Twice."

She remembered her sister's Eliot Ness comment. *A black ops agent is supposed to be for truth, justice, and the American way, right? Am I naïve to believe a man like Peel would hesitate to kill to get what he wanted?* If Gideon's hypothesis were true, that Peel had killed two people, perhaps that's why Dorcas was attracted to him. *Dorcas.* "Gideon, what can I say? I can't be a party to an affair. I don't want to be—"

He stopped her words with a burning kiss. When they broke apart he gasped, "God, it's been so long. I want you, Claire. I promise you my...problem will be resolved. I promise you"—his lips went to her hair so his words were muffled—"my heart."

Claire couldn't breathe. Gideon held up her hair and kissed the back of her neck, then planted kisses around to her throat. He continued down to the tiny hollow above her sternum. She closed her eyes, willing her mind to go blank. It worked. She dropped into a pool of sensation filled with the soft touch of lips, the sharp nip of teeth on flesh, the dibbling of fingers over skin. He tossed her blouse on the floor and pulled the bra down so it cupped her breasts. Cool air touched her nipples. They stiffened, dark with hot blood.

He bent to kiss them, then took each nipple and rolled it, squeezing lightly. Her whole torso bent to him. He slipped his hands under her arms and knees and hoisted her up, then strode to the stairs.

"No, Gideon, no."

He didn't respond.

Oh good, I didn't say that out loud.

At the top of the stair he kicked his door open, dropped her on the bed and landed heavily on top of her. She squirmed away. He grabbed her arms, pinning her, and rolled on top of her again. His eyes bored into her as he lowered his head, closer and closer to her mouth. Just before his lips reached hers, she heaved him off and scrambled to the other side of the bed. Misjudging the distance, she landed in a painful heap on the floor. She could hear Gideon panting, but he made no move to come after her.

After catching her breath, she decided to use the unexpected intermission to review her situation. Half naked, and therefore already compromised. *That doesn't give me carte blanche to encourage further misconduct.* On the other hand, he did promise to take care of the Dorcas issue. *Right, while simultaneously pulling my blouse off and snorting like a rutting boar.* Despite his macho behavior, she did believe him. *But what about the principle of the thing? He's still married.* Well, he couldn't be blamed for that. He'd tried everything to get Dorcas to sign the papers—including bringing in a Sherman tank in the form of his mother. Sooner or later she would have to cave. *It's really only a matter of time.*

All remained quiet on the bed. She began to wonder whether Gideon had given up, or fallen asleep, or, worse, lost interest. *I'll just take a quick peek.*

Her head came in contact with something both soft and hard.

"Ouch!" A head showed above hers, holding its nose. A drop of red splashed onto her breast.

"Oh, dear, did I hurt you?"

"Obbiously. Whaddid you do that for? I'b bleeding!"

Claire rose and looked around for a tissue.

"Id da batroom."

She retrieved a wad and returned to the scene of the crime. Pushing Gideon onto his back, she dabbed at his nose. He spent the time groaning dramatically. To distract him, she moved down his body with her free hand, landing on the top button of his trousers. She wiggled the zipper until it opened and slipped her hand inside. He stopped groaning.

His cock expanded under her fingers and batted against her palm. She tickled the head and leaned down to give it a quick lick. Before she could continue, fingers crawled under her waistband and pulled her skirt down. Gideon tore the silk bikini off, tossing the shreds on the floor. Taking hold of her hips, he moved her off him, rotating her so she kneeled on the bed, with his body curled over her. She thrust her pelvis back toward him and he insinuated his fingers into her vagina. She began to grunt, her juices dribbling out and pooling under her on the sheet. As her orgasm crackled upward, he released his fingers, leaving her on her knees, ass in midair. She couldn't see him, but the fragrance of his aftershave—a mixture of bay, lime, and mint—mingled with the scent of arousal. "No, Gideon! Don't leave me now!"

Putting a hand on the small of her back, he pushed her down on her stomach. "Wait."

Claire's mind was a whorl of red and blue waves running straight toward her feminine parts. She couldn't stop moving, rubbing her body on the sheet, trying to ease the ache. She heard Gideon yank his pants off. He held her shoulders and lay across her body. "Cross your ankles," he ordered. She did so. He spread her thighs slightly. His penis nudged against her, and with one great intake of breath, she sucked it all the way in. His hand slid under her and pressed on her belly button. "Do you feel it?"

A round, hard lump pulsed against his palm. His cock filled out the hollow channel and scraped the walls of her vagina. She didn't feel overstuffed, but more complete, as though an organ had been missing all her life and Gideon's penis filled the empty space and made her whole. "Yes. Oh…oh. Oh."

He began to pump. She grabbed the sheet with her hands and let the sensation take hold of her. To get closer she ground her bottom against his balls. His dick rolled into her like thunder and held her captive. His pistoning grew wilder and harder. "I'm coming! Claire!"

"Gimme it, gimme it. Oh God, me too!"

His last thrust sent her forward into the pillows. They rested, chest to back.

"Okay, now you may scold me."

Claire raised her head and stuck her tongue out at him. "There."

He kissed her forehead. "Duly chastened."

They were quiet for a while, neither wanting to break the peace. Just as Claire dropped off, Gideon rolled away to look at the clock. "Uh oh, I've got to get back to the temple."

"Why?"

"Remember, I promised Treadwater I'd come back and finalize arrangements for the donation ceremony."

Claire teased, "Oh yes, you were only going to escort me out."

He pretended to commiserate. "Poor Timothy, but I'm sure he's been dealing with the police since I left anyway."

"Oh, right. The tampered locks. Do you think it will delay the ceremony?"

"Not if the worshipful master has anything to do with it. He ordered Treadwater to polish out the marks and leave the rest to the police."

"So the ceremony is turning into a big event."

"Are you kidding? Treadwater's so excited he wet his pants twice yesterday. We're meeting with all the chairs tomorrow. Comfrey put Quinn in charge of publicity since he owns a public relations firm. So far Fox News, CSpan, and the local channel are planning to cover it, as well as the *Washington Times* and the *Alexandria Gazette*. They expect a huge crowd."

"Yes, I imagine both academics and Masons will be interested."

"Not to mention a good portion of my senate colleagues. Senator Allison canceled a hearing on that helicopter that entered Pentagon air space without authorization so he could be there. And Senator Hawke of West Virginia is bringing his entire staff. He considers himself the leading congressional expert on George Washington—"

"You mean, before you arrived?" Claire snickered.

Gideon shook his head. "I'm not in his league, but he did behave with uncharacteristic surliness at my swearing in. It could have been the fuss the vice president made over my reputation. He's come around since then—possibly because I asked him to give the keynote speech at the dedication."

"Very diplomatic."

"Yes, but I had an ulterior motive." Gideon rubbed her nose. "He's the ranking member on the Energy and Natural Resources Committee, which has jurisdiction over public lands. Mollifying him gives my request for added security funds for Fort Ellsworth a boost."

"Fort Ellsworth? You mean that little area on the temple grounds?"

"That, little lady, is the remains of a Civil War fort named for Elmer Ellsworth, the first Union casualty of the war. He was killed right here in Alexandria while attempting to improve the view from the White House."

"Huh?"

Gideon rose and began to pull his clothes on. "The story goes that an Old Town hotel owner named Jackson hung a Confederate flag from his roof, a flag so enormous that President Lincoln could see it from the White House. Ellsworth—who happened to be a good friend of Lincoln's—took it upon himself to remove the eyesore. Jackson did not take kindly to his redecorating efforts and shot him."

Claire sat up and pulled the sheet to her chin. "So why did they name a fort after him?"

"As the first casualty, he became a rallying cry for the Union troops. The President was grief-stricken by his death and ordered that the body lie in state at the White House. All of which conspired to turn him into a martyr."

Claire watched as he knotted his tie and shrugged on the navy suit jacket, his muscles rippling under the white shirt. To distract herself from the molten signals coming from her nether parts, she said, "You seem to have a taste for haute couture." She nodded at the paisley tie she knew cost at least two hundred dollars.

He held up the tip. "Dorcas again."

Shit. Change the subject. Change the subject. "Er...so why are you pushing for security for Fort

Ellsworth?"

Gideon seemed as eager as Claire to talk about something else. "It happens to be public property. If I can add funds for guards at the fort, there's a better chance that whoever is vandalizing the temple will be caught."

"Do you think you'll get it in time for the ceremony?"

"Unfortunately, no. We haven't even begun markup on the appropriations bill, but in light of recent events, as well as the addition of the Washington letters, I think I can make a good case for added security for the building. Let's hope the committee agrees."

Claire snuggled deeper into the pillow. She opened one eye to find a tourmaline green one about an inch away. "Ack!"

"My sweet, I must leave you. And…er…you must leave as well."

"Are you kicking me out?"

"Unless you want my mother to find you post in flagrante delicto. She's coming over for dinner."

Claire was up and out before Gideon could find his house keys.

****

"Thanks for coming in, Mr. White. Claire, would you please fill him in on the conversation you overheard between Mrs. Bliss and Peel?"

Was it her imagination or did Ernest lay particular emphasis on the word "Bliss"? "Certainly."

The three men listened to her story intently. In this, her fourth recitation, she presented a more coherent picture. When she had finished, White drew a hand across his brow.

"This is unfortunate."

Duh.

"Simon Peel may have gone renegade. I must find him."

Angle's resentful voice caught their attention. "Look, White, we need more information. We *are* investigating a murder you know."

"Two."

"What do you mean? One victim is an Italian criminal shot on the observation deck of the Masonic Memorial, and the other is a professor of history at Georgetown University, strangled in his own home. Where's the connection? It's not like we don't have our share of murders even here in Dogpatch, you know."

White shot a meaningful glance at Martingale. "I'm sure you do. Look, I'd better give you some background. In 1998 we received information that Truffatore had made a secret trip to Washington sometime in the eighties. He stayed a mere twenty-four hours, then headed back on a private jet to Argentina."

"Did Scordato accompany him?"

"No. In fact, Scordato arrived in Argentina a week after Truffatore's return. When Truffatore was extradited in 1987, most of his Italian minions followed him back to Europe. Except for Scordato."

Claire sat forward. "Wait, that's it!"

"What? You've solved the case?"

She looked around as though rediscovering her whereabouts. "Uh, no. It's just…well, Ernest, didn't you say Gasparo Scordato was an alias?"

"Y…yes." Angle nodded reluctantly. "His real name was Giuseppe Cuomo."

"Well, I looked it up. The alias, I mean. Gasparo means 'treasure bearer,' and Scordato means 'left behind.' " She stopped short of pumping her arm in triumph.

The pause lengthened while the men shifted uncomfortably. Finally Martingale cleared his throat. "Yes, good. Now, where were we?"

White studiously avoided Claire's crestfallen face. "Scordato seemed to be lying low, for what reason we weren't sure. But being the suspicious types"—he ignored Angle's snort—"the Bureau of Syndicate Operations figured he was waiting for something—a sign, a communication, something. When we learned of Truffatore's little junket we sent Peel to keep an eye on Scordato. Peel's been there ever since."

Claire spoke up. "He met Dorcas—Mrs. Bliss—there. She's the daughter of a wealthy rancher."

"Yes. I told you, we know all about Dorcas Bianchi Aguirre Hernandez Bliss. Her first husband, Eduardo Hernandez, is currently on the lam, accused of murdering her lover." He tasted his coffee and grimaced, set it down gently, and pulled a flask out of his inside pocket. In response to their shocked faces, he held it up. "Water. My own special blend." Taking a sip, he resumed. "Her father, Luis Bianchi, has been on our watch list for decades. Couldn't ever pin anything on him, but we're pretty sure he financed some of Perón's less savory exploits."

" 'Bianchi' doesn't sound Spanish to me."

"It's not, it's Italian. Around the turn of the twentieth century, Argentina—just like America—experienced a huge influx of Italian immigrants. More than fifty percent of the population is of Italian ancestry."

Martingale whistled. "So Truffatore and Scordato must have fit right in."

White stared at him until he subsided. "Yes, they did."

Better get this back on track. Claire broke the silence. "Did you know they went to Paris together?"

"Who? Peel and Mrs. Bliss? No, although that clears up one mystery. He claimed he heard a rumor that Scordato had been communicating with someone in Paris and went to check it out. A couple of weeks later he returned to Argentina and reported that it had been a red herring." He scowled. "Sounds like his excuse for a taxpayer-paid tryst."

"He left Dorcas in Paris."

"So you say. We had no interest in her at that point."

Claire remembered a tear-stained face and pleading voice. *Apparently neither did Peel.*

"In light of your revelation we will take another look at her. She could be a weak link." He swallowed another mouthful of water.

"So, Peel's in Argentina. Then what?" prompted the chief.

"Let me back up a bit. Over the years Peel insinuated himself into the underground Perónist lodge. He learned that, other than an initial set of instructions, Scordato had had no word from Truffatore since Truffatore's extradition. He seemed to be on hold. That is, except for a few coup plots and money scams…you know, just to keep his hand in." White's eyes crinkled in an unsuccessful show of humor.

"How long did this last?" Claire was beginning to

think the spy game could be rather tedious.

"About fifteen years. Then a month ago Peel informed us that Scordato had finally received the message he'd been waiting for. We told Peel to approach him and offer to help in exchange for a share in the profits. He didn't succeed in striking a deal, but he did manage to worm enough out of Scordato to learn he was heading to the District." White stopped and smiled thinly. "Peel is one of our best operatives."

No one asked for further detail on the methods Peel used for his worming. After a minute the chief leaned forward. "Well? What was his story?"

"The message ordered Scordato to go to Washington and pick up an object. Scordato intimated the item was very precious but gave no specifics. Peel planned to follow Scordato. That was the last we heard from our operative."

"And you still have no idea what the item is?"

"Not specifically, no. We assume it's of great value—"

"How?"

"I mean, it must be worth a lot of money to P2. When Truffatore fled his villa in 1998, the police found a cache of gold ingots worth two million dollars. That cache probably represented most of his assets. Since he could hardly have carried that much gold with him while he was on the run, we're guessing he took something small with him, something valuable that could be sold or bartered."

"Like a rare stamp?" Claire's eyes lit up. She'd seen that in some movie. *Now what was the name of it...*

White gave a disdainful sniff. "*Charade*. Yes. Even

though that particular plotline has been done to death, it's a plausible idea."

Angle spoke up. "The Italian police believed Scordato had access to funds from a secret cache. If Truffatore only fled with a small item, where did that money come from?"

Claire saw her opening. "Could it have come from Dorcas Bliss?"

"Perhaps. Or blackmail. Money laundering. Maybe he used the thing as collateral. We heard rumors that Truffatore was implicated in the sale of Juan Perón's hands. Who knows?" White shook his head, his face alight with pure admiration. "These guys are truly gifted. Truffatore and Scordato could talk a pig into frying his own bacon."

"Yeah, well." Ernest didn't seem to share his awe. "How come it took so long for Truffatore to get the message to Scordato?"

"We're not sure. He's been incarcerated for over ten years and any communication with his old colleagues would be monitored. He's nearing ninety now. Maybe the guards grew a bit lax."

"Or maybe, since Scordato hadn't been told what the object was—or even where he'd hidden it— Truffatore couldn't figure out how to convey the information to his man without the police intercepting his instructions."

Martingale had been doodling on his wrist. "Let's get back to what the item might be. How about stock certificates? They're lightweight."

"Possible, although how could he be sure they'd maintain their original value?"

The chief frowned. "I…er—"

"Or…" Claire jumped up, face flushed. "It could be the key to a Swiss bank account. Dorcas discussed a key with Peel."

"Not bad," said Angle slowly, "except it's not clear whether Scordato already had the key or was coming to Washington to get it. We found no key on his person."

"That's because Peel has it."

"Right—I'd forgotten." Angle checked his notes. "According to your story, Mrs. Bliss said something on the order of 'what good's the key to us?' Correct?"

Claire nodded, proud of herself. For a moment she saw her name in the headlines—Docent Solves Decades-Old Crime. Her fingers traced an imaginary autograph for an imaginary fan.

Ernest was still speaking. "Would that make sense, though? If it were a key to a bank account in Switzerland, why would they be looking for something here in the States?"

His puzzled face gave Claire pause. "*Erm*…it doesn't have to be Swiss, does it? It could belong to a safe deposit box here, couldn't it?"

"You may have something there, Claire. Well done." Martingale patted her hand like a proud father.

The police detective wasn't so easily impressed. "No, no. It doesn't work. If it's a key to a safe deposit box or locker or something, why is Peel trying to unlock cases in the temple?"

White started. "He's what?"

Ernest stopped in mid-pace. "You didn't know? Last Saturday the librarian at the Masonic Temple reported a case of vandalism. Someone's been trying to get into the cases on the fourth floor."

"And you think it was Peel?"

"Who else? Ordinary thieves would've grabbed something to sell. According to Treadwater, nothing was taken."

His lips as white as his name, the agent ground out in a low, rumbling voice, "Have you considered the possibility that Scordato may have had a partner?"

This idea struck everyone as unwelcome. Finally Chief Martingale muttered, "Do you have any evidence?"

White shook his head. "No, but it's worth considering all possibilities. As far as we know, Scordato worked alone. Truffatore's other associates had returned to Italy."

"Someone here then? On the inside?"

Claire thought of the absent Nigel. Somehow the pot-bellied hairless pornophile didn't seem the international criminal type.

The chief was speaking. "Sorry, that scenario doesn't fly. If Scordato had an accomplice, he'd have followed Truffatore's directions and be long gone with the treasure by now." He looked at White. "I think you just don't want to admit your man is AWOL."

Claire and Ernest pretended to weigh this idea while sneaking glances at White's expression or lack thereof. Finally the agent growled, "I need solid confirmation of that before I act. What we do know is that Peel"—here he glared at Ernest—"is now focusing his search on the memorial."

"And the extent of the damage means either he was testing the locks to see which one his key fit—or he didn't find what he was looking for."

"Or both." The chief peered over Angle's shoulder at his notebook. "How about the time line? When did the vandalism start?"

"Treadwater found it Saturday and believes it happened sometime after Thursday. If Peel has had the key since Scordato's death, what took him so long?"

Claire thought she had the answer. "He's been hanging around the temple for a month. Maybe he was scoping everything out before making his move."

"That makes sense." White seemed pleased.

"One thing to consider," said Ernest. "The vandalism began after Nutley's death. Could Peel have found something in Nutley's house that gave him a clue?"

"No." Claire spoke with assurance. "Nutley didn't have anything—not even the important historical document he claimed to have. Peel might have killed him, might have searched his house, but he wouldn't have found anything."

Ernest reread his notes. "Either way, we assume Peel took the key from Scordato."

Claire put a finger to her lips. "That means Peel killed Scordato."

"No, it doesn't." White's voice was firm.

All three turned to him. "Why not?"

Claire said, "I found Scordato dead on the observation platform. Scordato had no key on him then. Peel was not at the scene, but he has the key. What other explanation could there be?"

White cleared his throat. "For one thing, you haven't solved the question of how Scordato ended up on the platform. You didn't see Peel, did you?"

Claire shook her head reluctantly.

"Right. We can't build our entire hypothesis around one side of a whispered conversation. Especially as reported by a non-professional." His cold eyes swept over Claire. "The bureau is unwilling to presume the guilt of one of our operatives without incontrovertible proof."

Claire's cheeks burned. Angle took a step toward White, his arms rigid at his sides. "If you mean Claire, this *non-professional* has done more to clear up this mystery than you and all your special expertise has, *Mister* White."

White turned a slightly lighter shade of gray. His voice hummed with anger. "On the contrary, we still know very little—particularly whether Peel is continuing his mission or has gone rogue. My men are highly trained to infiltrate gangs and take on extremely believable personae. Nothing he has done so far contradicts that conclusion."

"Except," said Claire quietly, "that he has been incommunicado since he left Argentina."

White opened his mouth and closed it. Angle opened his mouth, but before he could say anything, Chief Martingale lowered his palm in a calming gesture. "Come on, everyone, let's not forget why we're all here." He leaned back in his chair and stuck a toothpick between his teeth like a paunchy Andy Griffith. "Two people are dead, and the killer or killers are on the loose. At least one is after something worth a great deal of money. We find it, we find him." He waited until the hubbub died down. "To move on, you have reason to think this item is hidden somewhere in the temple?"

White's face suddenly emptied of expression. *Just like Peel.* "Possibly, but we don't want hordes of people searching the place. It would be better to determine what we're looking for first."

Claire said slowly. "You don't have much time. There will be 'hordes' of people swarming the memorial next week."

"Why?"

"Because Senator Gideon Bliss is donating priceless documents—letters from George Washington—to the Alexandria-Washington Masonic Lodge next Thursday."

"Plus," put in Angle, "how do you propose to figure out what the item is, since the one man who knew the answer is dead? Obviously Peel has so far come up with squat."

The man tapped his temple. "We have an ace in the hole."

The others stared at him. "Ace?"

White unearthed a rusty attempt at enthusiasm. "Truffatore himself. He's still alive. I have people…er, discussing the matter with him as we speak."

The chief gazed reverently at the agent. "Wow. With or without the assistance of the Italian police?"

The operative took the opportunity to sip from his flask. Returning it to his pocket he remarked to the wall, "We have as much cooperation as we need. Mr. Truffatore is quite frail—"

"He's over ninety, isn't he?"

White ignored the interruption. "And so we are taking all suitable precautions to ensure his information is…accurate."

Ernest slammed his fist on the table. "If your guys injure him, it'll mean an international incident."

Menace leached from the black ops agent. He said nothing, but Angle must have sensed the dangerous rise in tension, for he moved closer to the door.

Chief Martingale broke the impasse. "I say, while we wait for developments from Italy, we can toss around ideas here. Let's put on our thinking caps, shall we?"

A few hours later all four people were unanimously agreed that the treasure must be behind a locked door.

"Or in a case."

"And it's small enough to fit under a jacket."

"And it's not of obvious monetary value."

"Like a jewel."

The chief rolled his eyes. "For the last time—" He stopped when the snickering grew too loud to be ignored.

"Okay. We know the searcher tried his key in locks on the fourth floor. Is there any evidence he went to other floors?"

Claire thought back. "Treadwater didn't say anything about other floors. I'm not sure he checked anywhere but the museum."

Ernest straightened. "Well, that's at least something we can do. I'll send a team over to the memorial to search all the floors for signs of forced entry."

"Good idea. We can trace the perp's failures."

"Let's hope we're there when he succeeds."

Chapter Fifteen
Interlinked

"The police found more evidence of mischief in the Knights Templar Chapel Room and the Cryptic Room, as well as the Royal Arch Chapter room."

Gideon handed his menu back to the waiter and leaned across the table. "Okay, so tell me what these rooms hold."

"The Knights Templar is on the eighth floor. It's a tiny space with four beautiful stained glass windows. The Cryptic Room, on the seventh floor, tells the story of the building of the second temple in Jerusalem. It's sponsored by the Royal, Select, and Super Excellent Masters." Claire sipped her water and tried to canvass the restaurant casually, as though she regularly ate in the private Senate dining room. She was sucking on a large piece of ice when the majority leader came up and high-fived Gideon. As she choked and spluttered, her companion jumped up and patted her back. "I'm...urk...fine. Please stop that, you're embarrassing me."

He sat down with a thump, his eyes worried. "Are you sure?"

Claire could feel the blush curl around her ears and head up her nose to her forehead, where it parked, heating the entire area. "Yes. Now, what was I saying?"

He gave her hand one last pat. "You were telling

me about the vandalized floors. The seventh and eighth floors I believe. And what was the other one? The Royal Arch?"

"That's on the fifth floor. It showcases the York Rite. There are murals depicting the building of Solomon's first temple and initiation rituals into the rite. Oh, and display cases holding more than seven thousand mark pennies."

Gideon accepted a plate from the waiter. "Pennies?"

"Tokens struck by a lodge and given to a Fellow Craftsman or Master Mason, who in turn puts his mark on it. Each one is unique. The collection holds pennies from lodges all over the world."

"Interesting." Gideon didn't sound very intrigued. He held a hamburger in one hand and a French fry in the other while he nodded at two men passing their table. "Orrin. Lindsey." Claire toyed with the idea of sprinting after the two senior senators and asking for their autographs, but had a feeling that would be considered bad form. The waiter brought her a bowl of navy bean soup. Gideon took a large bite of burger and washed it down with iced tea. "Anywhere else?"

"Treadwater found no evidence of tampering in the sixth floor library, but that's always kept locked. The librarian and the Worshipful Master have the only keys."

"Yes, I know. *Hmm*. Eighth, seventh, fifth, and fourth floors. Sounds like he's working his way down level by level. We know why he missed the sixth level, but why the ninth?"

"I'm not sure. Maybe because there aren't any display cases there."

"Of course. He's looking for something that requires a key to get into. Did it look like any of the cases had actually been opened? Remember, the vandal had managed to get into a few on the fourth floor."

"I don't know, but nothing seems to be missing." Claire tried not to gawk as she counted members of Congress and administration bigwigs sprinkled in with celebrities at the nearby tables. A buxom woman held court in the center of the room. "Is that…is that Dolly Parton?" she whispered.

Gideon didn't look up. "Probably. She's testifying at the Commerce Committee hearing today."

Claire tried to relax and took a spoonful of soup, nearly spitting it out. Famous or not, it tasted like insipid white bean puree. *Go figure.* She sprinkled salt in it and, after some thought, a lot of pepper. "The odd thing is it looks like Peel—if it is Peel—has hit each floor twice."

"Twice?"

"Yes. The first time the evidence was very slight— only someone as fastidious as Mr. Treadwater would have noticed. The second run-through the vandal did more serious damage. He even tried to open the Ark of the Covenant."

"Ark of the Covenant? Isn't that somewhere in Ethiopia?"

"What? I've no idea. This one's a replica. It's on the fifth floor along with the pennies."

Gideon leaned forward eagerly. "Is it gold—I mean, the Ark?"

Claire wiped the dribble of ketchup off his chin with her napkin. "Gold-en. I think it's gold-plated. Hardly priceless unless you're a Mason."

Gideon counted on his fingers, licking each as he went along. "He hasn't hit ground, main, or third yet. Why not?"

"I don't know—maybe he thinks he'd be more conspicuous there? If he's doing this during the day, that is. There are always more people around on the lower floors since they're open to the public."

"Perhaps. At any rate, he must not have found what he's looking for yet. We should keep an eye on those levels."

"For what?"

"Er…point taken. Maybe you should get your police friends to monitor the lower floors. They might catch him in the act."

"I gather that's their plan."

"Good, then we'll leave them to their work. Are you ready to go? I have something to show you."

Claire finished her soup, more out of homage to the United States Senate than out of hunger. "What?"

Gideon rose and took her hand. "Let's take a walk."

They wandered the halls of Congress for a while, admiring the statuary and the elaborately carved and painted ceilings. As they passed under the great dome of the Rotunda, Claire could swear she heard her own heart beating. Finally Gideon stopped at a door and inserted a key in the lock. They entered a small semi-circular room. Desks were set in rows, descending to a slightly raised platform and rostrum festooned with deep red curtains. A carpet of burgundy scattered with white stars covered the floor. No windows cut the gloom. Gideon turned on a wall sconce, illuminating the back row.

Claire touched a leather chair. "Where are we?"

"This is the old Senate chamber. The Senate met here from 1819 to 1859, when they moved to the present room. It's more private than my office, and you won't come to my house."

"You know why." Claire blushed at the memory of their lovemaking, then blushed deeper when the guilt set in.

"Claire." He set her down on a chair and kneeled before her. "I can't ask for your hand now, but I must tell you I love you. More than anything or anyone I've ever loved before."

"But Gideon—"

"Shush. I haven't finished. To prove my undying fealty, I have sought and received the consent of Mrs. Andromeda Bliss and Mrs. Letitia Canfield."

"Mother!" *That traitor.*

"I'm not sure if 'going steady' would constitute bigamy, so…will you do me the honor of"—he pulled a small velvet box out of his jacket pocket—"being my best friend?" He opened it to reveal a heavy gold class ring. A yellow topaz glistened in the middle. She made out the words Princeton University circling the gem and the date 1995 on one side.

Claire couldn't help it. She began to snicker, then to chortle, moving on to a snigger, sliding into home with a full-blown fit of giggles. Gideon waited patiently, although once or twice he shifted his knees on the hard floor. When she'd calmed down, he pushed the box at her. "Well?"

She took the ring and slipped it over her thumb. It fell off. Gideon picked it up, staring at it in consternation before perking up. "I almost forgot!

Mother said we'd probably need this." He pulled a second velvet box out of his other pocket, this one long and thin. She opened it. Inside lay a thick gold Figarro chain. Pavé diamonds encrusted the lobster claw clasp and tiny pearls gleamed at intervals between the links. "This belonged to my great-grandmother's sister. If it's as strong as she was, it should hold my class ring." He slipped it over her head. "There. Now, can I get up?"

She kissed the top of his head. "Rise, friend."

****

"We've got to catch Peel in the act. The ceremony's next week." Ernest paced the chief's office like a caged panther.

"In the act of what? Vandalism? Remember, we're after Truffatore's treasure, not my agent."

"Speak for yourself, White. My job is to find the murderer of two people."

The black ops agent put down his stylus. "You have no proof that Peel killed either one."

"Not yet." Angle held White's gaze as long as he could before the steel splinters shooting from those metallic gray eyes forced him to blink.

If White reveled in his victory, he didn't show it. "I would suggest that, Peel being the highly trained operative he is, you are likely to fail in your quest."

"Unless you help us."

"Ah."

The silence deepened. Finally the chief broke it. "We need this operation wound up before next week, however you manage it. Mr. Comfrey—the head of the lodge—has been most gracious up to now, but he wants nothing to interfere with the ceremony. At last count, they had fifteen senators, thirty congressmen, the

Secretary of the Interior, and the President's husband coming. Not to mention the masters of the grand lodges of Pennsylvania, Virginia, and New York."

Claire spoke for the first time. "Are they all Masons?"

"I have no idea." The chief ducked his head and checked for something in his desk drawer. They heard him mutter, "It's not something people announce in public."

"So it's true," she pressed, "that most of our prominent citizens are Masons?"

When the chief didn't respond, other than emitting a few grunts and harrumphs, White took the floor again. "Where are they holding the event, Martingale?"

"I believe in the Memorial Theatre. That's on the main floor."

"The vandals have already been there, correct?"

"No," said Ernest. "There's no evidence he—or they—have hit either the ground or the main levels. We found damage on the fourth, fifth, seventh, and eighth floors."

Martingale put his hand on the telephone. "So we'll need to have heightened security in the areas he hasn't searched."

White took the receiver from him. "I don't see why that's necessary. I've been monitoring the building."

Claire spoke up. "Peel could be planning to use the crowd as cover."

"I doubt it. Too much chance of being observed."

Angle said, "With such a mass of people, he...or they...might feel they can easily blend in. In that case, we'll need enough men to watch the perimeter."

White acknowledged the point grudgingly.

The chief steepled his fingers. "All right, to be safe, I'll post a couple of men in the building starting now."

White stood. "Let me know if and when you find anything on those lower floors." He began to leave, then stopped. Claire didn't see him move, but he suddenly appeared before Angle as if by magic, his face inches from the latter's.

The police detective held his ground. "What?"

Claire realized for the first time that White stood a good five inches shorter than Ernest. "I begin not to trust you, Angle. That you don't trust me is immaterial to the operation. However, to ensure your continued cooperation, I shall give you one more piece of information." He took a step back to take in the other two. "You wonder why I am not convinced that Peel is our suspect? Because there's another candidate for the position. A close associate of Truffatore's has arrived in Washington and is actively seeking the item."

"What!" Chief Martingale came around his desk and grabbed White's elbow. "Why didn't you tell us before?"

White glanced down with cold disdain, and Martingale's hand snapped back as if it had been bitten. When the chief had resumed his seat, White surveyed his audience. "Two days ago I tossed out the suggestion that Scordato had a confederate. However, in the latest interview with Lazio Truffatore, we learned that he sent the cable with the details of his mission to Scordato alone. A few days before Scordato's death Truffatore lost contact with him. He dispatched a second colleague to find out what happened and to retrieve his cache."

"Where did he send him?"

"Our regular informants report that the man arrived here from Buenos Aires a few days after Scordato's death, but I have reason to believe that's not true. One of my operatives says he came straight from Italy, and may have intercepted Scordato when he landed at Dulles Airport."

Angle barked, "You're saying even your own people can't keep track of these guys?"

Claire studied White. *What a difficult life it must be—not to trust anyone, not even your own informants.*

White said mildly, "I'm saying there seem to be several threads in play—some intersect, some don't. It's not clear which is which yet."

"Do we at least know who he is?"

"We have a partial description. A tall, thin man of about forty-five, clean-shaven, former military. He's not well enough known to Interpol to have much of a dossier."

Martingale hiccupped. "A tall Italian?"

White shook his head. "He's German...or possibly Swiss. We don't think he's a Mason, so we can't use their directories to locate him. On the other hand, that may work to our advantage. Since he's unfamiliar with masonic customs, he won't be able to insinuate himself easily."

"Meaning he'll stick out like a sore thumb if he tries to pass as a Mason?"

"Precisely."

"And where is this associate at present?"

For the first time since she'd known him, White hesitated and dropped his eyes. "We...don't know."

Three voices cried in unison. "Excuse me?"

"My agent...uh...lost track of him."

****

"Let me have a look at it." Claire pulled the chain over her head. Her mother hefted it. "Beautiful. I adore old gold. And look at those lovely seed pearls interlinked—I've never seen a design like that."

Andromeda took it from her. "It belonged to my great aunt Celestine. The man she almost married gave it to her."

"Almost? What happened?"

The old lady settled back with the air of someone who has told the story many times. "It was in 1865, a few months after the War of Northern Aggression— what our family calls 'The Late Unpleasantness'— ended." The old Southern euphemism for the Civil War always tickled Claire. "A band of former Confederate officers had been terrorizing our town, pillaging the stores, and beating the men. Joseph mustered out near Richmond and rode four days to fulfill his vow to wed Celestine, but when he arrived he found the gang in the street. He stood up to them while the whole town watched. They killed him."

"Oh dear." Claire pictured a beautiful young girl waving her kerchief as her hero went to his death. "Did she find the necklace in his effects?"

Andromeda smiled benignly. "Yes, and her last love letter to him."

Letitia heaved a delicate sigh. "I suppose Celestine never married, pining away for her Joseph."

"On the contrary, she married a Mr. Parsons and had ten children. She and her family traveled by prairie schooner to Arkansas, Texas, and finally Oregon in the 1870s. Her daughter rode the train alone across country to New York and graduate school, one of the first women to do so." The gauntlet was thrown.

Letitia picked it up with a wintry smile. "I guess some families never lose their wanderlust, do they? Now *my* family found the perfect spot right here in Virginia in 1607 and never saw any good reason to leave. Of course they were very successful farmers and statesman." She eyed Andromeda, braced for the response.

Her friend did not disappoint. "Well, I always say travel broadens the mind," she warbled airily. "One can become awfully…parochial if one nests in the same tree for generations." She checked the ceiling for cracks before delivering the coup de grace. "Everywhere they settled, *my* ancestors certainly flourished."

The two old ladies set their chins. Claire, squeezed between them on an uncomfortable antique settee, half expected them to leap up and start circling each other. She had been entertained for a few minutes, but it was time to revive their customary cordiality. "May I have my chain back?"

The interruption allowed the combatants to relax without losing face. "Oh, of course, dear." Gideon's mother handed it to Claire and picked up the teapot. "More tea?" As she poured, she remarked idly, "It's so delightful to see you two young people getting along. Despite the difficulties."

Letitia jumped in. "Certainly not difficulties of your own making." She threw a triumphant glance at Andromeda.

"Nor of Gideon's," retorted her friend.

"We understand Mr. Peel has parted company with Dorcas. That might make her more amenable."

"Or more recalcitrant."

Claire looked from one to the other. "How did you know that?"

The ladies exchanged looks. Andromeda murmured primly, "I think it's important to maintain acquaintance with people of all walks of life. Wanda at the Tivoli Tavern is a convivial hostess and a reliable font of information, don't you think, Lettie?"

Letitia nodded. "She certainly is."

Claire looked from one to the other. *The two Marples are at it again.* "What else have you dug up?"

"My dear, we're not snoops! If people wish to confide in us, it's the Christian thing to do to listen."

"You wouldn't want us to be rude, would you?" The Marples gazed like two bright-eyed budgies at their fidgeting guest.

"No…I guess not."

"There, there." Letitia patted her daughter's arm. "Andy here had seen a portrait of Dorcas's father when they visited him in Argentina and noticed he wore a Mason's apron and carried a square. So we thought it might behoove us—"

"Since Christie's had no scheduled auctions—"

"—to do a little research on the Masons in Argentina."

Claire almost hated to ask. "And what did you discover?"

The two women sat quite still, Letitia munching thoughtfully on a cookie. Evidently some communication passed between them, for Andromeda finally said, "There seems to be a lot of cross-cultural activity between Italy and Argentina. Rather curious."

Try as she might, Claire could get no more out of either one. Finally she rose. "Mrs. Bliss, I can't thank you enough for the beautiful chain. I love it. And thank you both for your support in all this...er, mess. You really are dears."

Both of her listeners contrived to look affronted. " 'Dears'? You make us sound like old biddies."

"If the shoes fit." Claire blew them both kisses, and hotfooted it out to her car.

****

The telephone rang at seven the next morning. Claire dropped it twice before finding the Talk button.

"Claire, is that you? I was about to leave a message."

"Mr. Quinn?"

"Yes. Could you please come to the lodge? Right away?"

Claire went over the To Do list for Thursday. Getting to work three hours early wasn't on it. "I suppose."

"Wonderful. It's an emergency."

Isn't that an oxymoron? "I'll be there as soon as I can."

Half an hour later, Mr. Quinn met her on the steps, a look of distress flushing his features. "Thanks for coming, Claire. There's been more vandalism."

"Oh no! Where?"

"They've now hit every floor except the main entrance and the library."

"Even the Cedars of Lebanon?"

He nodded. "Locks have been forced. In some cases the glass has actually been smashed."

"Was anything taken?"

"Not that we've determined, but so much is broken or destroyed, it will take us weeks to assess the damage.

The policeman arrived half an hour ago. He's with David."

Where is the guard Martingale ordered? "Hopefully he'll check for fingerprints. Why don't you show me what you found?"

"All right. The only floor they've missed is this one, but there's little of interest here except in the replica room. Perhaps that's too public for them—the monsters!" Quinn led her onto the elevator and pressed "5." "They went back to the Royal Arch room again. This time the Ark…" A tear welled up and bubbled in the corner of his eye.

On the fifth floor, the vandals had torn down the curtains that normally covered the golden depiction of the Ark of the Covenant, then dragged the chest from its niche and cracked it open. The head of one of the angels was missing. Quinn picked it up from a corner and carefully wrapped it in his handkerchief. Claire didn't have the heart to point out the police might want it for evidence.

On the left side of the room, the glass panes protecting the mark pennies were scored, but luckily not broken. The rest of the room was trashed.

Quinn turned his back on the wreckage. "They also pillaged the Cryptic Room, the Chapel, and the Cedars." In the Cryptic room, Claire put her foot down and quickly withdrew it. Shards of paint lay all over the floor. All the gold leaf had been scraped from the paintings and the heads of the figures gouged. Quinn took her arm and pulled her back onto the elevator. "There's nothing else here."

He pressed "8." A miniature Gothic-style room opened before them. Four tall stained glass windows depicted scenes from Jesus's life. The wood paneling had been ripped out and the small altar knocked onto the floor. A suit of armor lay on its back, its chest plate crushed.

The damage was even more severe on the ninth floor. Claire contemplated the ruins. "It almost feels as though he lashed out in frustration."

Quinn gave her a surprised look. "He? You think a single person did all this?"

"We think Pe—" Claire caught herself in time. Quinn had been told nothing of Peel and Operation Gladio, and White had made it clear that the circle of the informed should remain limited. "I have no idea. You're right. It could be a gang."

Quinn indicated the mess. "This doesn't look like frustration to me. It looks like wanton destruction. Don't vandals wreck things for the fun of it?"

Better just agree with him for now. "Yes, yes, you're right."

When they returned to the main floor the worshipful master greeted them. Quinn caught his elbow. "What did the police say?"

Comfrey's face sagged. "They only sent one man over. He took notes and said he'd get back to us."

For the first time since she'd known him, Quinn appeared genuinely angry. "What is going on? Don't they realize how serious this is? Don't they understand how crucial it is we stop these…these crimes, before the ceremony?"

Quinn's outburst seemed to boost Comfrey's spirits. He bestowed a resigned smile on his warden. "I'm sorry, Peter. I'm sure this will all be resolved in time. We must be patient." He walked off down the hall.

Claire made a mental note to inquire why Ernest had failed to post guards. *Is Anton White now in charge?* Why would they let him interfere with their investigation? *Is he merely protecting his operative? Or could he be in on it with Peel?* With an effort she returned her attention to Quinn. "I'll see if I can find out any more from the police. I have…I have some connections there." She patted him awkwardly.

Quinn shook his head, his lips set in a morose frown. "What possesses people to do this kind of thing, Claire? What is this country coming to? There's no respect for other people's property anymore."

****

"I don't know what to tell you, Claire. I posted three men in the temple, one in the main lobby and two to make regular rounds of the building. They claim my office called them off yesterday."

"You didn't?" The two knocked and entered Chief Martingale's office.

The chief looked from one to the other. "He didn't what?"

"Call my men off temple duty. No." Angle studiously avoided Claire's eyes. "We may have gotten some signals crossed. They were told to head over to the Nutley investigation."

The chief cleared his throat. "I sent them. Working on a fresh murder case seemed to be a better use of our limited resources." He too evaded Claire's glance. She looked from one policeman to the other, then at the shadowy man in the chief's chair. It seemed all too clear who ran the show now. And it wasn't the Alexandria Police Department.

White put in smoothly, "We're in luck. The destruction was extensive enough that Quinn didn't notice the locks were tampered with on every case and box. If he had, he might guess the truth—that someone is systematically searching the place and not simply running amok."

Claire regarded him with surprise. "How do you know Mr. Quinn hasn't figured that out?"

He paused. "I…we talked to Quinn. Naturally."

"After he and I toured the floors?"

"Yes. I wanted to gauge how much he had seen or understood so we can calculate how much to disclose about this whole operation." The vacant look returned. "It's amazing how unobservant some people are."

Claire felt she had to defend the senior warden. "Mr. Quinn knows every nook and cranny of the memorial. It's like his second home."

"Well, perhaps he can file a claim with his homeowner's insurance." White's tone was almost light. "You say the perpetrator tried twice to get inside the Ark of the Covenant?"

"That's what Mr. Quinn told me."

"*Hmm.*" White tapped his knuckles on the desk. "Peel has now tried every case in every exhibit in the temple except the main floor. What's there?"

Claire ticked off the list. "Several public rooms— the theatre, Memorial Hall, the gift shop—a couple of meeting rooms, and a replica of the original Alexandria lodge."

"The original lodge?"

"The first Alexandria Lodge as it looked in 1802 when Washington became its Charter Master."

"Are there any cases there? Anything locked?"

"Yes, there are a few mementos on display. You know—jewels—"

White almost rose out of his chair, but settled back quickly and assumed an air of calm. "Jewels?"

The chief held up a hand. "Not in the sense you think. Claire means the symbols of office for the different chairs, like the square and the plumb. They're not encrusted with precious stones or anything like that."

"I see, so the room contains nothing to attract an ordinary burglar?"

"I wouldn't say that," said Claire. "One case holds Washington's Masonic apron and the silver trowel he used to lay the cornerstone for the Capitol building. They're of great historical value."

"Hardly the Hope diamond though. Now, if Truffatore had hidden evidence of shenanigans—you know, Washington and his cronies stripping naked and indulging in orgies—that would be worth stealing."

Claire hoped he hadn't heard her gasp. Washington and sex scandals lay too close to the truth to be comfortable. *How much does White actually know? When did he show up anyway—before or after Nutley's death?* Trying to remember, she glanced furtively at the agent. *Did he talk to Nutley? Did he in fact murder Nutley?*

"Still, he's bound to search the room." White addressed Angle, "Didn't you say your witness heard Scordato and Peel talking about jewels in the Buenos Aires airport?"

Angle checked his notes. "Says here the witness saw Scordato and an unidentified man arguing and caught the words, 'jewel,' 'papers,' and 'box.' "

Martingale held up a hand. "Wait a minute—could Scordato's companion have been Truffatore's other colleague—the German? Didn't you say he met Scordato at the airport?"

White shook his head. "No, we believe they met at Dulles. We have no solid evidence the German was ever in Argentina."

Ernest muttered, "Seems you don't know a lot about this German—like even where he is."

White's body went so taut Claire could see the bones pressing through the skin of his cheeks and hands. He stayed rigid a full minute, then relaxed. "The second man is irrelevant until he reappears. If and when he does, we shall deal with him." He studied Ernest, apparently waiting for a reply. When none came, he leaned forward. "Okay, this is what I propose."

Chapter Sixteen
Chain Links

Claire didn't know how she managed to get through the next few days. She'd never been asked to do anything remotely clandestine before. Her one attempt at skipping high school had ended in disaster and at the time she vowed never to put herself on the wrong side of the law again. She longed for Gideon's calming presence, but Senate business kept him tied up all of Saturday. Late in the afternoon he managed to squeeze in a quick call from the cloak room.

"How are the preparations for the ceremony going?"

Claire waited for her heart to slow down. Would she ever get used to that melting voice, a voice like hot fudge sauce on a cool scoop of ice cream? "You'll have to ask Mr. Treadwater, although you're more likely to get an overwrought bleat than a lucid account of the current status of arrangements."

Gideon chuckled. "The majority leader hasn't scheduled any votes next week, so I'll have a little more time to come and help him. I gather the venue's been moved to the Memorial Hall from the theatre. Any idea why?"

"Um, no, no I don't. Maybe there's more room there." *For the undercover cops to reel in the net, that is.*

"I guess that makes sense. By the way, Timothy scheduled a press conference for Monday. Are you...uh...busy after that?"

Pride kept her from admitting she'd drop everything to see him, but something else nagged at her. *Oh yeah—I've got a heist on the docket.* "A little. There are a few things I have to do."

"Oh. Well, at least I'll see you at the press conference?"

"Of course."

Claire finished the laundry and checked the TV listings. *Oh goodie,* Iron Man *is on.* Robert Downey, Jr., had to be the sexiest man alive. She fingered Gideon's ring. *Or almost.* A check of the kitchen revealed a plethora of nothing. *If I could fit a full-size refrigerator in here I wouldn't have to replenish so often.* She got her purse and headed out to the store.

Hmm—Paw-lickin' Good or Fat Cat Food? She gave up and started to put four of each into her basket.

"Tell me that's not your dinner?"

She dropped all eight cans on her foot. "Gideon! What are you doing here?"

He got down on his knees and scrabbled around picking them up. Popping the cans into her basket, he grinned. "Well, let me see..." He made a show of sweeping the area. "I'm in a grocery store. Now whatever shall I do while I'm here..."

Claire stomped on his foot. As they both leaned against a shelf rubbing respective toes, a woman pushing a stroller walked by and shot them a suspicious glance. Claire straightened. "Aren't you supposed to be running the country?"

Gideon kissed her cheek. "I'm grabbing a premade sandwich. It's going to be a long night. Apparently all senators—even short-termers—are expected to know the rules and procedures of the Senate. I hear there's a pop quiz."

Claire knew from Lincoln's days as chief counsel just how critical a mastery of Senate rules could be in a legislative debate. "Oh, yes, a humdinger of a test. Study hard."

They paused, staring into each other's eyes. Gideon said, "Well, I'd better go."

Claire whispered, "Yes, me too."

They were still standing there when the lady with the stroller came back. Gideon noticed her and, turning to Claire, took her in his arms and gave her a flamboyant Valentino kiss. When Claire came up for air, the woman stood rooted, ignoring her yowling baby. Gideon raised his voice. "And *that*, Miss Feingold, is how we do it in Missouri!"

When Claire got home she fed the cat, poured a can of chicken noodle soup into a pot to simmer, and turned on the TV. Robert Downey, Jr., no longer seemed quite so appealing, so she settled for Maria Muldaur singing "Midnight at the Oasis" and mooning over Gideon.

****

Despite it being a Monday—not a working day for most Inside-the-Beltway types—a fairly decent number of reporters crowded into the Memorial Hall for the presser. Gideon and Treadwater stood behind the huge bronze statue of George Washington listening to the Worshipful Master. Comfrey droned on for just five minutes too long. When members of the audience started to drift away or pull out their tablets he wound up with a regretful, "Thank you all for your attention.

And now may I present Mr. Timothy Treadwater, Librarian of the Washington Memorial, who will introduce our distinguished donor."

The librarian quick-marched out to the dais and stumbled only once in his prepared speech. He waxed eloquent over Gideon's virtues and accomplishments, and thanked him profusely and repeatedly for the incredible gift to the memorial. Finally he turned in Gideon's direction. "Senator Bliss?"

Gideon came forward. Claire stood in the south aisle and scanned the crowd as it ebbed and flowed between the pillars. No one seemed familiar. She wondered if Ernest or White were around. Gideon began to call on reporters. Most of the questions concerned the discovery of the papers, since the press release had carefully avoided mention of the content. The Masons had no wish to confuse the fourth estate with a scandal concerning George Washington that wasn't really a scandal. Considering the demands of twenty-four-seven cable news, they feared the story would be instantly blown up out of all proportion. For his part, Gideon wanted time to finish his research and publish his findings.

One old fellow with a booming voice and unruly sideburns stood. "Senator Bliss, can you tell us anything about the murder of your colleague, Frederick Nutley? In your opinion, was it connected to the other recent murder that took place here in the temple?"

Gideon looked to Comfrey, who stepped forward. "These matters are under investigation by the police. You'll have to ask them about the status of the case, but at this time we have no reason to believe the murders are related."

"That's funny." The man scratched his head. "My sources tell me Nutley is…was…a person of interest in the prosecution of an Italian Mason named Lazio Truffatore, an associate of the first victim. Truffatore is a well-known crook, who used his Masonic lodge called P2 as a front for his illegal activities. Do you have any comment?"

Gideon's mouth opened and shut. "No comment."

"I also have information to the effect, Senator, that your wife, Dorcas Bliss, has been seen in the company of a dangerous American operative with connections to Truffatore. Sir, does Mrs. Bliss have anything to do with these murders?"

No one spoke.

In the silence, the reporter drawled, "I think my readers would like to know if the Masons are still involved in arcane, possibly nefarious activities. Especially if your wife is implicated, *Senator* Bliss. So, again, do you have any comment?"

Gideon's complexion had grown progressively darker and darker as the man went on. Finally he spat out, "I have nothing to say about my wife's relationship with either Truffatore or Peel. Her link, if any, to P2 does not concern me. I'm here to talk about the Washington letters and that's it."

The press conference dissolved into shouted questions and the click-clack of keyboard keys. The words "Dorcas Bliss" and "renegade Masons" could be heard coming from a hundred lips. Comfrey and Treadwater vanished into the north aisle.

Gideon stood stock still at the rostrum, a dazed look on his face. As Claire pushed toward him through the throng someone caught her wrist. A gaunt, blue-eyed man stared down at her. After a second he let her go, muttering, "So sorry, I thought you were someone else." As he melted back into the mass of salivating reporters, a whiff of a familiar scent floated past her. *Someone here smells like my grandmother.* She didn't have time to bother about it—she had to get to Gideon. The object of her quest was at the moment holding a hand to his ear and shaking his head, just the way President Reagan used to when he didn't want to answer questions from the paparazzi. He saw Claire and took a step toward her, but his way was barred by a tall woman in Dior and Jimmy Choo pumps, her ebony hair cascading over her shoulders in shimmering waves. Dorcas.

Just then a firm hand spun her around and Claire came face to face with a purple-veined, furious Angle. "What the hell did you tell Bliss?"

As they swam through the mob of reporters Claire frantically tried to remember when she'd told Gideon about Propaganda Due. She thought back. Yes—it was before the tampering began. She must have mentioned P2 then. Maybe the Marples discussed it with him. *I wouldn't put it past them to know all about Truffatore.*

Ernest led Claire down to his borrowed office and drew her inside, closing the door. "I assumed you knew everything I told you was in confidence. Now the entire press corps will be going after the story."

"But that's not Gideon's—I mean Senator Bliss's—fault."

"Are you kidding? It only takes one 'No comment' to get the hounds baying."

"Don't you think you should be more concerned about where that reporter got his information?"

"I'll have people follow up on that. Meanwhile, no more blabbing to Bliss. Got it?" His mouth was set in a grim line. "I'm not looking forward to what White will have to say about your loose lips."

"No one said anything about keeping it secret." She put on a brave face, but her lower lip threatened to betray her.

Ernest almost laughed. "I think we should assume that everything White says is supposed to be a secret. He probably only allots us a fraction of the intelligence he gets."

"Well, if he's so good at his job, how come he lost his operative? *Hmm*? And besides, if two little old ladies can find out about Peel, anyone can. That reporter's information was only partially correct after all. He must have gotten it from someone who didn't have all the facts."

Angle stared at her. "Little old ladies?"

Oops—now I've put our mothers in jeopardy. "Never mind. If our plan works, the press having an inkling of the affair isn't all that important, is it?"

"You don't understand. We don't want the press to have an inkling, a hint, a clue—anything." He checked his watch. "It's almost time. You'd better get going."

Claire left Ernest fuming in his broom closet and went back to the hall, only to find it empty. She wondered what Dorcas had said to Gideon and where they'd gone. Had she forced him to confess where he found the letters? With a sinking heart she realized if that were the case, Dorcas would never give Gideon a divorce. Something broke off from her heart and dribbled down to her stomach, where it lay like an undigested gummy bear. She deliberately emptied her mind of doubt. *I have a job to do.*

She checked to make sure all was clear, then walked quickly past the warden's office. Slipping into the janitor's closet, she picked the set of master keys off their hook and dropped them into her purse. Bill Overbrook, the junior warden, sat in Nigel's spot at the desk. He looked up and nodded casually. Harry called to her from the bookstore. Heart in throat, she gurgled, "Be there in a sec."

She turned left into the replica room and strolled up to the case that held Washington's trowel and apron. Tours had been cancelled for the press conference, so the only interruption she had to fear would be from Harry or Bill. She looked over her shoulder. Harry had disappeared and Bill was bent over his newspaper. She quickly unlocked the case, slipped a slim leather box about ten by twelve inches inside, and closed the case without relocking it. As White had instructed her, she wadded a bit of silly putty into the hole. "You see," he had explained, "when Peel turns the key in the lock the putty will impede it just enough to make him think he's unlocked it."

She backed out of the room and skipped toward the bookshop. Harry came out from the supply room. "There you are. That book you ordered finally came in. Sorry it took so long."

"Oh, how fabulous!" *Tone it down, Claire.* "So...er...how about those Redskins, eh?" As Harry rang her up she kept up a constant patter, all the while keeping an eye on the wall clock. After ten minutes she ostentatiously checked her watch. "*Oops,* I'm late. Gotta go!" She nipped across the lobby, skipped down the empty hall, slipped the keys over their hook and left by the north exit. Easing into the passenger side of the squad car, she breathed, "Done."

"Good girl. No one saw you?"

"I don't think so."

"We should know if White's plan is going to work in the next forty-eight hours." Angle made no move to start the car.

She turned to him. "What do you think he'll do if we discover Peel is after the treasure himself?"

"Good question. I don't trust him—he seems way more interested in protecting his agent than in pursuing justice for our victims."

"I think," she said slowly, "he may be concerned with a far bigger endeavor. Operation Gladio has been embedded in Europe for almost sixty years now. Propaganda Due is surely not the only cabal they're after. He may believe the death of one creep is a small price to pay for keeping Italy out of the hands of the Communists."

Ernest took a sip from his coffee and put the lid back on. "Yeah, well, this isn't 1945 anymore. These black ops may be a tad out of date. Me, I've got a real job to do. If he interferes with it, I have resources of my own. This is my turf after all."

Claire touched his cheek. "Ernest, Anton White is a very dangerous man—I can feel it. Don't do anything rash. If he felt he had to take another life in pursuit of his mission, I doubt he would hesitate."

Angle started to pat her hand, then suddenly bent toward her and kissed her full on the mouth.

The shock left Claire speechless. When she didn't respond, he turned on the engine. They drove in silence the few blocks to her house. He pulled up and sat, staring straight ahead. "Tell me that wasn't a mistake, Claire."

"I'm sorry, Ernest. Really."

He smiled—a lopsided, bittersweet smile. "Ah, well—it was worth a shot." He put the car in gear. "I'd better get back to the temple."

****

No one went near the replica room for the next two days. Claire volunteered to take over all the tours for Tuesday and Wednesday, and she successfully steered her groups away from the booby-trapped case so as to not interfere with the plainclothes police monitoring the room. Mr. Quinn had his hands full with arrangements for the ceremony and didn't notice her directing her people straight onto the elevator, bypassing the Memorial Hall and main floor entirely. Luckily she had a full roster of elementary school field trippers. A man—even one as nondescript as Peel—would have definitely stuck out in a swarm of third-graders.

The day of the ceremony dawned, gray and damp. Claire hadn't slept at all. Since there'd been no sign of Peel, White announced—without bothering to give credit to Claire or Angle—that he must intend to use the ceremony as a cover after all. Would the police be able to handle both him and the crowd of dignitaries? She wished she knew whose side White was really on. *Will he work with the police to catch the vandal, even if it's Peel?*

Gideon called. "The show begins at one. All right if I pick you up at noon?"

In a stew over Peel and White and the possibility of impending catastrophe, Claire had forgotten that it was Gideon's big day. "Oh, dear, that's way too late!"

"What? Why?"

"Um." She may have spilled the beans to Gideon about P2 and Peel, but telling him about the trap they'd set was definitely a no-no. White and Ernest had made that extremely clear. That is, before they fell to arguing about who would nab the culprit. "I promised Mr. Quinn I'd be there by eleven. I'll see you there, shall I?" She hung up before he could protest.

All righty then, what to wear for a sting? She checked the sky. Black clouds threatened and she heard rumbling in the distance. An autumn squall. Washington loved to tease her citizens with a brief cool spell in late September, then slam them with ninety-percent humidity just after they'd put their summer clothes away. Thumbing her nose at the weather demon, she pulled out a dark teal, short-sleeve linen dress that not only showed off her slim figure and perfect legs, but breathed. *Doesn't hurt that it matches my eyes either.* Her mother would be proud of her. "Dress for success, my dear," she always said.

Ernest appeared from the shadows when she came in from the parking lot. It had begun to drizzle and distant thunder rolled. "Everyone's in place."

Claire shivered involuntarily. "What do you want me to do?"

"You have to identify Peel. Except for White, you're the only one who knows what he looks like."

And the Marples. Thank God I talked them out of coming to the ceremony. "Where is Mr. White?"

The detective looked over his shoulder. "I have no idea. These spooks are worse than a white dog in a snowstorm. I hope to God he doesn't nab Peel and disappear."

"Why would he do that?"

Ernest pursed his lips. "Guys like him take care of their own. Peel will get justice, but not American-style. I don't approve of that. And we can't close the books on the murders until we have an arrest."

Claire agreed that would be very bad. He led her to the gift shop. Through the door she could see the replica room. "Why don't you wait here? I doubt anyone would think twice about you hanging around, since you're here almost every day. You can keep an eye on the entrance and the back of the hall as well." He hesitated a moment, then said in a subdued voice, "Is Bliss expecting you to be at the ceremony?"

"He didn't say." *Well, not in so many words.*

Ernest straightened. "If you have to be there, make sure you stand toward the back. We have men stationed both outside and in. If you see him, find me and do this." He stuck a thumb in the air.

Claire blinked at the lanky man posed with his finger aiming skyward. *Would pointing out how silly I'd look, not to mention conspicuous, be wasted on him? Nah.* "Um, Ernest, how about if I just scratch my head?"

"What? Oh sure, whatever." He left her and she settled against a counter and watched the front doors.

They had cancelled the tours and closed the building to all but invited guests and the local media. In order to appease the various politicians chafing to get a hand on the microphone, the master had scheduled a second press conference after the ceremony for all national press. He had expressly asked that Senator Bliss not answer any questions.

People were already trickling in, gawking at the

great murals lining the Memorial Hall, peeking into the North and South Lodge Rooms that were not normally open to the public. Claire saw Senator Strummond in his wheelchair, surrounded by aides. She wondered if the rumor that he ate five dozen oysters a day was true. *Aren't oysters supposed to be an aphrodisiac?* As she watched, he held out a hand to a young woman, squeezed it, and winked at her.

A hubbub in the vestibule drew her attention. *Ooh, there's Senator Hawke.* The man Gideon had replaced as resident expert on George Washington shook off a dripping raincoat and shot suspicious glances around. His tightly closed lips transformed into an artificial smile when he saw Gideon. He strode over, both hands held out. At that moment Gideon caught sight of her and raised an arm, nearly taking off Hawke's head. Claire shrugged as if to say, "You're busy. I'm fine." She hoped that would hold him.

A quick survey identified several cops. Most of them were obvious, dressed in rumpled suits you wouldn't even find at Goodwill. She kept an eye out for White, searching for a hint of movement in the shadows.

She checked her watch. Twelve-thirty. At the other end of the hall the worshipful master came out from behind the curtain and adjusted the microphone. One of the deacons set chairs out on either side of a makeshift rostrum. The master had decided not to display the box of letters, citing the lack of security in the more open hall. The change should work in their favor, since they wanted Peel to think the box in the replica room was the one he was after. That is, if he was indeed looking for a box.

Gideon had extricated himself from Hawke and was headed in her direction when Treadwater stepped off the elevator and accosted him. They held an animated conversation, Treadwater gesticulating wildly and Gideon's face alternating between annoyance and excitement. They got back on the elevator.

Claire didn't have time to speculate, since White had just materialized beside her and passed in a blur. He went through to the replica room, and then crossed to the South Lodge room. He did not acknowledge her. A minute later, Dorcas swept into the hall. She wore a magnificent sapphire silk qipao dress, the slit almost to her waist. Her ebony hair was folded into a complicated knot at the back of her neck. She looked neither right nor left, but marched to the front row, ignoring the reserved signs. No one complained.

Claire moved behind the cash register so she could see both the replica room and the entrance. Only one passageway led to the lodge room and that went through the gift shop. She'd spot Peel if he tried to come in. Of course, he could hardly miss her standing there, but as Ernest said, he wouldn't find it unusual.

Her purse slipped off her shoulder and she bent to retrieve it. Noise filled the hall. The audience settled in their seats and the curtain opened. The master came out, his face a mask of uncertainty. "Ladies and gentleman, the ceremony will begin shortly. Our guest of honor and most benevolent donor of long-lost papers of George Washington is on his way." He stepped back behind the curtain.

Five minutes later he returned, gave the identical speech, then droned on a bit about freemasonry and its proud association with George Washington. He pointed out the murals in the hall, describing them in detail. Then he stepped back behind the curtain.

Ten minutes later the crowd had grown restive. One doesn't keep senators, congressmen, and especially businessmen, waiting. The master appeared, this time bearing a shaky smile. He had also acquired a decided tick in his left eye. He launched into a recitative of the birth of the George Washington Masonic National Memorial, beginning with the original lodge chartered by the Grand Lodge of Pennsylvania. "That lodge, which became the Alexandria-Washington Lodge number 22, was housed in the market building on Cameron Street for over 140 years. When it burned down in 1871, we thought we'd lost all the documents and memorabilia donated to us by Washington's family. By sheer serendipity our illustrious patron, Senator Gideon Bliss—" He paused expectantly. Nothing happened. With a heavy sigh he resumed. "Senator Bliss discovered a box in the basement of his house, a box that he has generously offered to donate to the Masonic Memorial. In that box…"

Claire realized she'd been staring at the tiny man in the distance and had neglected to scan her area. No one had passed her so she checked the lobby. For the sake of thoroughness she turned to look into the replica room. Peel stood at the case. He opened the top, pulled the box out, closed the lid, and walked casually to the door.

Claire froze. She couldn't remember what hand gesture she was supposed to use. She couldn't remember where Angle or the other policemen were stationed. As Peel drifted past she stood awkwardly in front of the cash register, pretending to tidy up the counter.

He had reached the lobby when a shadow detached itself from the wall. *White.* She saw the gleam of a gun. Peel must have seen it too, for he whirled and leapt back to the gift shop. His eyes locked on his adversary, he muttered, "You'll do." He stuffed the box under his shirt and grabbed Claire, pulling her arms tightly behind her with one hand. With the other he proved he also was armed. He pointed the Glock at White, who now stood between him and the elevators.

White stood impassively, his gun at his side. Behind him, Comfrey continued his discourse to an audience rapidly losing interest. Several plainclothes officers rushed out from the north and south rooms but halted when they saw the two men with Claire. Angle barged in through the revolving door, followed by a sharp flash of lightning. "What the hell are you doing, White?" he yelled angrily, but made no further move.

Peel stepped forward, the pistol at Claire's head. "Execute the plan," he said. The other agent nodded.

Behind Peel the elevator door opened and Gideon and Treadwater stepped out. "What the—"

Both agents said in unison, "Get out of here." White waved them to one side.

Peel backed into the elevator, Claire pressed to his chest. As the doors closed, Gideon lunged at them. Behind him, White's pistol slashed down, striking the back of his head. Claire saw her lover tumble forward. As he fell, a shiny object dropped from his hand.

Peel held her in a vise-like grip.

"Where are we going?"

"Up."

Claire hardly felt it incumbent upon her to point

out that this was not a sensible move. *Unless black ops guys have wings surgically attached to their bodies. And maybe gills.* Wow, the six million dollar man. No wonder White let him go. *He couldn't very well mark him off on the budget as capital depreciation—even the Pentagon would notice.* Before Claire could bring up the topic of high tech appendages, the elevator stopped with a jolt. The doors did not open.

Peel snarled and jabbed at the buttons. Nothing happened. He pulled his belt off and tied Claire's hands with it. Then he took a small leather case from his jacket, chose an odd-looking metal instrument and inserted it in the lock. The elevator started up again. Peel gave her half a smile. "Old Boy Scout trick."

She doubted the average Boy Scout had sophisticated lock-picking tools, not to mention wings and gills, but said nothing. When they reached the ninth floor Peel dragged Claire off. A steady thrumming sounded overhead. *Oh perfect—a thunderstorm—just the finishing touch we needed. I sure hope Peel has a built-in lightning rod underneath the gills.*

He opened the door to the observation deck. The rumbling continued, but she saw no lightning. "What is that noise?"

"He'll be here any second. Sit tight."

"Who?"

Peel made no answer. As Claire watched, a blue and white helicopter hove into view, coming from the east. It circled the tower twice, then moved off. Peel shook his fist at it. "What the hell's he doing? We don't need fucking tactical maneuvers. I want to get the hell out of here."

She was afraid to ask what he planned to do with

her once they got the hell out.

The door to the Cedars room blew open. Peel took Claire and ran around the tower to the west side, scanning the skies. A crowd of policemen surged from both directions but stopped when they saw Peel's gun pressed into Claire's neck. Angle shouldered his way through the crowd. "Everyone, hold your fire." He put a hand up. "Peel, the jig's up. You might as well drop the gun."

Peel didn't respond. She noticed his hand remained steady, but she could feel his heart pounding. *He's worried.*

Pandemonium suddenly broke out in the back of the pack, and cops fell away like matchsticks, revealing a deliriously beautiful woman in a blue silk dress. Dorcas rose to her full six feet. For one crazy second Claire imagined that if this were a movie, fire would be spurting from her red-painted mouth and her hands would flash with scimitars. A hysterical giggle rattled in her throat.

The policemen receded, leaving Dorcas alone in a bubble of space. "Simon!"

Peel cringed—a reaction that would have been funny if the situation weren't so dangerous. "Dorcas, what are you doing here?"

"Never mind that, what is *she* doing here?" She pointed a long, sharp fingernail at Claire.

He tightened his grip and continued to focus on the angry woman. "Don't be ridiculous, Dorcas. She's my hostage. You're acting like a fool."

Dorcas took a step forward, bringing her within three feet of Peel and Claire. She began to wheedle. "Simon, let me go with you. You promised to share the treasure with me. You promised to take me back to Paris. We'll be safe there. Simon…please."

Her imploring face seemed to embolden Peel. He said crossly, "I did no such thing. Honestly, Dorcas, you only hear what you want to hear."

She drew back, lips and forehead pinched, her eyes closed to slits. Claire could have sworn laser beams streamed out between her lashes. "All right, then, we can go to Argentina. Or Belize. Wherever. Take me. Dump the girl."

Peel glared at her. "I don't think you quite grasp the situation, Dorcas. You are not hostage material."

She took another step toward him. "Why not? My husband will pay dearly to get me back." She called over her shoulder. "Won't you, Gideon?"

Claire followed her gaze to see the top of a beloved head moving toward them. She screamed, "No, Gideon!"

Dorcas turned amazed eyes on Claire. "You? You're his secret love? You're the one he's been mooning over? I assumed the old ladies dug you up on Craig's List to keep me from tracking down Gideon's real lover. How bizarre."

Given a free hand Claire would have slapped her. Failing that, she lobbed imaginary grenades at the woman.

Gideon had reached Angle's side. Behind him wiggled the little Treadwater. "Peel. Drop the gun. We have what you're looking for."

Peel dragged his eyes to something shiny in Gideon's hand. At that moment Dorcas leaped. She grabbed for Peel's arm, but before she could get a purchase on him, he turned the gun on her and shot her at point blank range. Dorcas halted and put a hand to her chest. She looked down at the blood, then up at Peel. He shot her again.

As the silent crowd watched her fall, the throb of a helicopter engine reached undeniable proportions. It appeared behind the pinnacle and slowed, hovering just above them. On its red side Claire could make out *EMERGENCY* in black letters. A man leaned out and dropped a rope ladder down the side. *White*. What was left of her courage took a nosedive. *Ernest was right. He can't be trusted. Saving his agent takes precedence over everything.*

They heard a flat voice, the words sliced into consonants by the rotating blades. "Come on, Peel."

Simon, who had kept a firm hold on Claire even while shooting his lover, shoved the gun under her ribs. "What took you so long, Anton? I've got the entire Alexandria police department down here."

The voice floated down. "Sorry—took a while to arrange for the helicopter." White paused. "Who's the woman?"

Peel held Claire tighter. "Hostage."

"No, I mean the other one. The dead one."

Peel glanced at Dorcas indifferently, although Claire felt his pulse quicken. "Collateral damage."

"Shit, Simon. Why do you always to have to make things more complicated? How am I going to get us out of here now?"

Peel's face hardened. He spat out, "If you'd been here on time I wouldn't have had to kill her."

"Okay, okay, let's just get this over with. Do you have the thing?"

"You mean the box?" Peel patted his shirt with his

gun. "Yup." He pushed Claire up a couple of rungs and began to climb after her. The wind from the propellers buffeted her, making her swing wildly in midair. She clung to the rope, too terrified to look down.

Gideon yelled, "Peel—listen. We have what you want. There's nothing of value in the box you stole."

Peel stopped in mid-rung. "What the hell are you talking about? Who are you, anyway?"

Gideon shook off Treadwater's clinging hand. "Bliss. Gideon Bliss."

Peel glanced at Dorcas' body. "Ah, the husband. Sorry about that." He didn't seem sorry at all.

With what Claire surmised was a supreme effort, Gideon did not follow his gaze. "Yeah, me too. Look, I don't know what you think is in that box, but it's not what you've been searching for." He cocked his head at Dorcas. "What you killed her for."

Peel hesitated a minute. He looked at Gideon. "All right, I'll bite. What is it?" He nodded at the thing in Gideon's hand.

Gideon held up a coin. The clouds parted and the afternoon light struck it, making it shimmer with a golden glow. "This is what Truffatore hid in the temple. This is the treasure."

Peel peered at it. "It's nothing but a penny!"

"Yes, but it's not your ordinary penny, Peel. It's a mark penny. Which happens to be worth two million dollars."

"Bullshit. I've got the box. Truffatore said to get the box in the lodge. I checked every fucking box in this fucking tower. This one fits the description. It was in the lodge."

"Not the right lodge, old buddy. Your Mr.

Truffatore meant the temporary lodge where the Alexandria Masons met after the old lodge burned down in 1871. Truffatore did his homework." Gideon managed to make him sound like the good student. "He found the nineteenth-century records of the Alexandria Lodge and located the Cameron Street site. He left instructions there on how to find the penny. This penny."

Peel hesitated. The helicopter bobbed overhead. Claire saw the glint of a gun barrel, trained on Gideon. Peel looked up. "Cover me." He stuck the Glock in his belt, hooked an arm into the ladder, and opened the box. He caught the manila envelope just before it fell. Keeping a wary eye on the bystanders, he pulled out a set of papers and began to read. Eyes widening, he scrabbled through page after page. When he reached the last one he began to laugh, his voice rising quickly to a maniacal screech. Tossing the papers in the air, he let the wind blow them away and, reaching up, shoved Claire off the ladder.

She fell, arms and legs flailing, and landed heavily on something squishy. Dorcas. Before she could scream, much less roll off the body, Ernest lifted her like a latter-day Baryshnikov and held her tightly. She heard a grunt from behind her. "Let her go, Angle." The police detective glared over her head at his rival.

"Not till I know she's safe, Bliss."

"You heard me, Angle. I—"

But Gideon didn't get to spell out what he planned to do as Treadwater yelled, "He's getting away!"

Peel had taken advantage of the testosterone-driven diversion to jump down, grab the coin from Gideon's grasp and swing back up the rope ladder as easily as a chimpanzee. Before he climbed into the helicopter, he shot a round over the heads of the spectators. "For good measure," he called.

Everyone ducked. The helicopter rose straight in the air, banked, and headed east. Angle set Claire down and pulled out his cell phone. She heard a click and a distant voice say something, the words rising at the end as if in a question. His voice calm, Ernest replied, "Yeah, they're on their way. We'll see you back at the station. Have security meet them at the helipad."

Claire, from the constricting comfort of Gideon's arms, wheezed, "Who's they?"

"White and his prisoner."

"White?"

Ernest smiled complacently. "The plan worked perfectly, didn't it?"

Chapter Seventeen
The German Link

"But... White?"

The lieutenant raised a hand for quiet and dialed another number. "Harry—we need a CSI unit at the Masonic Memorial. And an ambulance. Send 'em up to the observation platform. One corpse to go." He listened a minute, then laughed. "Yeah, I'd guess you'd say it's 'déjà vu all over again.' "

Gideon grabbed his arm. "Angle, what the hell just happened?"

The detective looked quite pleased with himself. "The chief, White, and I hatched this little addendum to the schedule last night. White knew Peel would trust him. Black ops stick together. So, just before the ceremony, he approached Peel with a plan to help him get away."

Claire tamped down her anger. She'd been duped, not just by White, but by Ernest. *He'll have to change his name after this.* "So that whole scene by the elevators—that was simply a masquerade for my benefit?"

"Uh huh." A quick gander at her expression and he continued hastily, "I mean for the whole audience. And the sergeants. You know, so you'd all be convincing." When she didn't seem mollified, he added wistfully, "It really did work after all. We'll be booking Mr. Peel on"—he gazed at the crumpled body of Dorcas, her beautiful legs twisted, her indigo dress blotched with red—"three counts of first-degree murder."

As if on cue, the policemen who had been listening to Angle's summation broke up and set about their work. An eddy swirled through the pack and a man cried out, "Hey! Watch where you're going!"

The door to the Cedars room opened and shut. Ernest yelled, "Who just left?" He parted the onlookers like the Red Sea, strode to the door, and wrenched it open. Claire followed him inside. The elevator doors were nearly closed and Claire only caught a glimpse of a man's profile. Angle stood uncertainly. "Did you get a good look at him? Was he a cop, Claire?"

"I…don't know, Ernest, but I think he was wearing a uniform."

Ernest nodded. "He must be one of the men I had stationed here. Maybe he didn't hear me shout. Probably went down to the lobby to direct the investigative team up here. I'm glad at least one of these guys has some initiative." He headed back to the observation deck.

As they emerged, one of the cops called, "Yo, Detective, you want we should collect these papers? We're losing them."

"Nah, they're only a copy of Truffatore's will." Angle chortled. "That's why Peel flipped his lid. It only added insult to injury."

"What do you mean?"

"Truffatore left all his assets—including the mark penny—to charity."

Somehow Claire didn't feel like laughing. The cops began running yellow tape around the area and she, Gideon, and Treadwater were dismissed.

When they reached the sixth floor, Treadwater unlocked the library door and ushered the two in. Gideon gave Claire a big, wet, smooch and tossed a coin in the air. She caught it. "I thought Peel took this."

"Not this one. You didn't think I'd let something worth that much money slip through my fingers, did you?"

She examined the penny. About an inch in diameter, it shone a deep yellow gold. "How did you substitute the fake one for the real one?"

"I didn't. I just brandished the phony one around and he took the bait."

"And this one is really valuable?" She held it up. "Or were you bluffing about that?"

"Me? *Pas du tout*. Treadwater?"

The little man shuffled forward, eyes downcast.

"Now, Timothy, we'll have none of that. You saved the day. Tell the little lady what you did."

Keeping his eyes on the ground, Treadwater began to speak, his voice muffled. "As you know, Senator Bliss gave me the box of letters for safekeeping until the ceremony. I…I am afraid I've never been very good at waiting. I couldn't help it. I had to know what was in the other documents. I *am* a trained conservator, and I would have looked at them after the official transfer anyway, and besides—"

"Treadwater."

"Yes, well. Most were letters written by George Washington concerning the bogus claims of one Eleanor Nutley that Washington had fathered her child. In fact, he hints that his brother John Augustine was the culprit, and that he'd seduced not Eleanor but her slave

Jane. This proves old Nutley once and for all dead wrong." His smirk of triumph quickly folded at his listeners' shocked expressions. "Er…anyway, under the letters I found a false bottom. In a small compartment lay a paper of more recent origin."

"Go on."

"It was a note signed by one Lazio Truffatore…By the way, I looked him up. He headed an illegitimate lodge called Propaganda Due in Italy. It—"

Gideon shook his head impatiently. "Yes, yes, we know all about that. Get to the story."

"All right, all right. On the sheet Truffatore had drawn a rough picture."

Claire straightened. "A map? A treasure map?"

"No, it looked more like a game board, or one of those word jumble puzzles. Just rows of empty circles."

"Except one." Gideon wandered to a bookshelf and pulled a book out. He glanced at the title and stuck it back on a different shelf, ignoring the librarian's chirp of dismay. "In one of the circles he'd drawn an 'x.' "

Treadwater skirted Gideon, retrieved the book and gently returned it to its proper place. Having righted the universe, he nodded in satisfaction. "Yes, an 'x.' "

Gideon gave him a sidelong look and resumed. "When Treadwater came to me this morning and confessed his sin he showed me the picture. I immediately guessed it referred to the wall of mark pennies in the Royal Arch room."

"How?" Claire's fingers tingled. *We're getting closer.*

"The letter included the word *mark* several times. To the casual reader it came across as senseless jibber-jabber. Truffatore used phrases like 'mark my words.'

And 'on your mark,' that sort of thing. He talked about loose change and mint condition. Your description of the collection of mark pennies in the memorial came to mind. So we popped up to the fifth floor, checked the cases against his chart, and voilà." He pulled the coin from behind her ear.

"Hey!" Claire took it from him. "So what makes this one so special?"

"It happens to be solid rhodium plated with twenty-four carat gold."

"That would still only make it worth a couple of thousand, wouldn't it?"

"Actually, we think the rhodium alone is worth almost $15,000 at today's prices," put in Treadwater.

Gideon added, "With the gold, you're up to about $25,000."

"Nevertheless, I doubt if even Peel would go to all this trouble for such a piddly sum." Claire handed the coin back to Gideon.

He rolled it in his palm, then stuck it between his teeth and chewed on it. "I saw that in an old movie. No idea why people do it."

Treadwater piped up, beaming. "To see if it's real—gold is so soft it will show dents if you bite it."

"Why, thank you, Treadwater. You're an invaluable source of trivia." Gideon slapped the little librarian on the back. He waited until the coughing fit subsided, and continued. "Value is often embedded more in rarity than in beauty, Claire, and that's the case here. Truffatore had this coin struck for P2. Since the Propaganda Due lodge was not only declared irregular, but erased and then dissolved, it becomes one of a kind and very precious indeed. Treadwater here estimates its worth at—"

"Two million dollars," the little man interjected happily.

****

The trio made their way down to the empty lobby. Comfrey came toward them, rubbing his hands. "There you are. I managed to assuage the ruffled egos of a hundred peacocks and sent them on their way with goodie bags. We'll have to reschedule the ceremony of course."

All three stared at him. Gideon found his voice first. "You do know what happened on the observation platform, don't you?"

"Yes, Peter Quinn told me. Quite a fiasco." He seemed no more upset by the appearance of two dead bodies in his memorial in as many months than if he'd been told a light bulb had burned out. "Oh, by the way, Timothy, Zoe asked if you had found that book on South American lodges yet. Her uncle wanted to come by and check something." He wandered off calling, "Bill? Bill, where are you?"

Treadwater's brow furrowed. "David never pays any attention. I told him I'd found the book weeks ago. Why—"

The elevator doors opened to reveal Angle, accompanied by several uniformed officers. As he approached the waiting group, his cell phone rang. "Angle...*What?* Okay, I'll be there as soon as I can...No, the CSI folks haven't shown up yet." The sound of a distant siren floated up the hill. "Sounds like the ambulance has made it anyway...What do you mean, lock down? Where's the chief? He's where? *Home?* God damn it! No, yes, I'm on my way." He flipped his phone closed and without another word stormed through the front door. Treadwater, Gideon, and Claire looked at each other. Claire was the first to react, racing after the detective. She caught up with him at his car. "What gives?"

Ernest shook his head, his lips tight shut. "That cop? The one who left here in such a hurry? You know where he went?"

Something told Claire all was not well in Wonderland. "Where?"

"To the police station. He met the chopper at the pad. With a gun. No, two guns."

Bewildered, Claire tapped her foot. "But, Ernest, I don't understand. If he's a cop, isn't that what he's supposed to do?"

"A cop is not supposed to take White and Peel hostage. He's not supposed to shoot another cop. He's not, definitely not, supposed to steal a helicopter and leave the premises without permission."

Claire ran around to the passenger side. "I'm coming with you." Angle nodded and she got in. As he pressed a foot to the accelerator, Gideon dragged open the rear door and jumped in.

As they roared up to the station in his squad car, they were forced to slow down and inch their way through a mob of police, FBI, CSI, and assorted other acronymic personnel. A second police car, siren blasting, pulled up behind them and the chief jumped out. Three helicopters circled overhead.

Martingale panted, "How far can they go in the bird? Does anyone know?"

Nobody answered him. A man in a windbreaker emblazoned with FBI came up. "Chief Martingale? I'm

Thompson, Washington bureau. Perps stole the copter from Mount Vernon Hospital. Pilot and medic found tied up in a supply closet."

Ernest and Martingale stared at each other. In unison they said, "That wasn't part of the plan."

The agent didn't blink. Without taking his eyes off Angle, he beckoned to a colleague. "Fred? Can you come here?" Another FBI agent came over and, at a signal from Thompson, took out a recorder and clicked it on. Thompson turned to the chief. "Plan?"

By dint of patience alternating with barking annoyance, the FBI agent managed to wring the story out of the embarrassed policemen. Meanwhile, the sky darkened and the streetlamps came on, flooding the police parking lot with light.

"So, let me get this straight. White was supposed to commandeer a police helicopter and pretend to help Peel escape from the tower—"

"Or to rescue him from the police, whichever worked best. We thought he should have some flexibility in dealing with his agent. White concurred. He—"

"I see. And what collateral did you have in case White and Peel actually did abscond with the stolen chopper, not to mention the million-dollar casino token?"

"Er."

"Er."

They were saved from having to come up with more creative excuses by a buzz. Thompson opened his cell phone. "Yeah? Okay." He gave a thumbs up to the little group. "Got 'em."

****

The tiny private airfield in western Fairfax County had rarely welcomed such a vast array of security personnel—although old Mr. Peabody, the janitor, claimed he'd escorted FDR to the hangar for a secret rendezvous with his mistress at the height of World War II. Police surrounded the high chain-link fence with two rings of squad cars, their headlights trained on the helipad. Claire got out, flanked by Gideon and Ernest. She felt a bit like the only sardine in the sandwich.

A helicopter stood in the center of the tarmac, its blades slowly rotating. FBI agents surrounded it, guns drawn. Claire whispered to Thompson, "Why doesn't it just fly away?"

For answer he pointed to the tail assembly. It hung by a wire, trailing sparks on the asphalt. Whenever the helicopter tried to lift off, the tail acted as a drag, making it skew at a forty-five degree angle.

"What do we do now?"

"We wait."

For a long few minutes the tableau remained static, like a television movie on pause. Claire felt a sudden craving for popcorn. Just then Ernest started and pointed. "Something's happening."

A light flashed on and off in the copter's interior. They heard a crash, and the helicopter tried again to rise. This time whoever was at the controls kept forcing it up, which only made the ship lean more precipitously until it finally fell over on its side. The thing scudded across the grass, scattering police and agents as it careened, its speed increasing. When it reached the fence it crashed through. Claire thought for a minute it might actually break out and keep moving, but the tail assembly caught on the post and the aircraft screeched to a halt, spinning wildly.

They heard a gunshot, and then another. The police rushed the ship. One put a bullet through the main motor. A puff of black smoke rose from the engine, and it lay still at last. Ernest began to run toward it, but Thompson held him back. "Not yet. Let my men secure the area first."

The door opened, and a hand, covered in blood, scrabbled around until it found a solid purchase. White pulled himself up and through. He slid off the machine and landed heavily on the ground. A minute later another bloody hand manifested itself, and Peel climbed out, holding his side and panting heavily. He made no attempt to escape when the police moved in and handcuffed him. One cop lowered himself into the helicopter. Another one signaled to the ambulance by the gate. Two medics pulled a gurney out of the back and rolled it toward him.

The chief, Thompson, Ernest, Gideon, and Claire trooped over to the two operatives. The chief spoke first. "White?"

The black ops agent made as if to stand, and his face twisted in pain.

Thompson asked gruffly, "You shot?"

White shook his head. "Aggravated an old ankle injury, that's all. I'm fine."

Martingale clapped a hand on his shoulder. "Take it easy, old boy. Tell us what happened."

White let his first real smile warm his features. "All went according to plan, Chief. All according to plan."

Angle gestured at the helicopter. "What happened

to the police copter you were supposed to use?"

The agent snorted. "You should have checked the roster. They were all out on call. Had to improvise."

Peel said nothing. Claire saw blood trickle out between his fingers, where they pressed into his side. "You're hurt."

White glanced at the other agent. His voice cold, he snapped, "It's only a scratch. I winged him. He's all right. For now."

"Hey, detective, I found the hijacker." The sergeant who had been searching the helicopter scrambled out, hauling a body after him. He laid it out on the tarmac. The little group stood in a ring, staring at the man who lay inert, eyes closed, blood pouring from his chest. He took one rattling breath, and his body relaxed.

Angle muttered under his breath, "The second shot."

Claire stared at him, trying to place him. "Who is he?"

White rasped, "The operative Truffatore sent after Scordato. The German."

Claire bent down and brushed the dead man's hair back. A familiar scent wafted up. *Clean. Pure. I've got it—4711. Grandmother's eau de cologne.* The man's stiff white collar, bloodstained now, had come unbuttoned. Without thinking she buttoned the top button, then closed the tight fitting black jacket. "Oh my God."

"Do you recognize him, Claire?"

"I think so. But...it's impossible." She splayed her fingers on the man's chin, simulating a scraggly beard. A wispy yellow beard to match his hair. She pulled her fingers away and stood up. "Yes, I know him. It's

Werner Kurtz. The Amish man who discovered Scordato's body."

The chief ground his teeth. "Something tells me he did more than 'discover' it."

Chapter Eighteen
Linksmanship

Gideon put the phone down. "That was Treadwater. The appraisal on the penny came back."

"And?"

"And, considering the historic value, its rarity, plus the actual metal content, its value is assessed at...one thousand dollars."

Claire looked up from her newspaper. "Really?" She sniggered. "All that fuss—"

"Not to mention all the taxpayer-funded operations."

"—over a nearly worthless penny."

"Hey, a thousand dollars isn't chump change."

"It's not two million dollars, either." She peered at Gideon's beaming face. "You knew it was worthless, didn't you?"

"I do now. White explained the whole scam to Angle, who told me. Truffatore confessed to his interrogators from the Bureau of Syndicate Operations that he'd sold Perón's hands to a collector for a million dollars, but he and Scordato ran through it in five years. Truffatore owed a lot of important people a lot of money. In order to continue in the lifestyle to which he was accustomed—"

"I.e., alive."

"Yes. He had to dig up some funds, and quickly.

I'm guessing he found a coin in his pocket one day and came up with the idea of claiming he possessed a rare and valuable mark penny. He probably loved the idea of claiming it came from the P2 lodge."

"So how did it get from Argentina to Alexandria?" Claire stopped. "Wait, White told us Truffatore made a clandestine trip to the States back in the eighties. That must have been when he hid the penny."

"Got it in one. He went to the temple claiming to be a visiting Mason and hid the mark penny in plain sight. He somehow learned of the existence of a temporary lodge, and broke in—this was back when the house had been vacant for several years. He found the box in the cellar and placed the map in it. Ironic, isn't it?" Gideon grunted. "If he'd only known how valuable those old blackened papers he hid his map under were, he would have been spared the whole elaborate swindle!"

"Swindle? What are you talking about?"

"He used the mythical existence of a million-dollar mark as collateral to hoodwink his…er…marks, assuming no one would find it." He shook his head admiringly. "Sheer genius."

"But what did he need the map for?"

"It was all part of an intricate maze of clues to keep any doubting Thomas from discovering the truth. Truffatore figured if anyone got that far and discovered his shell game he would be safe and sound in Bali…or prison."

"Or dead. Ernest told me Truffatore's still alive."

"That's right. Ninety-three and still pumping iron. Did you know he was nominated for the Nobel Prize for literature?"

"I'll bet he nominated himself."

"He's sure got enough ego." Gideon slapped his knee. "The guy's a classic. Amazing what a really good scam artist can get away with."

"White said as much the other day. I find it awfully hard to admire a man who created so much havoc."

"And from a jail cell no less." Gideon began to hum "Folsom Prison Blues."

To drown him out, Claire raised her voice. "If the penny is worthless, why would Scordato bother to come and get it?"

Gideon shrugged. "They'd probably lined up some poor rich slug to buy the coin. He kept stringing Peel along to help corroborate the hoax."

Claire reflected that she would never understand the devious mind of a charlatan and decided to change the subject. "Before I forget, they found Nigel."

"Oh? Where?"

"At his mother's house in Pennsylvania. Peel had filled his head with stories of P2 and gold ingots and Nazi fugitives. I guess they overshadowed the latest issue of *Penthouse*, since Peel succeeding in bribing him to swipe the master keys. He says Peel promised to return them, which he did, but when Nigel heard about the vandalism he freaked and fled. Comfrey pronounced his sentence—he's busted down to Entered Apprentice. It was all I could do not to cheer."

"Poor Nigel."

"Poor Nigel, my foot. He's a nasty little man. The one I feel sorry for is Peel."

Gideon drew back, shocked. "Peel? How can you possibly feel sympathy for a murderer and a traitor?"

Claire kissed his cheek. "It just seems as though

everyone came out of this so well—even Truffatore, the instigator of the whole mess. All but Peel. He lost everything—his job, the love of his life, his chance at a new life."

"I fail to see your point. What about Scordato? And Professor Nutley?"

"Did Peel kill them too?"

"The police are still working on the forensic evidence, but Kurtz's gun matches the one used to shoot Scordato. And *Ernest* told me"—he frowned at the name—"that his fingerprints were found all over Nutley's house. It's pretty clear Kurtz murdered them both."

Claire poured more coffee. "It's obvious how and why he killed Nutley, but how did he manage Scordato? I mean, there were ten of us standing on the deck. We'd have heard a shot."

"Silencer." Gideon snagged the last bite of egg from her plate.

She cuffed him, but her mind lay elsewhere. "The timeline doesn't work. When Mrs. Kurtz heard Scordato scream, we were still on the elevator, including Kurtz. Scordato had to have been dead before we got to the ninth floor. "

"He screamed when he fell, but according to the coroner, the fall didn't kill him. The bullet did."

"Fell? He fell? From what?"

"From the helicopter."

Helicopter. So that's how he got there. Claire remembered something. "When we first got on the elevator, it shook."

"Shook? Too many chubby tourists?"

"No, it was a real bone-rattling tremor. We thought

there'd been an earthquake."

"Why didn't you go down then?"

"It only lasted a couple of seconds. We were already headed up to the ninth floor and then, when Mrs. Kurtz heard the scream, Kurtz thought we should investigate. Gideon"—she laid a hand on his arm—"when I followed Kurtz around the corner I noticed a helicopter hovering in the distance. I didn't think anything of it at the time—there are so many around here, what with the Pentagon so close."

Gideon pursed his lips. "Senator Allison postponed his hearing on excessive use of helicopters in the area. If he hadn't, this whole exercise might have gone down differently."

"So, did Peel throw him out of the helicopter?"

"He claims it was an accident. The plan was to lower Scordato onto the deck and he'd sneak into the tower that way. No one would take notice of a man going *down*—they would assume they had merely missed him entering. Then—"

"That's it! Of course! Why didn't I think of that before?"

"I don't know—you were blind? Occupied? Or rather"—he pinched her bottom—"preoccupied?"

"Stop it, I have to think." She buttered a piece of toast and lavished cherry preserves on it.

Gideon watched her. He licked his lips. "You know how sensual this little scene is? First, you gently spread the soft, creamy butter over the toast, making little whorls with your delicate fingers. Then you spoon on luscious, deep red cherries swimming in thick, rich syrup. One cherry falls and you catch it with your tongue, sucking it down your waiting throat. You cradle the toast in both hands and lovingly carry it to your parted lips, where—"

Claire spoke to Ichabod. "Did I, you ask? Yes, I did. I said to him, 'Stop it.' I did. I remember distinctly."

Gideon threw up his hands. "I'm done." He grinned wickedly. "For now." He licked a drop of preserves off Claire's chin. "Now, you were saying?"

She put the toast down. "The vandal hit every level of the Temple twice, the second time wreaking much more damage than the first time. Peel had the master keys. So why would he smash the glass cases? Because he lost the keys? Lost his way? Lost his temper?"

Gideon nodded slowly. "No. A second person— one who didn't have the keys—must have also been looking for the treasure. Kurtz."

"That's right." Claire paused. "I think I've got it. It all seemed to revolve around a key, but we had one too many. Keys, that is."

"What do you mean?"

"Well, there was the key Scordato supposedly had, that Peel took. Then there were the master keys that Peel used to open the cases. But *then* there was the key Treadwater reported stolen. If Scordato brought a key with him, what did the key in the museum belong to, and who stole it?"

"The only explanation is that Scordato didn't bring one." Gideon picked up the jar of preserves, dipped a finger in, leaned over and drew a red moustache on Claire's upper lip. "Truffatore used the key as another stop on the labyrinthine path he had set up to keep his creditors from finding the fake collateral. Scordato must have told Peel the key lay in a case in the museum."

"Peel did open the cases looking for the key, but once he found it he closed them again—all with the correct keys. But that's not all." Claire licked the cherry moustache off. "Remember Washington's inkwell?"

"Inkwell? What…oh, that it had been pried open? So what?"

"Just before he took off in the helicopter, Peel yelled that he'd opened every box in the lodge."

"Right…So…once he found the key, he started looking for the 'box in the lodge.' That would explain some of the other minor damage to the collection."

"While the major damage was Kurtz's work." Gideon jotted notes on a pad of paper. "Poor Kurtz—he didn't have a Nigel and had to break into the cases. Which means…"

"That Peel didn't murder Scordato. He had no reason to. He believed they were working together."

Gideon finished his coffee. "So after Scordato fell, Peel hovered for a minute, saw you and your group come out on the platform, and hightailed it out of there."

"Yup. Do you think he recognized Kurtz?"

"I doubt it. White said Truffatore dispatched Kurtz from Italy. Peel would have no way of knowing who he was."

Claire cast her mind back over the last few weeks. A tall, thin, blond man cropped up at regular intervals—playing the fiddle at Tivoli Tavern. By the bench on the waterfront. *At the press conference.* And always accompanied by the scent of 4711. *The cologne I first smelled…when? The day of the murder. Why, oh why, didn't I put it all together?*

Rising to put his dishes in the sink, Gideon

knocked over the coffee pot. He mopped it up, then wrung the cloth into the sink. As he started to make more coffee, Claire put a hand on his arm. "Why?"

"Why what? Why did Kurtz kill Scordato?" He shook his head. "I don't know. White and Angle have hardly been forthcoming with me. The only reason I coaxed any information at all out of them is because I found the penny. And because they know you told me the background." He rubbed his chin thoughtfully. "Maybe I should hold a hearing." He went to the table and jotted down another note.

Claire folded the newspaper. "You said Kurtz used a silencer. That means he meant to kill someone. It had to be Scordato. But why? That left him without a guide to the treasure."

"Ah, that's another puzzler."

"Unless…I'm going to ask Ernest."

"What? You're not—" Gideon looked from the dirty dishes to Claire. "Not now, surely?"

"No time like the present." She got up, retrieved her purse and headed out the door.

****

"You have to tell me, Ernest. Why did Kurtz kill Scordato?"

"Just a minute." Ernest handed her a mug of coffee, then poured himself one, dropping three packets of sugar and two spoonfuls of creamer into it. He tasted, grimaced, ran his fingers through his hair, and set it down. "Okay, this is what I've pieced together from the few facts White has condescended to give us." He scowled. "Our system of justice seems to irritate him."

"Must be nice to be above the law."

"Ooh, if I had my way—well, enough of that. You

know Truffatore sent a message to Scordato, instructing him to come to Alexandria. He told him to retrieve a key from the temple, which would unlock the box with the map. Now, Peel had been monitoring Scordato in Argentina for over a decade. When he intercepted the message he guessed Scordato had finally received his instructions, but he couldn't decipher the code. So he cozied up to Scordato, winkled whatever he could get out of him, and asked to go in on it in exchange for all the resources a black ops agent has at hand. After some initial distrust, Scordato accepted Peel's offer, probably with some idea of using him as a shill."

"Shill?"

"Scordato could point to Peel's pursuit of it as proof that the coin was valuable should a potential buyer have doubts. Peel came up with the helicopter and the plan to drop Scordato off on the tower. Then things went awry."

"Scordato fell out of the helicopter."

"That's what Peel claims."

"Did Peel see Kurtz kill Scordato?"

"He says no and I believe him. If he had, it would be exculpatory evidence."

"Wait a minute." Claire blew on the hot coffee. "How did he get the key then?"

"Ah, that's where his story stumbles. He won't say how he got it. Probably thinks admitting how much he knew would undermine his defense. He claims he was laying a trap for Scordato, but your testimony, along with the dying words of Dorcas Bliss, should make short work of that alibi."

"Could he…" *Might as well spit it out.* "Could he have taken it from the museum? Remember, Mr.

Treadwater mentioned a missing key."

Ernest jumped up. "Yes, of course! I'd forgotten all about that. That makes sense. Yes." He sat back down abruptly. "That doesn't mean he didn't push Scordato out of the chopper. If he knew where the key was, he had probably extracted all the information he needed out of Scordato."

"But the fall didn't kill him, correct?"

"Correct. According to the medical examiner, Scordato suffered a broken leg, four broken ribs, and a dislocated shoulder from the fall."

Claire put the cup down. "Well, considering Peel had a gun and is a trained assassin, don't you think if he wanted to kill Scordato, he would have?"

Ernest fiddled with his pencil. He finally muttered, "Maybe. It's true that he would have survived if Kurtz hadn't shot him."

"Which brings us back to my initial question. Why did he shoot him? Weren't they both members of Truffatore's gang?"

"According to White, his agents are attempting to pump Truffatore for that information as we speak, but their working hypothesis is that Truffatore feared Scordato had betrayed him and gone in with Peel."

"So Kurtz came to America—or was sent—to kill Truffatore's trusted lieutenant. A lieutenant who had been in South America for many years. Wait a minute…*he* stole the book!"

"Scordato? He couldn't have. He never got below the ninth floor."

"No, no. Kurtz."

Ernest looked puzzled. "What book are we talking about?"

"The book on South American lodges. The one Mr. Treadwater accused Gideon of taking."

"Oh, yeah. The one he found in the museum. So why would Kurtz steal it?"

"I don't know—to look something up, or maybe Truffatore had left yet another clue in it. At any rate, I know it was Kurtz."

"And what makes you so sure?"

"He stole it the day of the murder. I'd forgotten until now, but while I called for the police he muttered something about Jemimah's hat…"

"Jemimah…his wife."

"Yes. By the way, was she his real wife?"

Ernest grinned. "Funny you should ask. When I dispatched an officer to notify her of Kurtz's death, he could find no trace of a Jemimah Kurtz at the address they'd given."

Claire remembered that sultry gleam in the woman's eye. *Not a very Amish look.* "Well, anyway, Kurtz went back up in the elevator for the hat and when he came down he had—"

"Let me guess. A book."

"And no hat. I didn't think anything of it at the time, but it should have rung bells all over the place. I'm sorry, Ernest. You might have given him greater scrutiny if I'd told you."

Ernest's color heightened and he blinked rapidly. "Claire, there's no need to apologize. You've been a paragon through all this—strong, intelligent, fearless. I couldn't have asked for a better helpmate wading through the morass of clues. It's been…it's been almost fun. I only wish—"

Uh oh. Claire hastily interrupted, "Don't be silly,

Ernest. You did all the heavy lifting. In fact, I still have questions. For instance, why didn't Peel knock Kurtz off?"

"He didn't know that Truffatore had sent another man. He would have acted differently if he knew someone was tracking him."

"Then he isn't as great an operative as White thinks he is."

"He may have been blinded by love."

"Dorcas?"

Ernest nodded. "It can happen." He gave Claire a meaningful look.

"How could he kill the woman he loved? It makes no sense."

"Not to us, perhaps. He followed her to Paris, didn't he? And here?"

"I did see him with her on several occasions. And, except for that last…er…bit—"

"The part where he shot her?"

"That part, yes. He always seemed smitten. So did she."

"Dorcas was incredibly beautiful." Ernest seemed unaffected by the words. He kept his gaze on Claire.

"Mrs. Bliss—Gideon's mother—told me she liked the danger, the potential for violence. That's why she fell for Peel."

"A perfect match."

Claire thought of the man waiting for her at home. "Love is a tricky thing, isn't it, Ernest?"

His shoulders slumped. "Yes, yes, it is."

****

"So Peel didn't kill anyone but Dorcas." Gideon mumbled something.

"What did you say?"

"I can't help it." His lips turned up. "Someone was bound to do it eventually. Just glad I didn't have to."

Claire frowned in disapproval. "There is nothing funny about murder. Simon's going to jail for a long time, isn't he?"

"Yup. Uncle Andrew called. The judge set bail at a million dollars."

"Which he doesn't have."

Gideon nodded. "Right, so the judge ordered him incarcerated until the trial."

"Too bad." Claire put her mug down. "If he had simply harvested the wall of pennies, maybe he would have had enough to post bail."

"Maybe, maybe not."

"I am so glad Anton White turned out to be a good guy."

"Oh, I don't know about that. His loyalty to the agency would have overridden his allegiance to his country if it weren't for your boyfriend."

"Ernest?" She ducked, avoiding the cushion. "What did he do?"

"He talked White out of unofficially extraditing Peel to Italy. Otherwise we'd never have closure. Peel would have disappeared into the bowels of Europe, never to haunt halls or shadow people again."

Claire let her eyes go dreamy. "Ernest is a very good policeman, isn't he?" This time the cushion hit its mark.

When she'd rewarded her tormentor with a sloppy kiss, he consented to sit down and snuggle. Mid-cuddle he broke off. "You know, we've treated this whole brouhaha as so complicated, but it really boils down to an erroneous mixing of missions—an inappropriate linking of intentions as it were."

"How's that?"

"Think about it. Two unconnected sets of individuals were focused on two completely different goals. Here Fred and I were pursuing the George Washington letters—"

"Which are of inordinate value."

"Yes, and Peel, Dorcas, and Scordato were after a totally different treasure."

"Which, as it turns out, was of no value whatsoever."

"And somehow our paths crossed in the memorial and our fates intertwined."

"With tragic results. If it hadn't happened, Professor Nutley wouldn't be dead today."

Gideon pursed his lips. "Unfortunate, but he brought it on himself. If he hadn't been so quick to steal the credit, Kurtz wouldn't have mistakenly believed he had Truffatore's penny." He sat absentmindedly caressing Claire's hair. "Strange, isn't it? Everything to do with this Truffatore is fake from beginning to end."

Claire thought of another man who had turned out to be a fake, and gazed at her lover, affection, pride, and happiness streaming into every air pocket in her body. "I'm so glad you're not," she whispered.

A little while later Gideon murmured, "Have you heard from your mother?"

"Me? No. How about you?"

"No, and it's making me very nervous. Andromeda Miller Bliss is not one to hide under a lily pad when the game's afoot. You don't suppose they're unaware of the latest incident?"

Claire laughed. "By no means. The Marples have been on the case, according to my sister."

Gideon cocked an eyebrow. "Marples?"

"It's what I call them. Your mother and mine are two of the finest sleuths since Agatha Christie invented the little old lady crime solver. Did you know they knew who Peel was all along?"

Gideon's mouth fell open, and he tumbled off the couch. His head popped up. "Why didn't they go to the police?"

Claire pulled him up with some effort. "With what? They were unaware of Scordato and the mark penny. Their only interest lay in getting rid of Dorcas so you and I could be together. Like Sherlock Holmes, they ignored the irrelevant."

"They must have been shocked to hear of her death."

"On the contrary. Edwina says they sent a dozen white roses to the morgue and asked that they be laid on the slab next to Dorcas."

"Somehow that comforts me." Gideon began a cursory search of the contents of Claire's bra. "Hmm, both there." He pinched one breast. "Good tone." He flicked a nipple. "Nice and perky." His hand moved lower, fingers sliding down the breastbone to her belly button.

Claire let him continue. They had all afternoon. The Senate was in recess and the memorial closed down for cleaning. She'd sent Ichabod to explore Gideon's garden, where he quickly established dominance among the neighborhood cats. One finger reached the sweet spot.

"Do you want to go upstairs?" Gideon's voice,

thickened with desire, dropped an octave.

"No, I don't think so." Claire stood up and shimmied out of her skirt. Gideon drew down the silk panties, now soaking with her juices. She opened her thighs to allow him better access. When she felt the orgasm growing she pushed him away.

Going down on her knees, she pulled his pants down to his ankles, then climbed on his lap. Staring into his eyes hungrily, she lowered herself onto his thick, hard prick. Once he'd reached the point of no return, she leaned back and away from him until she lay almost flat, resting on his knees. He began to thrust. In that position, his penis filled the channel completely, scraping deliciously against the sucking walls of her vagina. He threw his head back and groaned. "Claire, this is it! Do it for me, baby. *Ahhhh*."

He slid out, and she crawled up his chest and laid her head on his shoulder. She felt both sated and comfortable. *All is well.*

A faint scratching came from the garden door. Ichabod peered at her through the pane. As she scrambled up, the phone rang. "Hello, Edwina…What? They both do? Tonight? I'll check with…I see. It's an order. All right. Morrison House. Eight o'clock. Got it."

Gideon had pulled his pants back on and was buttoning his shirt. "Your sister?"

"The Marples want us to escort them tonight. Apparently there's an open mike party in the bar of the Morrison House. They have a pianist who plays show tunes and anyone can step up to sing."

"Show tunes, huh? My mother's a real aficionado."

"And my mother knows the lyrics to every Cole Porter or Steven Sondheim song ever written."

"What? No Lerner and Lowe? No Rodgers and Hammerstein?"

"She turns her nose up at them—musical plays for the common man, she sniffs."

"Would she be amenable to a little Gilbert and Sullivan?"

"Perchance."

"I suppose the ladies are already bickering over which song each gets."

"How did you know?"

****

"Gideon! We're going to be late. Where are you?" A man's voice sounded faintly from a distance. "What?"

"I'm in the cellar. I found another box!"

Claire wasn't sure whether this cheered or depressed her. "Bring it up."

"No, I think you'd better come down."

She felt her way carefully down the damp stairs, catching her best silk dress on a splinter. *Phooey, I hope it's not ruined. Edwina says this coppery color is so becoming on me.* She had planned to descend from on high to enthusiastic applause. These were not the stairs she had intended to use.

"Gideon?" She saw light flickering in the far corner. A flutter in her heart reminded her of the terror she'd felt in Peel's grip. "Gideon!"

Suddenly another candle lit up, revealing her lover in the center. He held out a small box. "Look what I found."

She took a step toward him, but tripped on a loose board and fell into his arms. He kissed the top of her head and sat her down on a packing crate. "Feels just like home, doesn't it?"

"Gideon, do get on with it."

"Okay, okay. Now I doubt whether this new discovery will cause Treadwater's heart to palpitate, but I'm hoping yours will." He opened the little box. In it lay a ring. Two pear-shaped diamonds sparkled on each side, setting off a large, emerald-cut ruby in the center. Claire put a hand to her neck. "Oh, it's beautiful. Do you suppose it belonged to Martha?"

He stared at her. "Martha? Who's Martha?"

"Martha Washington. Who else?"

His brow furrowed for an instant before he threw back his head and roared. "Oh my love," he finally panted. "No, this ring—if you'll take it—belongs only to you."

Still somewhat befuddled, Claire touched the chain around her neck. "Does this mean I have to give back your class ring?"

"Oh no. That's to signify we're best friends. This"—he held out the ring—"this represents my undying love. I want you to be my wife, Claire. And my best friend."

If anyone had looked for them later that night, they would have found the happy couple lustily singing "It's Too Darn Hot," accompanied on the triangle and cymbals by two radiant old ladies.

A word about the author...

M. S. Spencer has ten romantic suspense/mystery novels published.

Although she has lived or traveled in every continent except Antarctica and Australia, Ms. Spencer spent most of the last thirty years in Washington, D.C. as a Congressional staff assistant, speechwriter, librarian, editor, birdwatcher, kayaker, policy wonk, non-profit director, and parent.

She has two fabulous grown children, a perfect granddaughter, and currently divides her time between the Gulf coast of Florida and a tiny village in Maine.

http://msspencertalespinner.blogspot.com